MW00411684

FRANKENSTEIN:

THE DAWNING AND THE PASSING

FRANKENSTEIN:
THE DAWNING AND THE PASSING

• BY MARIO MARCEL SALAS •

A SEQUEL

THE WATERCRESS PRESS • SAN ANTONIO

2000

First Edition

Library of Congress Catalog Card Number 00-190920
ISBN 0-934955-42-5

Book design by Paul Hudgins

Graphics by Lenella Meister

Manufactured in the United States of America

This poem is dedicated to my husband,
my soulmate, Mario Marcel Salas

UP FROM THE ASHES

Up from the ashes
Arose my soul
Free to soar high
Straightway for the sky.
Far, far away from the memories that stole
All semblance of sanity, partial or whole.

Far from the images
That once engulfed my very being,
And tightened the chains
Of a lifetime of wretchedness and pain.
Far, far away from an abyss of fragmented thoughts
Where demons and spirits of skeletons were caught.

Up from the ashes
Though covered with soot,
A purging of mind
Caused my spirit to bind
To a force, to a strength, far greater than I.
To this Force, to this Strength, will I ever draw nigh!

Edwina Lacy Salas
October 15, 1999

CONTENTS

FRANKENSTEIN:

THE DAWNING AND THE PASSING

"He sprang from the cabin window . . . upon the ice raft which lay close to the vessel. He was soon borne away by the waves and lost in darkness and distance."

—Mary Shelley

THE LEGEND, 1850

It has been said that a man named Victor Frankenstein created a life form from human remains. This creature murdered Frankenstein's family and friends, and in a duel dance of revenge they pursued one another to the ends of the earth, to the icy regions of the north where the creature was impervious to the terrible extremes of temperature.

There was reputed to be only one witness to the climax of the story, a Captain Robert Walton who was driven insane and raved for all the years of his life. It was said that he could be heard from the forlorn walls of an asylum screaming: "The monster lives! My God, the monster lives!"

Two doctors, surgeons, Sir Astley Golem and Joshua Hamel, heard of the legend of the monster. They had experimented with the effects of freezing on humans to preserve life. They sought the truth of the legend for they suspected that Frankenstein had found the secret of immortality, and to this ungodly aim they had dedicated their science and their very lives.

They began a search for the record of the voyage of Captain Walton but could find nothing in the official accounts of the maritime office. Finally they discovered a fragment of the ship's log of a Captain Solomon Amos, who had entered the tale of a strange incident dated September 11th, 1831. The latitude and longitude of the event were obliterated, as was the rest of the document. Only two words were legible: "The monster . . .". With this clue, they pursued the story.

No one knows if the two surgeons ever found the creature, for they disappeared without a trace, and their laboratory was destroyed by fire.

BOOK I

THE DAWNING

Prologue

A.D. 2351 — The Dawning

London was now barren. London Bridge spanned a dried riverbed. The skyline that once caught the eye of the world was reduced to jagged and crumpled piles of concrete and steel. The dreaded hot wind whipped against the rubble of London like a continuous blast from some kind of explosion. The temperature hovered at 118 degrees Fahrenheit and the wind blew constantly at eighty miles per hour, with gusts to one hundred.

London had once been known as a city of cemeteries. Now not even those remained. Hundreds of gravestones lay in the bed of the Thames. The rise in temperature produced melting of the polar regions, which in turn shifted the earth's mass. These shifts put extreme pressure on the earth's crust, causing tremendous earthquakes all over England. The earth rose and sank in London, destroying buildings and graveyards alike.

There were roving clans of people, but as the years progressed they were dying out. One group built a large brick structure and was able to grow some vegetables for a while. Another clan found a well that still contained water; it did not last long.

Once a year the leaders would meet and exchange information about food stores, water, and shelter. The meeting was held in the Thames riverbed beneath the remains of London Bridge, but these meetings had become sad affairs. Each year the clans were smaller. By 2340, only 22 groups were known to exist. The birth rate was dropping as many of the mothers and children died in childbirth from the heat. The clans were never able to join forces for they disagreed with each other on religious grounds. Some of them even praised their own leader as a god.

A clan leader was one who knew the terrain. It was absolutely necessary that water and food be found. The leader had to know where food stores had been exhausted and where they remained. Children who showed ability to lead were groomed from an early age. They were trained in the art of survival to eventually lead a new clan forward. At the age of twenty, a prospective leader would take the excess numbers and establish a new group. The new clan then searched out and found individual survivors and incorporated them into their group.

Ransom was born into the Williams-Fernandez clan in the year 2301. There were many families in the group, which ensured a greater chance of survival. By the time Ransom was ten, the group had almost doubled in size from finding new families and from births within the clan. It now had seventy-three members.

In A.D. 2321, Ransom McDonald left the Williams-Fernandez clan with thirty-three followers. They were optimistic, having heard of sightings of other individuals. Early on, they had found a cool cave with water, but the water soon dried up, forcing them to move on. There had been at least a hundred roving clans in London, each made up of fifteen to forty members. By 2351, the McDonald Clan was the only group remaining in the London area.

The people did not have access to any literature. It was one of the problems that often plagued Ransom. *"There are no more books that I know of. Perhaps there is a great vault of buried books somewhere! If we could only find a Bible,"* he thought. He brooded constantly on his life-long quest. *"I have prayed and prayed that one day I will find a Bible. I have tried throughout my life to find the ruins of a library or a book market in London. When time permitted it I searched. I am fifty years of age now and have not seen another book except for the one my mother gave me."*

His book was a treasure but no one would listen to his readings or explanations of it. *"The others have thought me insane to be so concerned about books. It is said that before my birth the earth was quite cold. As it grew colder many of the books were used for fires. I have not met anyone who has actually seen one other than mine. I may be in possession of the last book in the world. My mother once told me that her mother had a Bible but it was lost in a terrible battle between two clans who were fighting over water. My mother read to me often from the only book she had. It was called* Pilgrim's Progress. *I do not know the name of the author for the cover of the book is gone and many pages are missing. I carry the book with me to this day, and I may be the only one left in the world who can read. I have tried to teach my son but it has been slow. We are always occupied with survival."*

Ransom thought on these things as the situation grew more desperate every day.

"When water is nowhere to be found, these words from Pilgrim's Progress *help:*

> *For my part I know not whether 'tis best to live thus, or to die out of hand. My Soul chooseth Strangling rather than Life, and the Grave is more easy for me than this Dungeon!*

And Hope replied:

> *My brother, said he, remembereth thou not how valiant thou hast been heretofore? Apollyon could not crush thee, nor could all that thou didst hear, or see, or feel, in the Valley of the Shadow of Death; what hardship, terror, and amazement hast thou already gone through!*

Ransom McDonald wanted a Bible. In his book were references to it. He had wanted one for as long as he could remember and he searched for a Bible at every opportunity. He could not afford to spend much of his time teaching his son. His mind turned to the horror at hand. There was a creature that roamed after the clan through the years. It preyed on the little ones and the weak. *"We have never seen it clearly,"* he thought. *"Through the blowing dust I have seen its form. My mother once said that hyenas roamed the countryside. She described one to me. She had said that the creatures were once kept in a zoo. On several occasions I saw more than one. They have followed us night and day."* Ransom McDonald grew angry as he spoke aloud; "I hate the creatures!" Ransom had tried to follow them to discover their water source but they were too fast and their tracks were always obliterated by the wind.

His thoughts were interrupted by the voice of his son. "Father!" asked his son, "What hope do we have?"

Ransom did not want to sadden the boy for he had suffered enough. When he was younger his mother had become too weak to walk and it was impossible to carry her. Ransom had to leave her for she was too sick to walk any farther and there was no water. They had been searching for three days. Ransom could not save them both. The boy's mother agreed to be left behind. She said goodbye as

Ransom pulled away his crying son. It was horrible! The horrendous gnawing and tearing still echoed in his mind.

It was time to answer his son. "There is always hope, my son," he said. "Hope never dies, even in this hell!"

Ransom turned away — and then it happened . . .

Diary of Ransom McDonald — A.D. 2351

The wind has blown this way for months. Across this desolate landscape, blowing dust saturates the sky. We have been wandering over the lifeless terrain for days. In my mind's eye I see myself and the others as small figures on a large canvas, some men, some women, and a few children. My clothes are tattered from the cutting, blowing dirt.

I went forward, barefooted, into the wind. There were rows of slanted, rectangular-shaped rocks, spreading outward over a long distance, out ahead of the endless unseen country. I waited for a break in the blowing dust to peer ahead as far as the break would allow. With my hand over the brow of my eyes I looked at the apparition ahead. I ordered the others to stop. Ghostly stones littered my path for as far as my shielded, squinting eye could see. In the presence of eternity, all of the haunting stones were strangely alike. The wind compelled me to look downward. I saw stones at my feet that appeared to be stepping-stones, of brick or concrete, of some abandoned walkway.

I have seen the remains of stone walkways before, but this was different. Their scattered checkerboard pattern disturbed me. I grew confused as I looked all around at the stone walkway that extended into the dusty distance ahead.

Farther ahead were more slanted stones. Some of them were shorter than the next and appeared to have been sheared off. As I led the group ahead there was in each eye a frightened look at the forlorn aspect of scattered ruins of unknown meaning. As we passed one slab there were a few scattered symbols on its face. Most of them were no longer legible. I instinctively placed my finger on the stone and rubbed over the indentations. We walked slowly ahead through the maze of stones until we saw an outcrop of exposed land. As we drew closer I saw two objects, undeterminable from the distance, but strongly attractive to my eye.

The objects were encased in a square opening whose visible side, now exposed as the result of ground shift, revealed three coffin-like vessels in the face of an outcropped cliff. The floor of the structure jutted out from the cliff wall, and part of it was filled with dirt which had collapsed inward.

This was where I came to know of a past and of a future.

"What is that?" said one of the men. He was pointing to the box-like objects as he squinted for a better view. We moved closer, and within a short time were able to peer through the flowing dust at three strangely-built boxes.

"Look, one of them is smoking!" said my son. We climbed up to the cliff face. Upon reaching the area immediately in front of the structure we noticed that the floor protruded out from the cliff. The floor had been sheered off making a ledge, but enough remained for us to grab and raise ourselves up into the structure. Having accomplished this I looked closely at the vaporous objects.

"What are these things?" Before some thought could enter my mind the earth began to tremble and shake violently. We waved the rest back away from the structure, and sought refuge under the tables that held the strange vessels. We swayed with the earth for a few seconds.

Part of the ceiling fell and struck one of the boxes causing part of its top to fracture. As it did, a rush of vapor escaped into the air, and when it cleared, the head of a corpse relaxed from the edge of its death bed. Its hair flowed in the blowing howling wind, which, for a moment, gave it a living macabre look.

"It is the corpse of a man!" We peered into the hollow tube and could see that on top of the corpse a bundle of papers lay across its bosom. Pages were strewn about. As I reached in I could taste the coldness. Small hisses of an icy mist continued to exit from tubes in the rear of the coffin. The opening was large enough for me to slip my head and arms into it to retrieve the papers. As I did, I noticed that one of the corpse's legs was missing. I sat down on the floor and looked intently at the papers.

One of the men soon joined us. I turned to him and spoke. "We must get out of this storm. Get the others. We can stay here for a few days until the storm eases." I glanced at the remaining coffins. They were still intact. I opened the first book. Although it was extremely dry the writing was still clear.

"What are these things? What is this place?" asked my son. Most of our small band had now entered the structure. "I do not know. A record has been left, an account it appears, of what happened here. In any event we must stay for a while out of the dust and heat. It is cool here, and from the vessel dewdrops have formed on its under side. Gather the containers, for precious water drips from this place."

The others pushed the damp and decayed dirt out and began stacking bricks up against the wind. The floor was littered with them, which was helpful in building a protective wall. As the bricks rose, the wind grew faint and we rested. We stayed here for several days, looking at the corpse and the remaining vessels, pondering where we would go when the water ran out.

It was during this interval that I began reading the papers I had taken from the corpse. "What does it say, Father?" my son asked. "What tale does it tell? I have watched you read those pages and your face has grown gloomy. You have said little and have been reading furiously. We have tried to break you from this trance, but you did not seem to hear. What have you found out? We are almost out of food and have been out looking. What is it, Father? Please talk to me!"

I raised my head and looked at the unbroken vessels in horror. I turned to my son and said, "We have been directed here by some unknown fate, the horror of which is yet to come. I have attempted to piece these pages together, in the correct order, as they were strewn about, and to name them as I saw fit. Listen to this horrible tale from the lips of the dead. Listen to what has happened here."

Hamel's Diary

February 2nd, 1849

I have decided to commit to paper the entire story as I know it, and as it has been told to me by Captain Solomon Amos, Captain Robert Walton, Sir Astley Golem, and the creature whose intent it is to destroy the world. I have resolved myself to record the words and events that took place as accurately as possible, for what has happened may have worldwide consequences.

I do not know if anyone will ever read the record contained within these pages, but as God is my witness, I have recorded what I know. I have included the writings of the creature and those of Dr. Golem as they were written, and have not so much as changed a single word. I have also kept with me the narration of Victor Frankenstein as told to Captain Walton.

It seemed to me that keeping a record of these events was of the utmost importance. I have written in my diary daily, and it now resembles more of a story. I have tried to record the events as accurately as possible and have written feverishly, each day recording the events as they unfolded and capturing my feelings before they could be lost. If for some reason I am unable to continue my tale I would hope that whoever may find this record continue the story, for the world must know what has happened. I was able to obtain many of Golem's notes as well as those of the monster, and though much will have happened in the interval of time between when I wrote these pages and whenever my body shall be found, the tale will not be lost.

I am afraid for mankind if it does not resolve itself to being more humane. The creature's dawning is upon us. Perhaps all is lost. If Captain Walton was correct then it shall not matter in any case. We are doomed. All of our hopes and dreams are blasted. May God have mercy on my soul.

Joshua Hamel

Hamel's Diary
July 13, 1848

I first met Sir Astley Golem when studying at the anatomy school where he was a respected professor and a surgeon, as had been his father before him. Soon he commended my skills, and after I obtained my degrees he invited me to work with him in his research and laboratory experiments. I accepted with pleasure and none of the sense of foreboding which should have warned me away from this evil man.

Gradually I was taken into his confidence and I began to realize that his obsessive desire was to discover the secret of immortality which he believed had been achieved by Victor Frankenstein when he created his infamous monster. Like most of my generation, I had regarded the story of Frankenstein and his creature as a legend, an apocryphyal tale perpetuated to frighten children on All Hallows' Eve.

But Professor Golem was convinced that Victor Frankenstein and his monster had lived, and he was determined to follow the trail which might lead him to their secrets. The first step led to an old ship captain named Solomon Amos, who had rescued a man named Walton, the last person to see Victor Frankenstein alive. And Doctor Golem had learned the whereabouts of Captain Amos and took me with him to interview the old man.

I remember his words well. He spoke thus: "I, Captain Solomon Amos, have become the unwilling caretaker of the story. I have not seen the record book for years, but I remember Walton's words — that those who have violated nature's laws and God's trust must not be told what has happened. I must ask you if your studies are a violation of God's trust and nature's laws?" I looked in Amos' eyes. I felt the weight of his words in my soul.

Golem answered him, "I can say that we are surgeons in search of the truth; a truth that must be told for future generations, so that God's will will be done."

Amos looked at us and seemed to notice something in my face, a recollection perhaps. He seemed to be reminded of something which I could not comprehend.

In a somber and grave voice, Amos continued."Well, gentlemen, I can tell you that Captain Walton lives. He is quite mad to be sure, and may be found at the London sanitarium. I have told you all I dare to. If you want more it will be for you to discover without my help. The records are sealed, and as to their location I will not contribute to portentous fate. I want to die with my thoughts. Captain Walton will tell you nothing. This story is a tale and no more. Nothing human could survive in the icy north; perhaps a fiend could tolerate the temperatures. As far as I am concerned it is only a tale of terror. Go! Hunt for your truth! Perhaps it will find you!"

We turned and walked back to our waiting carriage and looked ahead while conversing in low tones. We wanted nothing more than to immediately engage the services of the carriage to take us to the London sanitarium.

Golem seemed filled with a repressed excitement. As soon as we were seated, he said, "The story is true! I know that it is. We need the latitude and longitude of the ship, where it went down. Perhaps the body of the creature is on the ice, in which case we will have a preserved specimen."

At the time I shared his excitement at the prospect. "I agree, Dr. Golem. The remains may have survived the icy cold water long enough to make shore. If this is true then we will have a perfectly frozen specimen for our experiments."

"Yes, Hamel, we may be able to use such a specimen for the liquid nitrogen experiments. It may shed some light on the decay of the body, and the relationship between cold and the passing of time."

"Did Victor Frankenstein create such a creature?" I asked. "Nothing now exists of his records or his lab. The politicians and the fanatics of religious dogma saw to that. Yet, could you not see the hidden truth in the captain's face? This incredible story is true! We are faced with a dilemma, it seems. Can we as men take on the role of God? What lies at the end of such deeds? I would think hell, doctor, hell for sure."

Golem did not appear to appreciate my objections. He was stoney faced as usual."I see no dilemma, Mr. Hamel! You are a strange fellow, Joshua. Here we are about to embark on a journey to find a creature created by man, and, when we return, to continue our experiments in cold science, but you talk of hell! Is not immortality the realm of gods? Why trouble yourself if your beliefs tell you it is contrary to the laws of God?"

"I am not sure that it is, Dr. Golem. We do not know where our experiments will take us. We do not know the end. It seems to me that if good is accomplished we will not be violating the laws of God, but if evil results . . ."

Golem cut me off quite forcefully. "It sounds interesting, Hamel, but no one knows the end beyond all doubt. If we follow your logic, anything we do could turn to evil and we could be sent to hell, if one exists. Well, your concern does not seem sincere; you are just jousting with me, or with yourself. Come, let us make haste to the sanitarium." Golem gathered some notes, and we proceeded to the waiting carriage which he secured for the day.

The carriage lurched forward into the cold air. Dr. Golem sat there looking straight ahead. Outside, the blowing wind was bellowing from the north. It fluttered the ice-covered leaves of passing evergreens. Smoke blew from the nostrils of the trolley horses, and icy slush, deposited from sleet, was lifted from the roadway and slung all about. It plopped in clumps on the side of the roadway. The coachman looked ahead hardly moving from the sway and roll of the coach. It was this movement that perpetuated a disposition; I became lost in a reverie. I did not know why but I viewed our journey from above the frozen landscape. I saw as a winged creature would. I was viewing our forlorn carriage, driven by a coachman who was dressed in dark clothing. His figure painted the foreground onto a bleak canvas of blurred white wasteland. In my state of mind I imagined that time could be measured by the passing of the coach. I soon awoke in worry at the thought that no one viewed our journey crossing the countryside; we were totally alone. Yet, there was a presence measuring these fleeting moments. I hoped that perchance God was witnessing this crossing of the countryside, to measure these fleeting moments of eternity. I wondered if some evil followed us that day.

We sat inside the carriage silent. I did not feel like conversing. We were, it seemed, only a dark blur rolling across the white ground. The two horses pulling the carriage through the frozen air made me feel small and insignificant. Their hoofs pounded the frozen slush. I continued to wonder at the thought of who, besides ourselves, recorded this journey. Who would ever remember if this journey was for good or evil? The sky had darkened and was creeping behind us. It was following us like the empty shadow of oblivion, enveloping us. I saw a large black raven perched in a tree as we slowed for a bend in the road. It took on a strange appearance as I looked into its watery eyes. The creature's head moved erratically, reminding me of the floating feelings I have experienced over the years. I was reminded of death.

The approach to the sanitarium was on a steep incline. The horses exhaled warm vapors through their nostrils in the icy air as the last expanse of distance lay ahead. The sanitarium resembled a castle in the background, but the front of the structure lay stretched out as any present-day mansion. The entrance was marked by high walls and a gate at a cobblestone approach. The gate was locked, but from afar we could see a small figure approaching. He soon arrived, bid us welcome, and after we explained that we were surgeons he let us in. We were escorted to the head physician's office and shown in.

Upon entering the office the guide retreated from view and we were before a man of delicate build and an amicable face. We introduced ourselves, presented our credentials, and learned that he was a physician named Alexander Creda. As we did not wish to reveal our aims, we explained our presence was due to an interest in the ravings of the mind and declared that we had heard about the strange delusions of a Captain Walton and wanted to hear the poor man's story.

Dr. Creda was quite willing to accommodate us. He pointed us to a hallway which led to a descending staircase. As we journeyed downward faint screams echoed in the distance. The closer we approached our destination the louder were the screams. They began to echo in the outer chambers. This had a freezing effect upon my spirit. As the last terrible echoes sank to silence, an attendant joined us and produced a huge set of keys which he gave to Dr. Creda.

The doctor opened a large door, and then another just beyond the first. Inside we saw horrible things. The room was dark. There were more screams ahead of us and around us now. There were people walking in circles, moaning in agony. Some were clustered in the recesses, rocking and fixated at some unknown source. I grew fearful at the sight and soon wanted nothing more than to leave. There was something gnawing at me. It was a fear that I did not want to confront.

We were led past a group of inmates squatting and defecating on the floor. It was with relief that we soon approached a corridor away from the pathetic creatures. This hall was lined with a series of doors that punctuated the pale walls. The corridor extended beyond the range of my eye. After a short walk we came to a door with a sliding face-plate punched into it at eye level. Dr. Creda slid the metal plate to one side and peered in. He then instructed us to look.

"The poor old captain just sits there," he said. "He can sit and sit and never utter a word. We know he eats, but no one has ever actually seen him do so. I have tried to talk with him to break through whatever spirit holds him, but to no avail. At certain hours of the night, which I have documented, he cries out in such a shrill and horrid tone that all other sounds are drowned out. At first I could not make out what he was saying, for he often screams until he is hoarse. After several nights of this I finally deciphered that he was saying; 'We are doomed! Revenge!' which he repeats over and over again until he has exhausted himself. No one comes to see him anymore. His sister, Margaret, used to come and attend to his needs, but she has long since died after a tragic life. In fact, her life was as tragic as his. She once revealed that she had lost several children at birth and her husband to drowning. Nevertheless, she was able to communicate with him in such a way that I often suspected they were bonded together in some terrible secret. Whatever it was they concealed she would not communicate, nor would she cooperate with me. She took this secret with her to the grave, leaving her poor brother alone with whatever painful terror he holds inside. She once brought some old letters which she wanted him to have, but made me promise not to read them. I agreed to her request. These letters seemed to comfort him, but he never lets them out of his sight. I believe they are a record of one of his voyages to Archangel."

"May we see him alone for a time? It may be that we can find some common ground," said Golem in a reassuring tone.

"That will be fine, Sir Astley. Perhaps you could succeed, where all other attempts have failed, to communicate with him."

Dr. Creda stuck the huge metal key into the door. The metal hinges moaned from the rust as the door was opened. We walked in and Dr. Creda said "Call out when you are ready. I will inform the attendant. He will be close by." He gave us a half smile, sympathetic it seemed, as he backed out and closed the door behind us.

My attention was drawn to Captain Walton's appearance as he sat on the floor. He was dirty. His beard was unevenly grown and ragged; the ends had thickened into globs. His trousers were in tatters just below the knee. His clothes were filthy and smelled of excrement. The poor man looked deathly ill. Though he was not particularly thin his skin looked drawn and shriveled. It was like that of a dry wasted fruit having been tossed to the ground. At first he said nothing, but within a few seconds raised his head to stare at us, then dropped it again. I had never seen a man more pitiful; his condition held me immobile.

Golem spoke to him. "Hello, Captain Walton. I am Dr. Astley Golem and this is my assistant, Mr. Joshua Hamel. We would like to have a few words with you."

Captain Walton remained on the floor with his head between his knees and his hands grasping his shins.

I lowered myself to his level and began speaking. "We have come a long way to discuss Victor Frankenstein, and the monster he created."

Captain Walton's head moved and soon his sunken watery eyes were visible. His shirt was torn at the elbows, and where he held his arms across his legs, his veins bulged from the grip. I stood. His eyes slowly raised themselves up toward my face, and, as they came into contact with mine, a fear gripped and paralyzed me with horror. I glanced away, but the sensation persisted. I felt a cold shudder in my limbs. A weakness then came over me which I took for a fever. Why should a stare create such an insecurity in my emotional state? I had seen the stares of cadavers. I had seen the stares of people who had died in utter fear. The look in this man's eyes was not unlike that of such a corpse, yet he was alive! His gaze left a mark upon my soul; it ripped something away from me that was incomprehensible.

I managed to speak. "We have come to discuss with you the legend, or the reality of the account given to us by Captain Amos. We want to know of your extreme experience in the icy regions of the north, past Bear Island and beyond Novaya Zemlya."

Into my soul he looked for a time, but finally, after measuring me, turned toward Dr. Golem. Having somehow satisfied whatever spirits drove him, he turned back to me, and in a trembling fearful voice said, "Listen to me! The monster lives! We are all doomed! Revenge!"

He was able to gather himself rather quickly. His recovery was quite strange. It was as if we fulfilled some prophesy that he had been awaiting. He had a bundle of papers with him as Creda had mentioned, which he identified as the entire Frankenstein story. I carefully watched his face as fearful wrinkles formed in the creases next to his eyes.

"Listen, then! Listen to my story," he said.

We listened for hours to his story. From his diary he provided us with a tale I shall never forget.

Walton's Diary, 1831

It was several days after this horrendous incident, with most of the mountains of ice now split and cracked enough for our journey southward, that I spied the gigantic creature once more. His solemn asseverations, which, just two days before, had been filled with gloom and sorrow for his misdeeds, were now transformed to rage in my eyepiece. I cried to the men to hoist the mainsail, to begin moving as quickly as possible, despite the danger of ice still strong enough to breech our hull. After shouting these commands I returned to my eyepiece, and could see the hideous bestial rage on the monster's face. He had bestrode a circular-shaped piece of ice, and while lying on the bow of his craft, was striking his arms wildly into the water, propelling the ice sheet forward toward the ship.

It did not take long for the creature to traverse the distance between us, and, after realizing he had propelled the craft forward with enough thrust, he jumped up onto the ice, straddling it, and braced himself for the collision. I was frozen with fear; I knew that the fiend was endowed with superhuman strength. My thoughts were of the loaded pistols I kept in my chest. I felt the ice raft strike the starboard bow as I ran toward my cabin. I scrambled down the stairs so quickly that I fell and tumbled down the last set of steps. The pain from the fall was subdued by the terror that gripped me. I thought of Frankenstein's family and friends, murdered by the powerful arms of this fiend, who had now abandoned his remorse in favor of revenge upon us all.

Never could I forget the tenaciousness in his eyes, which struck out at me like steel projectiles, stabbing at me through my eyepiece. As I opened the chest I could hear the monster on deck.

"Revenge is all I possess! It is closer to my heart than my

most hopeless sorrows! I will live long enough to blast your hopes into oblivion! And your dreams of a bright future will be drowned in an ocean of blood and carnage! No other reason for living! You shall be cursed for your hypocrisy and inhumanity! Beware! This is only the beginning of your demise!"

I recognized these frightening words. They were words once directed at Victor Frankenstein. But Victor was dead, and the words that I now heard were directed at us all. I could hear screams of agony and thuds of bodies being slammed into the mast rigging and onto the deck. I was now shaking with fear. I fumbled for my two pistols.

I furtively moved up the stairs from my cabin and looked out onto the deck. There several of my crew had been impaled on whale hooks, while others were lying in pools of blood. The scene was fantastic! They seemed mere insects stuck on the point of a pin. I surreptitiously watched from my vantage point, but could not spy the malignant creature. I made my way out onto the deck and headed toward the bow. It was not long before I heard a crash. The coldness of the sound debilitated my spirit further. I determined that the noise had come from my cabin. I raised my weapons and held them at arm's length and slowly moved back in the direction from which I had come. I descended the stairs, but before I could get to my cabin entrance the ship began to sway from severe jolts that made the entire ship shudder. I lost my balance. I struggled back up the stairs against the rocking of the ship, fearing that we had drifted into an ice sheet that had pierced our hull. I could discern nothing, and so I again went down to my cabin. When I reached the cabin entrance I could see the monster standing in sea water which was now waist deep He was removing the body of Victor from his coffin which was floating in the rising water. The water was gushing into my cabin from a large gash in the floor.

The icy water filled the cabin rapidly as the fiend secured the corpse of his creator. Then, holding Victor's corpse over his shoulder he turned to face me. His hideous grin I shall never forget. He leaped out into the open sea swimming toward an island of ice. I could not for long concern myself with his departure as my ship was sinking.

The whole of the ship was going down into the icy waters. I hurried up to the deck in the hope that some of the crew had escaped the vengeful monster. I searched for them, but none had survived the terrible carnage. The ship was sinking rapidly. There was nothing I could do at this point. My only course of action was to throw myself overboard, on the very icy sheet that the creature had commanded. I fell very hard and almost lost consciousness, and lay face down on the icy raft for some time. During this frightful event I had somehow managed to clutch the ship's records and my diary which recorded the story of Frankenstein. I locked them in my hands with a grip that pained my arms. I remained there for a time, frozen and numb. I do not know how long I lay before I was awakened by a splash, which was a coffin that rose to the surface and turned out to be my salvation. Some days later I was rescued by Captain Solomon Amos.

On board Captain Amos' ship I was provided warmth and a bed. I lay in a state of torpor for days. Though my body began to warm, my thoughts remained locked in a frozen coma of fear. It was only after the low cold clouds of winter began to break that I felt enough courage to raise my head from the bed that was provided for me.

Captain Amos had a stern countenance. The lines in his face were wind-beaten and cracked by the many icy voyages he had made to the northern regions. His eyes were glassy—not of the glassiness associated with sleep and fatigue but of wisdom and hardness. His gaze was not unlike that of a bull. It was a window through which his strong will focused with penetrating savage depth.

When I first became fully aware of him, he was sitting beside my bed, staring intently into my face. Finally he spoke to me. "You have regained some spirit, Captain Walton," he said. "Here, drink some rum to quell your peripatetic soul."

I sat up and noticed that in my right hand I still clutched the narratives of this whole horror.

"You have held onto the ships records and your personal papers with such duty," Amos said, "that I could not but wonder what secrets are held within those leaves. I tried once to separate you from your burden, but your grip was like that of a vise. I made no further attempts. When we came upon you on the ice, and in a black coffin, my men became quite fearful. To see such a thing in the center of a floating ice raft, in this hell, struck terror into our hearts. Many thought that we should have left you there; my crew thought it was an omen of evil, a curse to be avoided. You could not have known the effect that was left upon the souls of my crew upon seeing you as you were! Many of them related to the first mate that they would never sail the ocean again. What has happened to your ship?"

I could not answer. My eyes sank to the papers in my hand and remembrance of the horrid events drowned my spirit. Soon, the images of the events grew vivid; I could see myself on the ice sheet. The events became clearer of the moments just before my rescue. I had tried to forget. I could see the aberration repeated. As the fog that covered my thoughts lifted I remembered what had occurred. The creature had bobbed his head up and out of the frigid water. He placed his hands on the ice raft, pitching it from side to side. I was awakened, and instinctively dug my frozen fingers into the ice as best as I could in an effort to hold on. Several times I almost lost my grip. Soon I was forced to let the bundle of papers go. I saw the papers slide towards the edge. I frantically crawled across the distance of ice, which was now sloped downward as a result of the creature's heaving. He was trying desperately to separate me from the bundle. I was fully conscious now and struggled toward the edge before the papers were lost to the depths. Just as the tottering records appeared to be lost, the crazed fiend placed his weight on the ice on the opposite side and with a heave caused them to slide back towards me. I seized my priceless papers and placed them inside my coat so that both of my hands would be free to hold on. Just then the rocking stopped. The monster, with the body of Frankenstein in his possession, swam away toward the icy land ahead.

My ship was gone. Only a few items remained afloat, none of which seemed of any use to me. My limbs began to shudder from the cold. I surveyed the floating objects, hoping to find something that would aid in my survival. I was almost overcome with fear at the thought of freezing to death when I heard air bubbles just next to the ice raft. Incredibly, the coffin that we had prepared for Victor Frankenstein erupted from the icy waters. It was now floating on the surface. I rushed over to the edge and with all of my strength pulled the death crib onto the ice. Miraculously, the bedding it contained was dry.

The coffin was a blessing. I climbed into it to protect

myself from the cold. I was forced to close myself in to escape the cold wind. I used pages from the ship's log to maintain a small crack through which to see. I looked out through the crack and prayed for a ship to rescue me; I prayed for warmth — or a speedy death.

My craft floated out farther from the island of ice, out into the open sea. I now only desired sleep, being completely exhausted. Despite my perilous condition I wondered what thoughts would cross the minds of seamen seeing a lonely black coffin resting upon a pure white sheet of floating ice. I soon resigned myself to hopelessness. I knew I was doomed. I prayed for forgiveness. I was totally alone. There was no other sound except the howl of an icy wind and the throbbing sea. I closed the crack in the coffin further, allowing only a few leaves of paper to separate me from the light outside. I lost consciousness and became one with the cold darkness within. I do not know how long I lay in this state before I was rescued.

After a time I awoke in the captain's quarter. I heard a distant voice which I later came to know as that of Captain Amos.

"Come to, man! Get a hold!" he implored.

My dark reverie subsided, and, as I raised my head and eyes to meet those of Captain Amos, I realized that the horror was real. My experience resembled a dream, a nightmare, and this nightmare produced a rolling viscous cloud that engulfed me in a maelstrom of terror; the confusion of my thoughts took on a gaseous quality which roiled around in my head like a fever.

"Get a hold mate, get a hold! You have miraculously escaped from certain death. Take hold!"

At first I could only scream from the depths of my horror, "He lives, sir, he lives! This is only the beginning of the terror! My life was spared to tell you that he lives! He is not finished with us. Set sail quickly or we will all perish! Perish! Perish!"

I could not untangle my fearful thoughts but nevertheless somehow managed to warn the captain. I gave him the ship's log and my diary. He went away and did not return for what seemed like an eternity. Finally he returned the papers to me and I remember fading into a trance. In my half-conscious state I released my records and let them drop to the floor. As they fell, my eyes opened slightly, and I could see the figure of Captain Amos standing near. His blurred form cleared, and it was then that these words parted my lips; "Tell no one what you have read. Have the records placed in a vault and sealed. I shall keep my diary, but take the logs! Confide only in the highest authority. These records must be secured and put away forever. Those who have violated the laws of nature and God's trust should never be able to come in contact with the creature. To all others let the account become a legend, a folk tale, passed on by an insane old sea captain whose tale of terror must be no more than an invention of the mind."

* * *

His story concluded, Walton took a deep breath, and, after a moment said, "Now, now you have it! It is true. The fiend lives! I am certain, even after all of this time that the fiend still lives, lives in those icy regions near Novaya Zemlya. It is a curse that has led you here to me."

His face turned to gloom as he leaned back against the wall and slowly slid to the floor.

We had come for only one reason — the coordinates. I remember asking him, "Can you tell us the latitude and longitude of the region where your ship went down?"

"I knew the day would come," he said. "Men strive for things they will never understand. We do not even understand ourselves!"

He gave us the headings which would put us just north of Novaya Zemlya. Within seconds after this he jerked his head back and forth, wide-eyed. He looked at me with a cutting stare that penetrated deep into my soul. He seemed to have awakened or surprised himself with his own words. He was calmed by taking deep breaths. Finally, he said, in a most normal tone, "Why? Why do you want to know? What do you plan on doing?"

Golem answered him. "We are going to recover the remains if we can. Perhaps the bodies are still intact, if they have not been ravaged by animals and are on solid ice. We will be able to help mankind rid itself of disease and perhaps increase our longevity by examining this creation."

"You are mad, Dr. Golem. You are as mad as Victor Frankenstein." He was becoming exercised with alarm again. "You will not find a corpse! You will not only destroy yourselves but all of us as well if you return the monster! Do you hear me! Do you hear me?"

Walton stared at us wildly, looking from Golem to me. Then he lurched up from the floor, clutched my throat, and screamed at me. I struggled, but his grip was like a vise. He would not relinquish his grasp. Golem just stood there frozen. I managed to wrest control of Walton's hands, forcing them downward until I was able to embrace him so that he could do no further harm. Then Golem approached Walton from behind and managed to pull him away. I gasped for breath.

As Walton's sudden frenzy ended, he suddenly went limp and slumped to the floor. I half stumbled as he fell and managed to scoop up his diary and papers and stuff them inside my coat. Poor Walton was not aware of my theft as he resumed his earlier posture; his head went between his knees as he was when we first arrived.

I struggled to gather my breath and my thoughts. Finally I said to Golem, "Let us go. We now have what we need. We can do nothing to help this poor devil. Let us make haste from this place before we fall victim to the horrors that lie here."

Dr. Golem seized my shoulder, directed me to the door, and called the attendant. I had second thoughts about the latitude and longitude and called out, "Are you sure, Captain Walton, about the location of the incident, are you sure?"

As Dr. Golem helped me out the door, Captain Walton looked up and said in a soft, haunting, barely audible voice, "I am sure. You have doomed us all. Your kind has doomed us all, if not you, then another like you. You have doomed the world." He fell into a stupor, whispering, "You have doomed the world." His whispers echoed down the hallway and finally sank to silence.

As we walked back toward the entrance I could hear the lock roll and the door shut, but its clank was over-powered by the echoes of Walton's whisper. We walked past the attendant's station and upstairs to thank Dr. Creda.

We soon found ourselves in the outer chamber of Dr. Creda's office where he was reading in a big chair by the window. The view from his window was splendid. It reminded me of a portal connecting us between here and forever. I was mesmerized by the sight. The distant sea could be seen from this vantage point. I once again pictured myself floating above the field of vision. I was adrift above the sea. The blue sky lay out ahead. I drifted out faster and faster toward a point beyond the horizon. My mind turned from these thoughts as I pondered on Captain Walton's writings, which I had taken during the scuffle. I pushed the papers deep into my coat as Dr. Creda addressed us.

"Ah, Doctor Golem and Mr. Hamel, I see you have completed your work. How was your visit?" said Dr. Creda.

"It was as you have told us. We were unable to unchain his spirit from the hell that holds him," Golem said.

"Then you will try again?"

"No, not at this time, Dr. Creda. I think perhaps we have seen enough. We want to thank you for your time and your cooperation in this matter."

Dr. Creda looked at us skeptically and asked, "What did you hope to learn, Dr. Golem?"

"I wanted to see the depths of despair firsthand. To see the manifestations of a troubled mind and to perhaps draw on my insights to explain such behavior as we have witnessed," said Golem. "We must reflect on the things we have seen and extrapolate. This will take time. I will be glad to share it with you when I have drawn on those insights and have made some connections. Now we really must be going as we have several appointments to keep. Again, I thank you, sir."

Creda said nothing, but his skeptical look did not subside as he bade us a cool farewell with the wave of a hand.

Out in the slush we tramped over to our carriage and boarded. I had pulled my overcoat tightly around me and felt the weight of Walton's papers against my body. I am not sure why I so mistrusted Dr. Golem, even at this early date, that I concealed from him my acquisition of these documents. Some inner prompting bade me keep them hidden from him.

The coachman tipped his hat and at once directed his horses out of the sanitarium entrance. We were soon on our way back to the city. We said very little to one another on the return trip. I kept my eyes focused on the surrounding countryside, on the desolate, cold, and windy landscape. The trees flashed by in a blur, and rocky crags jutted out of the white ice like darkened teeth. *"You have doomed the world!"* The words of Walton would not be subdued from my thoughts. I felt a deep pity for him while I looked out the coach window. I was unable to comprehend his experience and grasp its full meaning. How could an achievement as great as the making of such a creature be a bad omen? His thoughts must have come from his own ignorance, from his station in life. I thought he could not comprehend or appreciate the advances of mankind, or the desire of the learned to discover nature's laws. He could in no way understand the need to discover the secrets of life and to prolong the lives of men; his limited education would not permit it. It did trouble me that a man such as he, a sea captain, curious, adventurous, and experienced in foreign horizons even unknown to me, could have been so horrified at the creation. A little stoicism would have helped him. He gave in too easily to Frankenstein's advice; he should not have rejected ambition.

We arrived at our laboratory within several hours and immediately began to discuss what such a find would mean. Our experiments with cold would be aided in two areas. First, if the monster's remains could be recovered they should be well preserved given the extreme temperatures of the northern regions. We would be able to make comparisons on the length of time and the average temperature needed to maintain and best preserve tissues. Tissues that had become freeze burned could be compared with better samples from the same cadaver, and adjusted experimentally for the best temperature setting over time in the laboratory. We could study the formation of ice crystals in the blood and make adjustments in our methods. Through comparative analysis we would be able to compare tissue samples from the creature with frozen animal corpses. The possibilities were endless!

Secondly, if the monster could somehow be revived by use of artificial blood, we would have an experimental subject that would be more valuable than any animal. We could only hope for this scenario, since the body had first to be found and the temperature fluctuations had to be within certain limits.

These possibilities would have incomprehensible consequences but would also create problems if our aims were made known to the authorities. If the creature could be transported into the future along with us — which was Golem's intent — the general perception of men, I thought, would then be advanced enough for us to reveal our secrets and success with immortality. As time goes on diseases will have been cured at different intervals and thus life extended forever; I am confident that life will be extended until old age itself is conquered. With the future bright I could think of no reason why science would not develop to the stage of accepting our aims and goals. What is sacrilege now will be commonly accepted thought later; such is the way of history. I am sure of it.

* * *

We wanted to be certain that the coordinates given to us by Walton were accurate. We went again to Captain Amos. He reluctantly confirmed them by his records which he kept by his Bible near the mantel. At first his face was sullen, but as we were leaving it turned to darkened gloom. Having confirmed the coordinates we thanked Captain Amos and turned to leave. But before we did so, Amos moved to the door and momentarily blocked our retreat. I shall never forget the look in his eye, or the sound of his voice when he said, "I shall pray for you. When I came upon that dreadful black coffin, upon the ice, I should have known it was a terrible omen. Ambition is what I see in your eyes. I have seen the face of doom before. I shall pray for you!"

* * *

July 15, 1848

I was on my way, by carriage, to the laboratory to review some experimental notes, when an incident occurred, the memory of which would last forever.

There was a storm brewing and the skyhad darkened considerably. Lightning was flashing and was accompanied by loud, heavy thunder. The storm came upon the city rapidly. The horses became quite nervous. Upon our approach and turn down a narrow alleyway, the horses bolted as lightning struck a lamppost. The driver lost control, and as we raced down the street I heard a cry and looked out of the window to see a woman being thrown in the air. She had been struck by our horse. The driver regained control and brought us to a stop.

I jumped from the carriage and ran to where the poor woman had come to rest on the cobblestones. A quick inspection did not reveal any open wounds and she appeared to be in a semi-conscious state. I pulled out my handkerchief and gently wiped her face, which was now wet from the beginning rain.

She began to stir and soon opened her eyes. Though the lids fluttered and her gaze was uncertain, I could not help but notice how beautiful she was. She spoke to me thus, "What happened? I . . . was on my way. . .to my destination . . . before the storm broke, when . . . I am here, on the ground. . ."

Her voice was soft and melodious. Just then the rain began to pelt us with strength. "I must get you out of the rain," I said. "I am Joshua Hamel. I am a physician. Come, let me attend to you. I must get you to a dry place."

She nodded her head slightly and closed her eyes. I carried her to my coach and the driver opened the door. I gently laid her across the seat and instructed the coachman to drive to my apartment. My medicines and physician's bag were there. I could thus provide her with the help that she needed.

Upon arrival I carried her inside and laid her upon the bed in the guest room. I obtained a towel which I placed on her forehead. She now felt warm when I checked for fever. Within moments she awakened.

"Where am I?" she asked.

"You were unconscious and could not be left upon the street in such condition," I said. Her eyes now seemed a little brighter and I do not believe I had ever seen such perfectly round eyes. They were beautiful. "I am a physician and you are in my apartment. Please do not be concerned about being here alone. This is my attendant." I introduced the female servant as she returned with some warm water and fresh towels. The invalid's face relaxed and a lock of her hair fell across her forehead. Her hair was a dark auburn and her long eyelashes swept her lovely face. I was completely hypnotized by her beauty. The frightful pallor which had covered her face was now completely lifted.

"You told me your name. Was it Joshua I heard?" she asked.

"Yes, it is Joshua Hamel. I am a surgeon at the anatomy school of Sir Astley Golem," I responded.

She looked off and grimaced as she tried to sit up. She was about to say something when there passed between us that magic current which sometimes flows from eye to eye. It was without any known reason that our eyes mingled. She looked at me with the sweetness of a loving heart. I looked back into her eyes and could only smile. I did not want her to think wrongful things of me, and so moved away to prepare a sedative for her to sleep through the night. As I did so, I asked her to move her limbs, which she did, so that I might be assured that no bones were broken.

"Please drink this. It will help you to recover. Rest, and I will send word to your relatives as to your condition."

I instructed the housemaid to obtain her name and address. As she was doing so, my patient said to me in a soft voice, "My name is Jane Singleton."

I looked upon her once more, for her eyes were like magnets to me. I tried not to look too long and instructed her to drink the sedative. She did and turned on her side. I retreated from the room, leaving her in the care of the housemaid.

As I would need to be at my laboratory quite early the following day, I instructed the coachman, who had waited below, to drive her home when she had rested, if she felt well enough to leave. The next day the coachman informed me that Jane was taken home in good health and had left a letter. It read thus:

Dear Joshua Hamel,

I thank you for your kindness. I am sorry that we had to meet this way, for you are a gentleman. Your kindness will be remembered. If by chance you are free from your obligations tomorrow, I would like for you to dine with me and my uncle. He will want to meet the man who saved his niece.

Please do come, so that I may repay your kindness.

Sincerely,
Jane Singleton

I was happy. I would not miss this appointment for anything.

The following day I concluded my work at the laboratory and hurried to my apartment to make myself ready for my engagement with Jane. I put on my best clothes and spent a great deal of time at the mirror. I had not done such a thing for a very long time.

Upon arrival at Jane's home, I was greeted by a friendly house servant who said I was expected. She took my hat and cloak and ushered me in. As soon as I crossed the threshhold I beheld the beautiful Jane waiting on the staircase. Her eyes were as beautiful as before, and that magical feeling of electricity once again sparked the space between us.

"It is so good to see you," she said.

"It is my pleasure. I wanted nothing more than to be here. I . . ." I wanted to say more. I wanted to express the fact that she was beautiful beyond words but I felt so awkward. I was so unlike others. I could not throw myself into making advances with women as I had seen so many other men do. Most men disrespect the lovely essence of women. As much as I wanted to, I could not say anything else. I could only stand there.

"Come," she said. "Come into the dining room with me. My uncle wants to meet you."

In the dining room, Jane's uncle sat at the head of the table. He was very old but with the kindest of faces.

"I am Paul Singleton, Jane's uncle," he said. "I have been informed that you saved my niece's life."

"I am not sure that I did all of that, sir," I answered. "She is a strong young woman. I am truly sorry for what has happened. My horse bolted and . . ."

"You need not explain," Mr. Singleton said. "An act of God cannot be determined. Things happen for a reason. We do not always know the reason why things happen."

We sat down for dinner and enjoyed talking about science and the nature of things. Mr. Singleton was quite knowledgeable. After a time, he began to ask me about my work. I did not want to go into details and was relieved when he changed the subject. I was, however, in for a surprise.

"I understand that you work with Sir Astley," he said in a grim voice.

"Yes, I do. He is a doctor of great knowledge. He . . ." I was cut short.

"I will leave you," Singleton said. "You and my niece may want to get more acquainted. I must say that I do not approve of Sir Astley Golem. He is a monster! I know this. It is well known by many citizens of London. You had better be warned. Your relationship with Sir Astley can only lead to disaster for you."

I said nothing, as the thought of being alone with Jane was the foremost thing on my mind. Mr. Singleton left us.

"Jane," I said, "you look well. I am happy that you are recovered."

"I am well," she said. "I am pleased that you came to dine with us."

My lips could not hold back the feelings I had. My smile came so quickly that I felt embarrassed. "I saw the beauty in your eyes last evening and I see it still. You are as an angel to me," I said.

I thank God that she saw the humility on my face. Instead of being taken aback by my bluntness she smiled and said, "You are a gentleman. My eyes felt your heart. Do not be ashamed. You are wonderfully clumsy with women, it would appear. It is nice to see a man with a sincere heart."

She smiled, looking down for a moment. As she raised her head she said this to me, "I am free. I would like to become better acquainted with you."

I am sure my face was beaming with pleasure at her remark, and she returned my smile in kind. However, she walked away from me, and I wondered if I had said or done something wrong. As she looked out of the window with her back to me, she said, "There is one thing. How can you work with Doctor Golem? He is a dangerous man. Many have heard of his belligerence. He has hurt many."

Jane related how Golem had used the services of solicitors to evict people from their homes. I did not want to believe these things. Doctor Golem was an ambitious and intelligent man. He was the most intelligent individual I had ever met. Perhaps he had a few flaws in his character but his scientific wisdom was priceless.

Before I could say another word Jane broke in. "Enough of this. I would llike it very much if I could see you again." I would never forget these words. It was difficult to say goodbye.

In the ensuing days, our relationship blossomed, and the Void that made me feel empty inside subsided for a time. I told her about the upcoming journey to the North. Though we had only known each other for a short time, our love grew very rapidly.

Golem's Research Journal

I became interested in anatomy at an early age. My father, a surgeon by profession, was not a loquacious man. However, he did demonstrate to me the importance of science. He often without a word took me to his laboratory where I watched him dissect bodies. My mother and father were divorced when I was a small child. It was my father who raised me. He introduced me to sound financial practices and early on started me to a life of success.

I have studied cold and its effects on the human body for some time. I decided that since my studies were ongoing, consistent, and my commitment strong, a name for this old but new science was needed. Since biological organisms and cold were being studied together, I decided to call this new science "Kryology" and "Biokryology." Kryology would be the study of cold and Biokryology the study of cold as it relates to living organisms.

I became quite interested in this study as a result of first reading a translation from the Egyptians that I ran across by accident, and then the hypothermic recommendations of Hippocrates. These were my predecessors. Thomas Bartholini whose master was Severno of Italy wrote the first book of Kryology in 1661. His *Refrigeranda* provided me with some ideas on how ice could be used in the treatment of various medical problems such as hemorrhaging. I was particularly interested in the anesthetic use of cold that Bartholini wrote about so wonderfully.

More recent investigators, such as Baron Larrey who wrote his *Surgical Memoirs* of military campaigns of Russia, Germany, and France, gave me more insight. I read about how pain could be reduced in amputation with the application of cold. But most importantly, a surgeon at Middlesex Hospital discovered that by freezing some eggs at a temperature of almost zero, and then defrosting them, they could be conserved. It was with this research that I realized the prospects of immortality through freezing.

I set out to experiment on cadavers and smaller creatures. I was aided in my efforts when some very critical discoveries were made in regard to the microscope. Lenses have been recently improved, as well as higher powers of magnification. The studies of cells by various experts were made available to me, and with this knowledge I was able to overcome several difficulties.

Science has discovered the nucleus and the living substance called protoplasm. This stream of life, as I call it, is at the core of my theories. Under the microscope I discovered that the cells of most mammals were almost entirely made up of water. I was able to calculate the water content, which prompted me to study how freezing actually affected it. Through a microscope I observed that when an animal was frostbitten the cells and stream of life around them were crystallized.

At first, the cells of blood were found freely floating in their fluids. When these cells were subjected to cold, ice formations or crystals created channels between cells. When this occurred it caused the blood cells to diffuse along the channels. Cellular destruction could then be seen as adjacent cells collapsed into unorganized globs of blood. Cell destruction from freezing could not be stopped. The degenerative changes caused by the formation of ice crystals would not allow for revival of life after freezing. It was at this point that I began to experiment with colder and colder temperatures.

During my quest for immortality I discovered that the killing of cells could be propitious in cases where diseased skin needed removal. I was not interested in this aspect, however, and decided that I would pass on this information to Joshua Hamel. Later, Hamel used this knowledge to reattach severed limbs. I proceeded in my efforts and discovered that the biological systems of animals could be returned to normal function if the surrounding fluids did not freeze. I studied the prolonged effects of this as a function of temperature. I realized that a cadaver frozen over a long period would be an ideal subject if it could be restored or part of the cells revived. This discovery is what made it necessary to search for the being created by Frankenstein. The creature's blood and cell structure must somehow be different to have been impervious to cold. It would provide the resources needed to complete my work.

My experiments with cooling and thawing were not in vain. I realized that the survival of the cell depended on the rate at which cooling and thawing occurred. I was able to establish that rapid cooling produced fewer ice crystals, and that rapid warming caused the ice between the cells to melt so quickly that damage could be avoided. At first, I could only freeze cells at -20 degrees centigrade, using a salt and ice mixture. My findings led me to the conclusion that lower temperatures were needed if preservation was to be accomplished for long periods of time. The cooling velocity and thawing velocities were crucial in this preservation, as was the temperature. I discovered that I could best freeze cells — and prevent destruction most — by rapid cooling and slow thawing. My studies showed that the survival or destruction of cells depended on these factors. I was at a loss, however, to achieve temperatures colder than -20 degrees centigrade until I returned to past studies.

I found that Boyle and Gary-Lussac discovered that gases heat up when compressed and cool down when expanded. I was able to liquefy air by passing compressed air through a cooler and throttling it through valves. The air then drained out in a receptacle as a liquid. My goal was to achieve temperatures near or below -150 degrees centigrade. This temperature does not occur even in the coldest regions of the earth. I had calculated that -150 degrees was the barrier I needed to cross in order to freeze cells without large amounts of ice crystals forming in the blood.

After long hours of toil, both day and night, I was finally able to construct a device to liquefy nitrogen. I was overjoyed when my measurements were complete and the temperature of my liquid was -210 degrees Fahrenheit (-195 C). At this temperature cell activity ceased, and no biologic functions took place. The cell itself ceased to age. Most importantly, ice crystals were at a minimum at this temperature.

As my work progressed I created a silver-tipped kyroprobe which I called "The Wand." I could pour the liquid nitrogen into the top of it and then probe into diseased tissue to remove it. My "wand" was like magic. It fused diseased tissue and allowed for the rapid recovery of the area affected. The device was as large as a hunting knife, but could be held comfortably in one hand.

It was a marvelous stroke of fortune that I obtained some information about frogs that completely freeze during the winter months, and I was able to acquire a few specimens. I discovered that three species of frog found in the north of America could tolerate temperatures below freezing for over six months with almost all of their body fluids frozen. Under the microscope I discovered large amounts of glycerol in their body tissues and fluids that were not present in the warmer months. I was able to keep the creatures alive long enough to measure the glycerol levels in the summer. To my surprise, this level changed drastically in the summer to almost zero. In the organs, especially in the liver, the glycerol increased in the fall and then dropped off in the spring. In fact, I have proven this in the lab by lowering a specimen's temperature and recording the glycerol levels and their variations when the temperatures returned to normal.

I also created a preservative, whose ingredients I kept secret, that preserved tissue after death, which allowed greater time for dissections. After further study I realized that this solution lowered the freezing point of blood and would therefore act as a deterrent to the formation of ice in the body and in the cell. I deduced that all of a man's blood could be removed and this special solution introduced into the body for freezing at the liquid nitrogen level.

It was by such experimentation that I was able to achieve partial success in recovering viable tissue, after freezing, with the aid of glycerol. The recovery of red cells after freezing was accomplished with some degree of success by varying the rate of freezing and thawing as well as varying the glycerol concentrations between thirty and fifty percent. The liver of the frog provided the best clues for my discoveries. I came to understand that when seasons changed, the general size, pigmentation, and the cell contents changed. In the summer the liver of most northern specimens was quite large and light in color, while in the winter the liver became smaller and dark. I was able to construct a chart of the variations which showed that in the spring glycerol was often at trace amounts, but in the fall it would increase to 1.44 percent of the frog's body weight.

Soon thereafter I began experimenting with blood. I used various sugar solutions to freeze blood at a variety of temperatures. I discovered that with the right solution, at a temperature of -196 degrees centigrade, I could recover blood after three years. After these successes came more important discoveries with spermatozoa. I used goat, pig, cow, horse, and sheep spermatozoa, and was successful in yielding mobile sperm after freezing. Without the kryo-protective action of my sugar solution none of the frozen cells yielded a recoverable spermatozoa.

How then did Frankenstein's monster survive? Was his biological system capable of producing large amounts of glycerol? If I could study his biological system perhaps I could duplicate the change in man, either making the changing of the blood with a glycerol solution unnecessary or enhancing it with another solution.

I moved ahead. Little did I know at the time that more remarkable discoveries lay ahead. Spermatozoa were easy to obtain. After first using animal spermatozoa, I began to use my own for experiments on human sperm. To obtain ova, however, I had to pay resurrection men to bring in fresh cadavers for extraction of ova from the womb. I had discovered these disgusting people known as resurrectionists when I was a young student and happened to see my father pay them for their service on several occasions. Repulsive as was their activity, their ability to obtain cadavers on demand was needed for the advancement of science.

I was aided by the 1776 work of Lazzaro Spallanzani on the kryopreservation of human sperm, but for ova no one possessed the knowledge of manipulation until now.

It became necessary for me to invent several micro-tools for manipulation of the ova in order to study fertilized eggs. I wanted to confirm my belief that fertilized eggs would be more resistant to low temperatures with the proper solution of protective agents. Finally, I was able to obtain a young female cadaver. It was difficult to get one fresh enough for my needs. I was bound by science to do what had to be done. The young female was a burden upon society and her sacrifice was necessary. I put her to sleep after the abduction outside one of the poorhouses. It was then that necessity became the mother of invention. I not only developed a mouth-controlled suction device for extraction, but discovered how to fertilize ova in a small dish. I developed a microsurgical apparatus to accomplish this goal. I was able to obtain the services of a manufacturer to develop tiny needles, scissors, and scalpels, which I fitted to a screw-controlled apparatus that I could manipulate under a microscope. It was necessary to put the woman out of her misery. She had been a waste until now.

The area around the ova was at first very difficult to penetrate by needle. The zone around the egg was resilient and spongy, helping it to resist penetration. I soon learned that microscopic glass needles were better suited for penetrating the plasma membrane surrounding the egg. I was able to penetrate the egg with a microneedle, hollow inside, and inject sperm. I was, however, in for a disappointment. I discovered that developing embryos outside of the reproductive tract were subject to destruction by white blood cells unless they were immersed in a stabilizing agent. I experimented with many agents before realizing that the jellylike substance in red albumin would stabilize the egg while it developed.

It was by accident that I learned to fertilize a human ova outside of the body and to freeze it for later retrieval. From the cadavers of pregnant women I extracted ova and fertilized it with my own sperm. I froze these products and placed them in storage for later studies. On one occasion I found a fertilized egg in a cadaver which I was able to rescue by freezing. I was able to observe and sustain the development of an embryo for thirty weeks after freezing. When the products ceased to function I placed them in small kryo-containers for later use. I was thus able to grow human beings up to eight months for my use in the laboratory.

I discovered that all freezing protective agents should contain protein to control the variations in alkalinity and acidity within the cells. During experiments I used various water-soluble proteins of bovine blood, milk, egg whites, and other suitable substances. It was later that I discovered that my fluid contained some extracted solutions which, when mixed with glycerol, proved to be a better freezing agent for immersion in liquid nitrogen and the final freezing phase.

It soon became possible to fertilize embryos and implant them into other human beings. I was able to begin experiments with freezing embryos at different stages of development. These life forms made it possible for me to envision a future earth made up of children from the scientific community, frozen and implanted into specially chosen women. Not only will we be able to repopulate the earth with immortals but with the immortals of choice.

I am perhaps the first to use such a technical procedure for scientific manipulation of life. It would be well for me to develop the ethical issues at stake before people like Hamel begin their wailing against it. Embryos removed through the skill of a surgeon should be the property of the surgeon who removed them, to use as he deems necessary. To bring mankind to the threshold of immortality I will need frozen fertilized ova. Each failure must be preserved for experimentation.

The fear of death, which haunts us all like a spectre, is the wellspring of all of life's activities; these are activities often designed to ignore and avoid the inescapable hand of death. I have never come to terms with death nor will I ever accept its ultimate victory. In fact, I have rejected its final claim. With the kryo-unit I can stop the decay of the body. I have always been disgusted at the morbid feeling that overcomes me when I go to a cemetery. I have always been intensely conscious of the fact that after a time even the tombstones will be gone. The extreme morbidity that I have always felt for death drives me to defeat it. I will do so at all costs.

There will be those who say that the embryos I experiment with should be respected. I say that they are from cadavers and as such were destined to die. I have plucked them from certain death and so they are my property by right. The right of scientific research cannot be hindered by those seeking consent. If we were to wait for the consent of the relatives — or of Parliament — we would never be able to conduct procedures that clearly will benefit all. The humanization of medicine is impossible, for our aims are different from those who live ordinary lives.

We surgeons are not at the service and whims of human religious belief or doctrine. We must have the authority to use embryos and human tissue as we see fit. It is the surgeons and medical researchers that know the real issues of life and death. We are responsible for such decisions. We must be ultimately responsible for the freezing of embryos and the repopulation of the world with immortals. If we can obtain immortality it will not be necessary to procreate, but, if we find it necessary to do so, we can simply grow the children we want for specific purposes. Some will claim that this type of procreation constitutes the demoralization of sexuality, but sperm from the dead can procreate again, and the life of an individual be continued.

Science *can* conquer all. The causes of war and poverty can all be eliminated with the reorganization of the earth. The earth can live in peace with the advent of Kryogenics; the earth can be populated with a kryo-population, free from the evils of mortality. There is nothing immoral in what I am attempting to do. I will resist all attempts to hinder my progress! I will be the first to live forever!

Hamel's Diary
August 1848

Dr. Golem and I were able to secure passage for the polar regions with an adventurous captain named Joel. He had posted news of his departure throughout London in the usual form of solicitation for a crew. We saw the advertisement on Jamaica Street, which was often plastered with posters of solicitation of departures. We went there to secure such information. We could not reveal our true intentions and agreed upon a ploy. We wrote down the information and on the following day we dispatched a letter, by courier, to Captain Artemus Joel. It read:

Dear Captain Joel,

I understand that you will be departing for the icy regions within the month and are presently looking for a crew. We seek to travel to the arctic region. If this is possible and within the range of your exploration we would like to accompany you there. We are looking for the remains of our dear cousins who sailed on the Romanov some years ago. As you may know, their ship was met with disaster as it was trapped in the ice, forcing the crew to abandon ship. Survivors have informed us that our cousins perished on the ice near Novaya Zemyla. Our relations desire that their bodies be returned to England so that they may be interred in the family vault.

We will pay you a handsome fee. No price would be too much to accomplish our family duty. We will compensate you for the passage and time needed as well as any additional equipment that we may need. We can provide compensation for any manual labor that may be required to retrieve the bodies.

We realize that this proposal may sound odd, but recovery of the bodies is of extreme importance to our family. Please consider this offer.

Sincerely,
Joshua Hamel, Surgeon
Astley Golem, M.D., M.R.C.S.

We soon received a short reply. It read:

Dear Drs. Hamel and Golem,

I am pleased to inform you that I would be more than happy to provide facility to undertake such an honorable mission. You may indeed book passage. We will be going to Archangel and will pass the area you indicate while looking for the Northeast Passage. We can work out suitable arrangements that I am sure will be to your liking. Please be at the Jamaica Street wharf this Friday by noon for discussion. Departure will be the following Friday.

Sincerely,
Captain Artemus Joel

We were elated and decided to celebrate our good fortune with a trip to a tavern. We acted like schoolboys, and when it became apparent that we had become a spectacle, we retired.

On Friday we went to the wharf and made all the necessary arrangements. Dr. Golem insisted that the captain take more than enough to cover our expenses. He forcefully told the captain not to make any inquiries of me concerning the retrieval of the bodies. The captain was made to understand that I would become very distraught if questioned in any way. The captain said, "I will ask no questions. The sum you have paid me is enough to quiet a storm."

On the following Friday we arrived for departure. The ship was named the *Loshkin*. It was to be our home for a considerable time. We noticed that the crew was loading some whiskey and rum barrels. We laughed together as we remembered our high-spirited celebration of the acceptance of our proposal and the large amounts of whisky we had consumed.

We went up the plank and onto the deck where the first officer greeted us. He was a friendly man, and in a most gentlemanly manner escorted us below to the captain's quarters. The captain's chamber was superior in orderliness. It was enhanced by rows of properly shelved books by some of the greatest authors. We noticed that he had books by Shakespeare, Newton, Pythagoras, Milton, and others.

On his table were his instruments of navigation: his telescope, maps, writing instruments, sextant. As we lowered ourselves down the last steps into his cabin he greeted us with a hearty handshake and a hug. We were quite pleased with his welcome, and, by and by, worked our way over to the maps.

"Tell me, can you gentlemen read maps?" Captain Joel asked.

"Yes, and able to help calculate our position. Ha! Look here, Hamel, Archangel and beyond," said Golem.

"Yes, Dr. Golem, I see. Perhaps we can show the good captain the intended course we wish to steer," I responded.

"Yes, I think we can," said Golem. "Captain, here we have Archangel. We will need to look at this north and east latitude. Yes . . . yes, we will be north of Novaya Zemlya at these coordinates. Novaya Zemlya lies here, between the Barents and Kara seas. Here, Barents on the west and Kara on the east. It is very cold there!"

"I am prepared to sail as far north as eighty degrees," Captain Joel said. "Novaya is indeed very cold. Its southern parts were cruised in 1556 and eventually circumnavigated. Part of the island was explored recently. The east coast was mapped as far as seventy-four degrees north. So you can see, gentlemen, we are going where few have preceded. A Captain Walton and a Captain Amos are said to have explored these extremes, but little has been reported about their voyages. I plan to make history, gentlemen, by sailing north of Novaya and beyond. When we arrive the snows will have abated and some of the northern water will be free of ice. We will explore north of the island, and perhaps the bodies you seek will show up there. If the bodies are close to land perhaps they escaped the currents. The winters have been cold for several years and perhaps the ice has become stable. It just depends on where the bodies are. Unfortunately, the wolves and bears may have devoured them."

"We can only hope, Captain," I said.

"How long were your cousins seamen? Who told you of the disaster? The captain of the *Romanov* has been dead for some time now."

We said nothing immediately. Golem looked stern-faced at the captain while slightly shaking his head. Fortunately, the captain remembered his vow of silence and went on.

"Ah, yes, I have seen fossils of gigantic creatures long disappeared from the earth, still as they were when they roamed the planet," said Captain Joel. "Is there some other marker that may help, for the bodies would most probably be completely covered over from continuous snowfall?"

"Yes, Captain. They were on two sleds which the men constructed. These might still be above the snow," said Dr. Golem. Fortunately, Captain Amos had told us of the sleds that were used when Victor Frankenstein chased the creature.

"Not much to look for. Let us hope that the coordinates are accurate. The ship is most probably sunk by this time," said the captain in an unsure voice. It was obvious to us that he was growing uneasy. Dr. Golem diverted the captain's thoughts by reminding him of the large sum of money that we had already paid.

* * *

We set sail and eased out of the Thames toward the North Sea. Our voyage was long and the wind grew colder as we sailed up the eastern coast. The clouds thundered, and from time to time sleet whitened the deck. This white frozen rain fell all day and night for weeks, and the arctic winds grew more bitter. Sleet soon turned to ice.

We had extensive conversations during this time with Captain Joel and exchanged ideas about human life and death. On one particular night, with plenty of rum to warm our bodies, we discussed the idea of immortality. Captain Joel's argument was that only God had such power, and if one were a Christian, immortality could be gained through faith and in belief in God.

I asserted that God has given us the wisdom to make ships and to heal the sick. I argued that all we need do is expand our knowledge to know the secrets of life. One of Golem's most precious ideas was of immortality. If men could live forever, he argued, there then would no longer be any secret or scientific problem that could not be solved. There would be no final end to life, and therefore man would have unlimited time to ponder the enigmas of existence. Growing old, suffering, and gloom over the loss of loved ones would no longer drag the human spirit to despair.

Golem forcefully asserted that explorers and scientists would contribute to world knowledge without end. "The essence of what a man is would never be lost to worms," he said. Golem felt that it was a waste for intellectuals such as ourselves to be lost to the world. "Why should a mind that takes years to cultivate and train be allowed to vanish?" he pleaded. "Why would God create man, let him prosper and create new things, and then before he has a chance to perfect his knowledge doom him to the grave?" I joined in the discourse and said, "I say that God created us as intelligent creatures, capable of discovering ways to change the world. I think God would approve of anything we do as long as it is for good."

Captain Joel looked at me strangely and commented, "Anything? What about the body snatchers? The surgeons claim that what they do is for the good of mankind!" I glanced at the Captain and at Golem and said nothing.

The captain sat down and stared at us intently. His mood changed and he began to ask questions. "Why now? Why has your family just now decided to recover the bodies?" he demanded.

Golem tried to explain that it was a matter of family custom. "Our cousins have to be buried in the family plot as it is the custom of our order," said Golem in an irritable voice. I turned away, pretending that I did not want to hear, as was planned. The captain looked at us with skepticism. He rose from his chair and looked out at the waves. In the sky was a blanket of low clouds that were now dropping large snowflakes. He stood there, quiet, as if pondering our path ahead. Taking his Bible from the table, he read:

The earth shall quake before them;
the heavens shall tremble:
the sun and the moon shall be dark, and
the stars shall withdraw their shining.

I looked out past him and for reasons unknown felt strangely cold and lonely. I did not know why I felt so cold. Perhaps it was the anticipation of what lay ahead. Perhaps it was the idea of immortality and our continuous conversations about it. I had begun to have the distinct feeling of being tightly sealed. I did not know if the long journey, with so much of it spent in the tight quarter of the cabin, was the reason for my claustrophobia. I attempted to distract myself by making my way to the map table to check our position, and soon the feeling subsided.

* * *

The further north we went the colder it became. I was calmed somewhat by the hope that what we were doing would be for the good of man . . . that our journey was for good. We wanted to help mankind. I worried myself with the thought that men can do dreadful things with the best of goals; that in the name of what is right men can commit horrible crimes. My thoughts were directed away from these troubling problems when I began to consider that the bodies we sought might no longer be intact. They might have been eaten by wolves or bears as the Captain mentioned. It was very likely that their bodies might not be on permanent ice. I was wholly aware of the fact that they might have drifted out to sea on ice rafts, where they would have either been eaten by creatures or lost to the depths. I hoped that the sleds that they used in their chase of one another would still be above the ice to serve as a marker.

Captain Walton's remark about the monster being alive had distressed me. Though I thought from treating frostbite and experiencing the results of exposure to cold that the creature could not have survived, the idea lingered in my mind. Was not the very premise of Golem's theory based on life being sustained in the cold! What was the glycerol level in the creature's blood? Walton said that the creature swam away in the icy water. Though I had been numb to the idea before, it suddenly dawned upon me, *The notes from Walton indicate that the creature is immune to the cold!* Nature did not provide the necessary anti-freezing elements needed to survive. How was it possible for Frankenstein to develop blood with a proper glycerol content? How could the creature have survived? Hope and fear played with me that day.

My mind drifted to the terrible shrieks of Captain Walton, which echoed through my head as I pondered our journey. Once, when lying in my cabin ready for a night's slumber, the echo returned. I had been asleep for but a short time when I saw a roiling cloud coming at me. It contained the ghostly howls of Walton. I awoke in terror, dripping all over in sweat. I screamed and held my hands to my ears, but the howls of Walton did not subside. It was only after wildly looking about, and satisfied that no one was present, that I regained my composure.

I had experienced night terrors before but none measured up to this one. In my confused state I remembered that these terrors were associated with the first time I saw a dissection. I was ten years of age. My father never noticed my fear at being at the dissection table. During these early years I remember not being able to sleep for fear of having a nightmare. Often, after sleep finally came, I awoke totally confused and terror-stricken at the dark clouds that entered my dreams. All of my night terrors as a youth were filled with these roily suffocating clouds. It was a feeling of death. I never was able to comprehend their meaning.

The calmness of the sea did not prevail upon me. It only aggravated my disturbed state. The creaking of the ship and the calmness of the sea worked together to haunt me. As I lay in my bed a fear swelled in me that I was at a loss to explain. Whenever I closed my eyes I felt as if I were drifting toward death. I was unable to awake as I slid toward oblivion. I wrestled with myself to live. I barely awoke in time to save myself. I could not tell which was at work, my imagination, or death itself. Why would I be dying? I was not ill, nor had I been recently! Why was death trying to abduct me and carry me away? I could not fathom an answer.

Now I started up again in terror and sat beside my bed trying to understand what had happened. Perhaps it was the way I had stretched out. I had lain down flat on my back and for some reason found it comfortable to cross my hands across my bosom. Perchance this posture struck at an unconscious reflection of how bodies are often laid out in death for final burial. There seemed to be a strange connection between the way I felt and my childhood dreams. I was unable to return to sleep until the early hours of the morning.

At dawn, after conferring with Captain Joel as to our coordinates and making a few notes on plans for retrieval of the bodies from the ice, I went out on the deck. The crew were going about their duties. The sun was now rising over the sea. For a time I tried to relax my spirit by watching the waves rise and break. The sea was vast and majestic. The low clouds which had followed us for days now gave way to an ocean highlighted by the glittering sun. Those rays of light blanketed the blue sea in a glorious scene. My mind was diverted from its disorientation and the heaviness of my task. This sight was sufficient to redirect me to the sublime aspects of immortality. The melancholy of the night before was dissipated as I contemplated eternity. Perhaps Golem was correct.

The thought occurred to me that oblivion was not the same as eternity. I did not want to forfeit the essence of myself. Death was surely the end of this essence. Why are we born to die? Why must the quintessence of who we are be reduced to dust? That it takes a lifetime to understand reality, and then to be left to the grave, to worms and putrescence, makes no sense whatsoever.

Why does this happen to us? What is our ultimate purpose? Is our consciousness of death an attribute? We have built cemeteries and erected monuments because we refuse to recognize the finality of death. Our refusal has created gods, heaven, hell, and other places where the essence of what we are lives on. Why? Who knows if there is a heaven or a hell? I want to believe in God and heaven but these nagging questions will not go away.

There are rules to follow and doctrines to adhere to, which, if obeyed, lead to everlasting happiness, or if violated lead to everlasting hell. Every religion in the world claims to be right. Who really knows? With all religions eternity is the reward. It is an eternity of bliss, or an eternity of suffering, but still we do not go to oblivion. Oblivion is the true hell for those of us obsessed with life. I thought that going to hell for my efforts was a better prospect than total oblivion, for at least the essence of my being would not be lost in hell.

I have reconciled my undertakings with my beliefs. If there was a heaven, then my work would be rewarded, for what I do is grounded in my love for mankind. If my creator judges my work to be evil, at least my essence will live, even in the fiery reaches of hell. If heaven and hell did not exist, with the only compensation being the grave and oblivion, then my attempts at immortality will be more than justified. If I can defeat death and its empty regions I will have given man a reason for it all. The questions of existence can be answered by the same thinkers who pondered it thousands of years before.

I accept the challenge of finding a solution to nature's greatest enigmas. The thought of living long enough to answer our own questions will be a satisfaction undreamed of. The secrets of medicine can be taught to everyone. What we could accomplish would be greater than all of the existing accomplishments by men through all of the previous ages. What troubles me is Golem's beliefs. He does not want certain members of society to be given these privileges. Those whom Golem identify with limited intelligence would not be allowed immortality. He wants to rid the world of cemeteries but his generosity does not extend to the poor. Golem does not want to share immortality with everyone.

I looked out toward the northern horizon and the everlasting sea. I felt as if time were slipping past me. I thought of recovering the bodies and returning to London, to examine them and record our observations. We would need to conduct experiments on the effects of freezing. I am not sure if this journey will lead to progress. Who knows what will be? What will the world be like in five hundred years? I wish I knew. If only I could be assured that there is a heaven perhaps I would never have embarked on this hellish journey.

Amid these foreboding thoughts my mind turned to Jane. I missed her terribly. I wrote her many letters that expressed my love for her. They became so much a part of me that I could not bear to send a single one, even if there had been a way to do so. I kept these letters close to me and bore the pain of knowing that she would not be aware of why I had not sent her a letter.

I recalled the sad story Jane told. As I thought about it, tears flowed from my eyes. She had been separated from her family when only two years of age. There had been a flood and Jane was swept into a swollen stream after their carriage turned over. A Mr. John Singleton had saved the child and brought her up as his own. Singleton tried to find Jane's family but to no avail, and so the child, who became the woman I loved, was given the name Jane Singleton.

Tragedy struck again when John Singleton was killed after he fell from his horse when Jane was but ten years old. John's brother Paul raised Jane. Over the years, Jane searched across England for her family but in vain. She learned that an old family, which had died away, had lost a small child in a flood, and there was an older brother to the child, but no one knew what had become of him. She only knew his last name was Wallace but did not know if this person was in any way connected to her. This was her only hope. I made plans to help her find this man once I returned to England.

* * *

October 1848

After several weeks of sailing toward the north we finally arrived at the Barents Sea. There we saw the wonders of the ice as we passed several small ice islands which glittered like polished marble. We anchored near one of these islands and rowed over to its shore. Captain Joel needed to take on fresh water. He explained that the older ice was salt free, and, when melted, it could be drunk. The older ice was a pale blue while the new ice was gray.

We cut several blocks of pale blue ice with axes and loaded them in our craft. While there, on this island of ice, I climbed up a small hill to get a better view of the landscape. The hill was difficult to climb as the snow on its slope was loose, having dropped from the heavens just the night before. When I arrived at the top I looked back at the men below and then turned to the north. Out beyond me were mountains of blizzard blue ice. This scene impressed upon me a disposition. I felt empty when I thought of the incomprehensible amount of time that must have passed here. The ice mountains were streaked by a blowing cold mist of icy air that obscured parts of their summits. The beauty of the view was striking. It also had the power to bestow upon the mind a harsh blunt reality. The reality of incomprehensible time and desolation made me shudder.

The beauty was offset by the loneliness and unvarying aspect of the landscape. The blowing icy air reminded me that human life could not exist in such a climate for long, and that the howls of these icy winds had remained unheard by anyone for unbelievable amounts of time. I stood for a moment, stunned, and hypnotized by the forlorn aspect of the frozen landscape.

Having secured enough ice, we boarded our small vessel and returned to the ship. Several other trips were made as I observed from the deck. The captain stood with me and joined me in conversation.

"Ice and more ice," he said. "Never-ending ice. Hyperboreans lived here beyond the northern west winds. They are said to have enjoyed the peaceful tranquility of light everlasting."

"Are these legends true, Captain?"

"There is nothing in this hell but a few creatures and ice, unending ice! I have been here before and have been trapped in the ice and have lost many crewmen. I have been forced to abandon ship and go overboard. I remember well how my men froze to death while trying to make it to safety. We never made it beyond the northern winds nor found everlasting peace." He turned and looked beyond with lonely eyes.

As we spoke the wind began to rise, and from the distant western horizon we could see a storm brewing. We pulled anchor and immediately set sail north by northwest. The seas grew rough, and as the ice storm approached the crewmen had worried looks on their faces. I knew from the stories they told that the wind could toss the ship like a piece of paper to an icy grave.

Captain Joel raised his eyeglass toward the approaching storm. After a few seconds he began giving orders to the crew to secure all rigging and to make haste. Finally, we were under way.

"With good fortune we might be able to navigate beyond the reach of the storm and closer to Novaya Zemlya," the captain said. I thought of drowning. I wondered if we were fated to die here.

After several hours of sailing in a northeasterly direction it became apparent that we had sailed beyond the reach of the storm. Soon, land was sighted. We all breathed a sigh of relief and prepared to land on the northwestern coast of Novaya Zemlya. I was overjoyed. I tried to share my joy with Golem, but he never lost his cold demeanor. If the bodies could be found they would be just north of where we were.

On the icy island I was surprised to see life. There were foxes, reindeer, bears, ducks, geese, and swans. Snow began to fall as was common from October to May. The beginning of colder weather was near, however, and if we were going to find the bodies we would need to search for them before the seas completely froze. My hope was that they were at the northernmost tip of the island which would not have broken up during the summers unless it was uncommonly warm.

After a few days of surveying, Captain Joel informed us that we would be headed for the coordinates given to him. I made ready the axes, picks, and firewood for the stay on the ice. Golem was not much help. He complained of the bitter cold from the time we first spotted the island. It was not long before the day arrived for our expedition. Captain Joel said we had plenty of provisions but would not stay very long as he wanted to get as far as possible before the ice began to freeze.

Golem and I decided to first head south for one half mile at most. We theorized that the creature would not have been able to continue very far in these temperatures despite the possibility of high glycerol levels in his blood. We also knew that the body would be covered with snow, but that some part of the sleds would perhaps not be completely covered and might give us a clue as to their location.

As I looked out on the frozen landscape I grew despondent. The chance of finding the bodies seemed quite remote. Day after day the search continued. On the fifth day our situation seemed hopeless, as nothing had been found that would indicate any creature had passed through this wilderness.

Then one day we saw what first looked like a rock sticking up from the snow. Next to it was a snow-covered mound. When we closed the distance I realized that it was the foot of a man lying in the ice! The mound was the sled the monster had used. As soon as I was able to push away the loose snow I saw the entire length of his body. It was in a solid block of ice. I knew from its size and bulk that this had to be the creature that we sought.

I grabbed my pick and immediately began chipping away at the ice while Dr. Golem summoned our helpers to assist me. I could see a small portion of the creature's eyes which were partially open. It was lying on its back fully stretched out. Even through the pale ice I could see its disfigured face. I thought it best to cover it with loose snow as best as I could, not wanting the retrieval to be jeopardized. I feigned sorrow and respect by covering the face with a cloth that I carried in my satchel. Before anyone had the opportunity to see, I ordered the men to secure some canvas to cover the body.

Dr. Golem waited at this spot while I accompanied the crewmen.

Upon arrival at the cabin I instructed the first mate to notify Captain Joel that our search was over and to send more crewmen to help with the excavation. Within a short time, a crew of six returned with picks and axes. While they were digging, Golem and I constructed a makeshift stretcher. To my delight the crew found another body next to the creature, which I took for Victor Frankenstein. I instructed the crew to concentrate on Frankenstein's body while Golem and I worked on the excavation of the creature. Golem almost gave us away when he tried to hurry the crewmen in their excavation of Frankenstein so that they could help us with the creature. He stood directly on top of the creature's resting place barking orders. I handed him an axe and whispered to him that we had to do most of the excavation ourselves so that the crew would have as little contact with the creature as possible. This forced him to work.

Having completed the digging around the bodies, we exhumed them in complete rectangular-shaped pieces of ice. I instructed the crew to maintain as much ice as possible for preservation of the bodies on the return trip. I anticipated our return to London during the winter which would greatly aid in preservation. If we left the bodies in as much ice as possible we could hide the view of the creature as well as preserve its flesh. In the event they thawed out before reaching the laboratory, Dr. Golem was prepared to inject a glycerol solution. He explained that it would help preserve the bodies until we could transport them to our laboratory. However, we could not hide the fact that the creature was huge. The crew began commenting on this fact with one another.

We secured our cargo and rowed back to the ship where the bodies were lifted by means of blocks and pulleys. As they were being secured into the hold, a crewman who stood beneath the ice blocks and was directing the blocks into the hold let out a shriek that sent terror into me. He screamed again and pointed up to the ice block dangling on the ropes. We scrambled to his position. To my dismay the block had turned around so that the creature's face was entirely visible. Dr. Golem and I looked up and saw the hideous face of the monster through the dull glassy ice.

My immediate response was to get the body lowered as quickly as possible before anyone else had a chance to see the face of the creature. I quickly pushed the man aside and directed the lowering of the ice blocks myself. The crewman backed away with glaring eyes. I saw him running up on deck and alerting the rest of the crew. He looked down at us from the entrance to the hold above. I feared the worst.

The next day I awoke early. I could not sleep as I was anxious about what might happen. I tried to pass the time by reading the notes of Captain Walton. The papers described the creature as hideous. I studied again Walton's report that Frankenstein said the creature had superhuman strength and was not affected by extreme cold. I arose from my reading, dressed myself, and made my way to the ship's hold. Upon arrival I saw the two blocks of ice next to one another on wooden bracing, each covered with a tightly drawn canvas. I looked all around the hold making sure that no one was present. I went over to the ice blocks and pulled back the canvas that covered the creature, hoping to get a better look. A piece of ice cracked and fell from its face. Though the creature was horribly disfigured I did not think him so hideous. During my years as a surgeon I had seen much worse disfigurement from various diseases and birth defects.

The ice was still thick in most places. The creature was indeed a giant. The block in which he was entombed was well over the average length of a tall man. I was amazed at the creature's structure which implied great strength. I looked down into its face and felt sorrow at what had transpired. The epic of the creature and its creator was not yet done. I knew more about what had happened during its sad life than did Golem. I did not reveal what I knew to Golem. I still had not revealed to him that I had taken Walton's papers.

* * *

October 31st, 1848

The animals of the arctic were unusual. My observations of their behavior left a lasting impression upon me. I came to understand nature's cruelty in these regions. There were birds who used the treacherous cliffs to rest and raise their young. I noticed thousands of them caring for their newborn offspring. These black-headed birds scurried here and there bringing food or encouraging their fledglings to fly.

I witnessed many pitiful events while in these cold regions. Foxes had succeeded in overcoming the treacherous precipitous cliffs and were moving through the craggy slopes to corner their prey. The entire flock of birds numbering in the thousands abandoned the site, leaving in a great flutter. They doomed their tiny helpless offspring to the carnivorous creatures of the ice; within several hours many foxes came and devoured the helpless creatures.

Strange it was to see the foxes themselves leave their young. I witnessed this sad affair, taking notes of the event. There was a shortage of food for the cubs, and as it grew colder the parents would leave their den for long periods of time. They left daily, searching frantically for food to feed their young. The frozen landscape provided some mice and small shrubs, but this was not enough. The male fox left first. The female soon followed. Within a week I visited the den to see what had become of the small creatures. Not one of them survived. They were all starved and frozen to death.

These cold regions strike into the heart of all who stay here. It is as if life were not meant to be here, to prosper, but instead must fight with the extremes and abandon even those things that by all natural rights should be loved. I had seen enough of this hell! This place was cold in every respect. I was chilled by the depth of this coldness.

We had delayed our departure for too long to go any further north. Captain Joel decided that any further search for a passage across the top of the world would have to wait. We headed south, toward England, just escaping being frozen in the ice. As the weeks moved ahead, the seas and the climate worked on my state of being in such a way as to release locked memories of my early life. It was during such reflection that I experienced a most pitiful event. We had only just set out southward when I saw a large block of ice drifting south. I had seen ice sheets break and then drift south where in the open sea they would melt. Aboard this particular ice raft was a polar bear. The creature had apparently stayed on the floating ice too long and had drifted too far out to swim back.

My thoughts were broken when the captain came to stand beside me at the rail and addressed me thus: "I have seen the poor creatures do this before. They stay too long on the floating ice. I have seen drowned bears floating in the seas and have wondered why they ventured so far out. Their ability to know when to abandon their adventure seemed to have deserted them. Out of pity I have slain the creatures when circumstance presented itself."

"Why do you think the animals do this?" I asked.

"Who knows, Mr. Hamel? Perhaps exposure to a sun of long duration, or crazed by the isolation in some way. I do not know," mused the captain. He called for his musket.

"The weapon is loaded and ready, sir," said the first mate.

Captain Joel raised his weapon and took careful aim. He caught me off guard when he suddenly said; "You have brought coffins for the cadavers, but yet you have not attempted to place the bodies in them. Why?" I said nothing. I looked out over the seas and felt a sorrow in my heart for the bear. It would now die for a mistake that its feeble mind most probably did not contemplate. Why did it not return to solid ice when it had the chance? It did not appear to be ill. Creatures like this have lived thousands of years in these regions. There seemed to be no logical reason for the bear to have stayed on the ice. I wondered why these beasts, who have lived here so long, did not know when the dangers of the ice would imperil their existence. I thought of myself at that moment, of my lack of religious faith, and how long men have heard about God.

I looked over at the captain. He was adjusting his aim. I looked out at the bear, white, huge, and majestic. It was going from one end of the ice to the other in a panic, looking for some way to avoid its fate with the sea. As it grew more and more anxious, the icy vapors from its nose belched out at a faster rate.

I looked back at the island and thought of Loshkin, the man after whom the ship was named. I had learned from the captain that in 1760, Loshkin had spent two winters at Novaya Zemlya and was the first to completely circumnavigate the island. His records and the account of the journey have since disappeared. Though only a few seconds could have passed during my thoughts, it felt much longer. I grew extremely anxious in the moments before hearing the thunderous clap of Captain Joel's weapon. I did not look. The clap of death was not final, for it could not persuade me to part with the sadness that overcame me. Looking out over the calm sea, a feeling of extreme loneliness took hold upon my soul.

The captain broke my train of thought when he said, "I have asked you a question. Why have you not broken the ice around their bodies and placed them in the coffins?"

"Because the ice will better preserve them for a funeral," I said. I knew what the next question would be. He would ask about the height of the creature. I thought in vain for some quick response but I could not think of one. How could I have been so stupid? I had not thought of it — the coffin would not be large enough, for I knew from Walton's notes that the creature was gigantic. The captain never asked the next question. He measured me with his stern wandering eyes and then abruptly lowered his brows in anger. He turned and walked swiftly away toward his cabin.

* * *

We sailed farther and farther south, heading for England. Although it remained cold the temperature rose enough for us to be concerned about the ice blocks that entombed our cargo. Day after day Golem and I checked the ice, hoping that it would maintain itself at least until we entered English waters.

On one serene day the temperature rose above the freezing point and we grew quite worried. Below the ice blocks, drops of water began to appear. I feared that unless a coldness once again descended upon us we would lose our cadavers to putrescence. Slowly but steadily the ice blocks began to lose their density and shape. It was with great trepidation that I informed Captain Joel.

"I do not think we are going to make it, Captain. The climate has grown too warm to sustain them. At this point we will probably need to consider some alternative."

Dr. Golem joined us on deck and we proceeded down to the hold. There we noticed that the ice blocks had melted even more than we feared. The shape of each body was now partially visible as an outline under the canvas sheets that covered them.

"Though we are only a day out from the dock I think it is safe to say that most of the ice will be melted by then," said Captain Joel. Dr. Golem's face grew dark as he looked at a segment of the creature's arm that was now exposed to the air. Captain Joel noticed the arm also. The skin of the arm was drawn tight revealing muscles and veins which were huge by human comparison.

"Are there any ice blocks remaining from the supply that was loaded on for water? If so, then we might encircle the cadavers with what ice we have and tightly wrap them in canvas," Golem said.

"I do not think there is enough ice to completely cover them, but I will do what I can, Dr. Golem," said the captain in a very perturbed voice. He turned abruptly and left us.

When the captain had departed Golem immediately took interest in the exposed arm.

"This is a very good specimen, Mr. Hamel. Look here, under my glass! Look at the tautness of the skin. It has survived quite well!"

I looked at the skin in disbelief and turned to Golem. "I am still astonished, Dr. Golem, at what we have found. I am amazed at the size of the frame! Frankenstein did create a life! This is an astonishing find!"

"Hamel, get my instrument bag from the table. If the monster survived the icy regions for as long as it did then its blood might contain fluids that will support my theories. Even though the outer skin is frozen solid I suspect the inner blood will still be in a fluid state. Stand aside and hand me a small scalpel so that I might cut the hardened skin to plunge a syringe deep into the arm."

I handed Golem the scalpel and observed him cut a small lateral incision. He forced the slit open and inserted the needle. There were a few tense moments before he began to pull back on the syringe. I looked at the contents of the syringe in utter amazement.

"My God, the blood flows! It is unfrozen!" I said.

"Yes, Hamel, and I will wager you that when we analyze it we will find glycerol in high percentages."

"Glycerol? Are you sure?" I said.

"I will show you, Mr. Hamel. It is the secret to immortality!"

I stood back and looked at the monster. Its frame was at least eight feet in length. I could now see its face clearly. There was a saddened bitter and dejected look upon its countenance. These expressions stood out through the disfigurement. One of the creature's eyes was partially open with half of the pupil exposed.

The captain had the ice blocks delivered by his first mate and several crewmen and soon followed himself. I quickly drew the canvas over the creature's face. I thanked the crewmen and urged them away, and we hastily surrounded the bodies with ice. Dr. Golem left us to return to his cabin to store the blood sample. Captain Joel looked at me with a solemn face, then he pushed me aside and pulled the canvas away from the creature's face.

With a heavy sigh the captain gazed down at the creature and asked, "What sort of monster have I helped you to retrieve? My men have been fearful for some time now. I ask you, what is that? What evil have you brought aboard this ship? I have heard of a legend that a man by the name of Victor Frankenstein created a monster from the scraps of the dead, and that he and his creation chased each other to the ends of the world. The legend appears true. If I had known that you sought to find such a monstrosity I would not have brought you!"

"Think again, Captain Joel. You have only thought it a legend before now. We have paid you quite well for your troubles!"

"If I had known, I might have taken greater precautions to shield my crew from what you have found. They are alarmed, and there is now talk of throwing the bodies overboard and you along with them." I was horrified as the captain continued. "Even as we speak, my first mate is assembling the crew on deck for a meeting which the men have requested. I am afraid that if we do not go along with their wishes to dispose of the corpses your lives will be in jeopardy."

"Have you told Dr. Golem yet?"

"No, I leave that to you. I will be quite blunt, Mr. Hamel. If throwing the bodies overboard satisfies my men," he said, "I will comply with their wishes."

"But you cannot do that, Captain!" I rejoined. "We have paid you for the passage, and you have agreed to our request!"

The captain did not blink as his eyes bored into mine. "I agreed to bring back your cousins! I did not agree to bring back a curse, a monster, which could destroy my ability to garner future crews. I will not let you destroy my future! What I have said stands!"

I looked into the captain's eyes and saw that he would not retreat from his position. I walked around him and proceeded up to the deck where I found the men in an agitated state. They were clenching their fists, and although I could not hear their words I could see they were mumbling curses. I quickly descended to our cabin to tell Dr. Golem of the unfolding events. I found him making notes.

"The crew is threatening to throw the bodies overboard," I said. "The captain has informed me that if we do not go along with the crew our own lives could be in danger. He has made it clear that he will support the crew!"

Golem answered me in a calm voice. "Then I will have to address the crew, Mr. Hamel. Notify the captain that I will address the crew on deck within ten minutes."

"But what will you say? These men are superstitious, uneducated, and Christian. There is nothing that you could say to them!"

"We shall see, Mr. Hamel."

I became extremely agitated at Golem's calmness. I felt that his proposal was ridiculous. I left him and proceeded to the captain's cabin, informing him of Golem's request to which he reluctantly agreed. I returned to where Golem was waiting. He was standing before his table talking to himself when I entered.

"Yes, can we proceed?" he asked.

"The captain will assemble the men for your address," I said.

"Good. I think they will change their minds when they have heard me out."

Golem turned and shouted. "Do not concern yourself, Hamel!" With these words he proceeded to the deck. I followed along, fearful of the anticipated response of the crew to Golem's remarks. We walked out on deck and joined the captain and first mate. The crew looked on. There was anger in their eyes, but they were reticent. In fact, it was so quiet that the sea could be heard with crystal clarity, brushing and stroking the fears of my soul. Golem appeared alert and steady. He was extremely stoic as he began.

"I know you men have expressed concern for the cargo we are bringing back to London. It is understandable. The bodies we are bringing back will help us to help you, to help all people. I am a surgeon. I am skilled in my work. One of the bodies is that of a normal man. The other body is that of a circus freak. It is an abnormality!

That is all. The creature that you fear is only the body of a deformed man who suffered from some disease at birth. He lived until he met his fate on the ice. The bodies will be useful to us to study. We want to find a cause and a cure for such deformities! We want to study the effects of cold. We want to know how to better treat frostbite. These bodies might be beneficial to mankind! We need these cadavers for our research, and . . ."

"Lies! All lies!" clamored one of the crewmen. There was a chorus of rumblings and shouts.

"Throw the bodies overboard! They are a curse upon man!" they shouted.

One of the crew, who I recognized as the man who first saw the creature's face broke in. "This monster is a curse upon the world! The man is Victor Frankenstein!" He now turned to address the crew. "The other body is that of the monster he created! Frankenstein violated the laws of God by bestowing life upon the dead! You have all heard the tale! This is what remains of Satan and his monstrosity. We cannot allow these men to take back the remains of evil to the shores of England! All traces of this curse must be destroyed!"

The crew set up a loud wild roar of approval. The captain came forward and informed his men that he wanted to know the will of the crew.

They were furious as they shouted, "Throw the curse overboard!" They were delirious and had become a mob.

"Throw the surgeons in with them!" someone shouted, at which Captain Joel immediately intervened.

"This I will not allow! I will not allow murder aboard my ship! These men have made a mistake, but it would be just as bad a mistake for you to murder them! I agree with you otherwise. The bodies will be cast out to sea, but not without a decent burial. Make them ready for burial!"

Golem tried to intervene but I seized his arm and whispered, "We have a sample of its blood. That should be enough for what we need to do! I know it is not the optimum situation, but under the circumstances we cannot fare any better. Do not press these men further. They are determined." Golem relaxed his stand, turned around abruptly, and quickly exited the deck. I turned to the captain and shook my head in disgust.

I was about to give thanks to the captain when I noticed one of the crewman. He was the one who had rallied the crowd. He glared at me in a most evil manner. His eyes slashed at me with hatred. I could do nothing. He turned and walked away. Before he was out of sight he glanced again with horrid deadly eyes.

I broke away from the events on deck and returned to my cabin. I sat on the edge of my bed and was lost in a blank numbness. I stayed this way for an hour or so. When Dr. Golem returned he informed me that the burial would commence within the half hour, and that we should stay below during the ceremony. Captain Joel had threatened us with confinement if we appeared on deck again. I wanted to witness the ceremony and planned to watch it surreptitiously.

Dr. Golem was quite indifferent to the whole affair and went to his desk to write. He had simply resigned himself to the matter. "They are but ignorant rabble!" he said. I took leave of him and headed for the deck to look for a suitable place from which to watch.

On deck I found a group of water barrels which I used to conceal my presence. Shortly I saw Captain Joel appear, Bible in hand, together with the first mate. The bodies had already been brought on deck and placed upon planks from which they would be cast into the sea. They were still wrapped in canvas which was dripping water. The men gathered around as Captain Joel began the service.

"It is with deep concern that we gather here to commit these bodies to the sea. Lord, forgive them for their sins, and deliver them from the suffering that they may have caused. We do not know the souls that we commit to Thy mercy, but receive them, and deliver them into Your kingdom, if it is Your will. No man knows whether love or hate awaits him. All men share a common destiny. From the Bible it is said: 'There is an evil among all things that are done under the sun. . . . the heart of the sons of men is full of evil, and madness is in their heart while they live, and after that they go to the dead. For the living know that they shall die: but the dead know not anything, neither have they any more a reward; for the memory of them is forgotten. Also their love, and their hatred, and their envy, is now perished.' All come from dust, and to dust all return. Commit their bodies to the eternal sea! May God have mercy on their souls."

The planks were raised. Victor's body plunged into the sea immediately, but his creation did not budge. To my horror, I looked at the side of the canvas wrapping and saw the monster's hand gripping the plank! I squinted for a better view but as I did, the corpse slid into the sea. I scrambled to the side of the ship and looked at the bodies floating away and watched them drift off, bubbling as they sank. I struggled to see some sign, some further movement, but there was nothing.

I did not think that I imagined the incident. Benumbed, I struggled with myself for a moment until I resolved that it must have been my imagination. When I thought back on it however, it seemed to me certain that I saw the veins in his hand bulge as one would under strain. Still, I could not be sure.

I went below deck and headed for our cabin. When I entered, Golem was reading his notes. "I thought I saw the creature move!" I told him. "Its hand was grasping the plank!"

"Well, no matter now. I think if we can keep this vial of blood cool we will be able to analyze its components," Golem said with great indifference.

I was angered. "Do you not understand," I asked "that the monster is, or was, alive?"

"It is no longer our concern," he said.

I could not believe the indifference with which Golem spoke. I shouted at him. "It *is* our concern! If the monster was alive, then that means it lived through the cold. Its life-giving blood helped it to survive! It may still be alive floating there in the sea!"

Golem only slightly raised his head from his notes. "I am not concerned, Hamel! Even if we could somehow retrieve the creature it would only complicate matters. Suspicions could destroy my plans. We might not be so fortunate as we are at the present time. We would be under constant threat of discovery. We cannot allow anything to become an obstacle! I have the precious blood! That is all I need!"

"But the creature may still be alive!" I screamed. "It lived! It possesses superhuman strength. It could *still* be alive!"

"Superhuman strength? How could you know that, Hamel? Have you been attending to the superstitious gossip of these ignorant sailors?"

I said nothing. Golem still did not know that I was in possession of Walton's papers. I had read them. The creature did indeed possess superhuman strength. It had on more than one occasion survived when an ordinary man would have succumbed. The creature had been shot, wounded in the shoulder, and yet it survived without treatment. The creature lived by eating herbs and berries. It sustained itself on these few morsels. From the account of Walton, the creature had said, "I seek the everlasting ices of the north, where you will feel the misery of cold and frost to which I am impassive." I was now sure as I thought on it — sure that the monster had survived the cold waves of the seas.

I went up to the deck to look out at the far-reaching sea. I looked down into the cold waters and felt lost in their undulations. My reticent numbness was broken by Captain Joel's hand, which he had placed on my shoulder. He gently moved my shoulder in a comradely way. As he did he said to me, "I saw the creature's hand move!

It sounds incredible, but my eye did not deceive me. You saw it also, for I saw you leap from your hiding place as the bodies floated away." He turned and looked out to sea and in a solemn manner prayed these words. "It is close at hand — a day of darkness and gloom, a day of clouds and blackness."

BOOK II

THE BURIAL

The Creature's Notes
November 1848

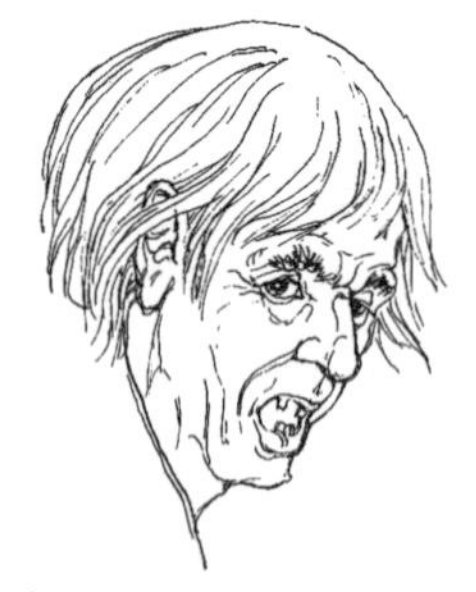

Against a tumult of cold seas and cold winds I swam toward what I later learned to be the English shore. I towed my creator with me, keeping his head above water as one would for a living man. I swam for the better part of eight hours before reaching shore, then lay at the water line with the surf just touching the soles of my feet. As I pulled my creator next to me, I felt the coldness of his body and thought it best that I embrace him. It was but a short time after this that I lost my will to think and fell into complete exhaustion. Before I fell into a deep sleep I looked up at the setting sun as its reddish rays passed through the clouds and a hazy sky.

When I awoke the sun had set. The stars were visible and a crescent moon was in the mid-sky. I stood and looked into the sky, feeling the pain and agony of loneliness. Loneliness was a sharp pain in the core of my being and throbbed in my bosom. I fixed my eyes on the heavens for a time and soon found myself chained to the twinkle of the emerging stars. I shook my head, feeling gored by the horn of gloom. A small stream of sadness left my eye. I fell to my knees in a deep depression. All seemed hopeless. It was better for me to think of nothing, though nothing was as painful. Tears dropped to the wet rocks. The stars were my only witness on this night.

"Why must I bear this pain alone?" I screamed. My shouts died into the darkness.

I looked over at the lifeless body of my creator. I reached out to touch his head, to stroke his hair. "Why have you done this to me? Why did you bring me into this world only to be where I now find myself?" I shouted. I could not control myself and wept violently as I held my face in my hands. I raved into the darkness.

"You created me! I have suffered beyond belief, and now you have left me in this world that has only shown me hatred. You have left me! Curse you! Curse you! You abandoned me to the hatreds of your world! Why did you make me like this, horrid to sight, detested, hunted, and ruined? Curse you, Frankenstein! Curse your kind!" Though no one was present to hear my woes I spoke into the night.

I fell into a rage that aroused my strength. It was most satisfying to feel the power of my body. Without thought I seized the doctor's head by his hair and pounded it into the sand. I lost consciousness after a few minutes and remember falling face down into the wet pebbles with my creator's head in my hand. Sometime in the night my hand slipped around his shoulder.

It was dawn when I awakened. The sky had a blood-red hue to it as the sun made its approach toward the horizon. I carried Frankenstein, cradling him in my arms, and began walking toward a hill. I was within a few yards of its crest when a vast wasteland came into view. A cemetery lay beneath us, and gravestones littered the field as far as the eye could see. I readjusted my burden and began my descent from the hill. The grass on its slope was brown and matted. Dried stalks brushed my knee, and among the shoots were dried twigs of different thickness and shapes. I looked ahead at the desolation. A stone wasteland lay before me. Though the graveyard sustained evergreen plant life it was suppressed by the hardness of the stones whose statues gaped at me.

The dead were buried here. Their remains lay beneath the stone slabs. As I approached the boundaries of this lonely place I noticed that the name and the date of death were chiseled into the face of each stone. I stopped to touch these markings and was immediately left with the impression of a permanence, a lasting reality that would outlive memory. I felt enlightened at the thought and laid Frankenstein's body down against one of the stones to contemplate this further.

They have had their names carved into stone. Stone has been here forever; it is everlasting! I glanced around in every direction noticing the names of unknown people; they were William and Mary, Thomas, Johnson — stones and stones of names and names. Though they were unknown to me, I knew that they had once existed, and that they were born and died. Some of them had left words behind, and I spoke them aloud; "Rest in peace, " and "ashes to ashes," and "dust to dust." I looked down in melancholy as these words died from my lips.

Left with a profound and fearful reverence, I looked out in every direction to see what was written on the stones. I resumed walking ahead reading the inscriptions as I went. ". . . for death is the destiny of every man . . ." All of the stones said something about the past of the humans buried there, or gave words of wisdom. This place was a memorial. It was a lasting monument to the lives of the people interred here. They have expected these monuments to last beyond them. I struggled to come to some other conclusion as to why stones should be left to mark a grave, but no ideas surfaced. What good was it? It was to leave a lasting presence. I was so deeply excited by this proposition that my melancholy disposition dissipated. It was a form of immortality.

I looked around this vast wasteland, and beheld the wide expanse of stone that beloved ones appropriated to the dead. My sadness soon returned as I thought that such a memory would never be given to me. I thought it appropriate that my creator have such a place assigned to him. With this in mind I went searching for a place to bury him.

Along the way I saw a caretaker's shack. I entered through its creaky doors and noticed a mat and pillow but no one was around. I found some tools and a few stone slabs that would serve my purpose. I proceeded toward a large tree and found a space available under the canopy of its branches. Surveying the area, I satisfied myself that this would be an appropriate place for Victor's burial and went to retrieve the body.

I threw his limp body over my shoulder and returned to the site I had chosen. I laid his body underneath the tree with it propped up against its trunk and returned to the shack, but along the way varied my path, and it happened that I came upon a view I shall never forget. There were large houses, crypts, and catacombs. It was a city of tombs in a valley below. It was a city built for the dead. These magnificent structures were not as numerous as the others, but they stood out on the landscape as a city would from atop a hill. With a shovel, a hammer, and a chisel from the shed, I started back to the tree, carrying with me the tools and the slab of stone I had taken.

On my way one of the crypts caught my attention. Its haunting gloss was enhanced by the silent words it spoke. Suddenly I heard music! I stopped and turned to listen as strange melodies played in my head. The sounds were from a flute, yet I saw no one! The music was suggestive, alluring, and soon flooded my mind. I altered my path through the grave rows until I was at the front of a tomb. This crypt resembled a house. It was like a small mansion. I read the inscription which said "The Lamar Tomb." The haunting music ceased as the wind rose. Having a hammer in hand I struck the lock and broke the bolt that secured the entrance.

I touched the door slightly, feeling its cold metallic designs, and felt a need to caress the ornate indentations carved into it. I pushed open the heavy door, and before me was a stone coffin that lay on a slab which was raised above the floor. I moved into an ancient vault now filled with dust and spider webs and crept around its perimeter reverently watching through the rays of light that now struck the sepulchre. I was unable to draw away. There was an eerie majesty about this place that forced slow movements.

At the head of the coffin was inscribed the words: "For what is your life? It is even a vapour that appeareth for a little time, and then vanisheth away." I had looked steadily at the inscription for a few minutes when my foot collided with an object on the floor. It was a steel hoop which was fastened with a chain. The chain was broken on one end, and upon further investigation I could see where it had been connected to a pulley system that hung from the ceiling.

Through the rays of light that penetrated the partially opened door I could see the outline of a door in the floor of the crypt. I bent down and grabbed the metal hoop and pulled it up with all of my strength. It was extremely heavy, but I managed to raise the broken chain to catch part of a dangling hook from the ceiling. The stone and steel moaned and creaked but it held. I looked into the darkness and could see a staircase. After pausing for a moment for my eyes to adjust, I made my descent into the tomb.

It was necessary to take small steps for the end was not in sight and I had to feel my way. Soon I could see a large room with what looked like cabinets on the wall. There were enough rays from the sun penetrating the sunken vault to make out the entire structure.

Upon reaching the last step I clearly saw cabinets of stone. Each of them had a name on it. I sat on the last step and my wonder grew as I began to fully grasp the efforts of man to gain immortality. Here before me lay an entire family from this generation and past ones. As my eyes surveyed the room I could see the birth and death dates of those entombed.

It was not long before I spied several unmarked crypts, or drawers, recessed into the wall, obviously meant for family members not yet dead. I stood up and walked over to one of the drawers to peruse the inscriptions. I saw a handle which I used to extract the drawer. It was difficult, but the drawer finally gave way. The ancient stones groaned as I pulled.

As the stone slab rolled out of its compartment, there, lying on it, were the bones of a dead man, mouth agape. I looked down into the eye sockets of the skull and deeply into its vacant head. A strange feeling came over me. I felt warm and cold at the same moment. I felt something move inside me that made me sit and tremble.

The shallow breaths of my lungs became audible, and in the faint distance I became aware of a haunting wind. It echoed through the upper chamber. I began to hear an approaching gale and the distant rustle of leaves moving upon the ground. I glanced at the bones before me and felt a strangeness that I had never experienced before.

Here, men tried to make the memory of their lives last forever. For what purpose? Only to become bones and dust? A bitter despondency grew in me, choking my spirit to emptiness. Men and their relatives could come to this place, read the inscriptions, and know that these people once existed. But only the stone remained unscathed! The vault I opened had only bones, and these too would disappear. I jumped up and went to another drawer. It was an older one. It was dated 1527. I forced it open. As I did a gust of cold wind found its way down the stairs. While I looked at the open slab and the pile of dust before me, the wind which had stolen down the stairs blew the dust off of the slab and into the chamber. When the wind subsided I could see the fine dust grains moving up into the sunlight and out of the vault. The entire room was filled with dust. Each ray of light was saturated with it, and as it moved up and off, a ghostly cloud of fine twinkling dust appeared to form some human-like shape. I fell back. It was a faceless thing made of dust. It moved so slowly that it appeared to be death itself. I was stunned at the apparition which disappeared in the blink of an eye.

There was nothing left. When I had gained my composure I was overcome with sadness. I began to weep until my body shook. Finally, my melancholy train of thought subsided and I was able to think again. The tombs were all that remained here. Is this all that is left of a life? This is only the remembrance of an inexplicable existence! There is nothing but these stones!

As I pondered on this fact my eye worked its way across the room to the rear of the staircase. For the first time, I saw that there were stone shelves with tiny crypts embedded into an entire wall. I went over to the shelves and blew dust from one of the crypts and discoverd that each tiny crypt was a cabinet, or drawer. I blew dust from one of them and noticed that the names were engraved onto each stone, just above a small handle. I pulled on one of the handles and was amazed to find a book inside. I was astonished at the condition of it, and I handled it with care, discovering that it was constructed of black leather. I opened the leaves of the book and the first few pages fell apart. The rest, however, were in remarkably good condition. It was a Bible.

I thumbed through the book and noticed a perfectly preserved leaf from some tree. The leaf was desiccated, but in good form. The pages of the book had held it there in complete peace. The leaf's edge was well defined, and its veins of life could be seen quite clearly. The leaf had accomplished between the pages of a book what the human body could not.

I placed the Bible on the floor and went looking at the other drawers. Blowing the dust from each stone crypt so that I might read the name, I discovered that each tiny vault was inscribed with the last name of the author of the book it contained. One stone drawer was engraved with the name Shakespeare. I thought the name strange, and proceeded to remove the volume. I thumbed through the pages looking for some words or thoughts to comfort me. There were several references about death which I thought interesting, but none moved me as much as these words:

Tomorrow, and tomorrow, and tomorrow,
Creeps in this petty pace from day to day,
To the last syllable of recorded time.
And all our yesterdays have lighted fools
The way to dusty death. Out, out, brief candle!
Life's but a walking shadow, a poor player
That struts and frets his hour upon the stage
And then is heard no more: it is a tale
Told by an idiot, full of sound and fury,
Signifying nothing.

The book was titled Macbeth. I was struck by the words in such a way that I could not immediately explain. I went through the leaves of this book until I came across another writing.

That skull had a tongue in it, and could sing once.
How the knave jowls it to the ground, as if it
were Cain's jaw-bone, that did the first murder,

This might be the pate of a politician, which this ass now o'erreaches one that would circumvent God, might it not?

My arm dropped with the book still in my hand, and as I contemplated the meaning of what I read my sadness returned. I could not contain the extreme melancholy that overtook me. If these stones were all that could be preserved then what was the point of living! I had been created only to end up here. My end would be like this! It would not even be as good! I had no one to see to it that my memory would live on. I had no one in the world to record my birth and death. I had not even a name for an inscription!

Victor Frankenstein, my creator, lay dead above. He had been my last hope! My existence died with him. I have been hunted and cursed, tortured and chased, shot and beaten, and could therefore expect no burial or gravestone from these accursed beings. It was in this saddened state that I felt compassion for Frankenstein.

He now had no one to construct a tomb or bury his remains. He only had me! My heavy compunctious heart turned toward the task that was left to be done. I resolved myself to bury Victor, and to construct a gravestone for him. Even though the thought of how I was abandoned weighed heavily upon my heart, it lightened my temper to supply my creator with the very thing that could never be given to me — a blessed burial.

I stood and proceeded up the stairs and left the vault knowing that it would serve as my home. This vault would provide protection from the cold wind and rain. It would be my sanctuary. I went out of the crypt and closed the door gently behind me, then turned in the direction where I had left Victor's body. I walked through the maze of gravestones toward the tree where the body lay. When I finally passed a rather large stone obstructing my view, my eyes spied several wild dogs tearing away at the body of Frankenstein. My rage was instant. I ran toward the beasts, but before I could close the distance my creator's arm was ripped from his body. The animals were fighting over this piece of flesh. As I approached they let go of their prize, and the angry beasts turned their fury toward me.

I was within but a few feet of the body when one of the creatures charged me and attempted to bite my leg. I snatched the creature by his leg as his teeth tore into my arm. I felt his bite. It was strong. I felt the creatures sharp teeth ripping at my flesh. I caught the dog by the neck, and when I had a good grip I tore off the creature's leg. The growling ceased, and it fell to the ground, losing most of its blood within a few seconds. The rage within me now boiled. I turned to confront the others. I raged at them, but they quickly withdrew.

I went to Frankenstein's arm and picked it up. Carrying it over to him, I placed the arm in his lap and looked at him for a time. "Why did you do this to me? Why? Why am I the only creature in the world without hope, without a future, and now without a past? Why? Why did you bring me into this world?" I began to rage at the heavens and sob uncontrollably. My head fell downward under the weight of my gloom.

I raised the shovel that I had brought with me and in a frenzy began to dig, raving as I lifted each shovelful of dirt. I went on in this way until my shoulders were level with the earth. Finally, I climbed from the pit and looked at my creator. I spoke aloud these words: "Ashes to ashes and dust to dust, so it is, even for you, Frankenstein. You are committed to the earth."

I raised his body and lowered it into the pit, being careful to place his detached arm across his bosom. Before covering him I decided to retrieve my Bible so that he might be buried properly. The little black book expressed words that would be appropriate to the burial. There were words in it that would adorn his gravestone.

I returned with the book and opened it to a chapter named James. My eye fell upon these words which I read aloud: "Whereas ye know not what shall be on the morrow. For what is your life? It is even a vapour, that appeareth for a little time, and then vanisheth away." These were the very same words that were on the tomb at the Lamar vault.

I picked a few leaves from an evergreen and threw them into the grave and onto his chest. I heaved in the first shovelful of dirt which landed on his face. I did not want to see his face disappear so soon, so I redirected my efforts toward his feet, legs, and torso. The hole began to fill, and as it did dirt slid onto his face from the pile at the other end of his body. Gradually dirt rolled onto the sides of his head and finally up to his eyes. Slowly, I lost sight of my creator as he vanished beneath the sliding slope of dirt.

The grave was filled. I stood. I could not control my gloom. I wept and fell upon the ground allowing death to court me once again. I buried the side of my face in the loose dirt. After a time I rolled over and stared into the sky. Tears rolled down the side of my nose and across my face and onto the ground. I lay this way for a long time until the clouds of the evening sun began to roll in. The ground had grown cold and when I awoke my eye noticed a small ant crawling across the dirt in front of me. I watched it move its head here and there, aimlessly it seemed. Suddenly I pounded the small creature into the earth until it disappeared from my sight.

I walked back toward my vaulted home with my Bible under my arm. For a moment I felt like a man returning from the burial of a loved one. I was lonely and unsure of my feelings at the loss of my creator. Each step gave me a feeling of worthlessness. It was not until I opened the door and saw the stone slabs and chisels on the workbench that the direction of my mind changed. I now focused on the task of what to put on the stone.

I did not know Frankenstein's birthday, or his death date. I decided on putting his name on the top of the stone. I chose the largest stone available with a rounded top. I wanted his memory to last and so needed words that best fit the everlasting nature of stone. I went down into the vault to look again through the interred books. Though there was some encrustation on the inscriptions the names were still visible.

Inside my cadaverous concrete vault I sought the words of men whose thoughts survived the years. As I looked at the interred books my feelings of fear and anger, hatred and love, were with me like an inconceivable distant echo. The loneliness of my existence was stronger than the task at hand.

I read once again from the Bible. These were the words that would adorn my creator's grave; I was struck by them:

For thou hast possessed my reins:
thou hast covered me in my mother's womb
I will praise thee;
for I am fearfully and wonderfully made:
marvelous are thy works; and that
my soul knoweth right well.
My substance was not hid from thee,
when I was made in secret,
and curiously wrought in the lowest parts of the earth.
Thine eyes did see my substance, yet being unperfect;
and in thy book all my members were written,
which in continuance were fashioned,
when as yet there was none of them.

I discovered other works that gave many details for the burial of a man. I read about putting the head of the body to the north or the right side to the east. I began to understand that parts of animals should be thrown in, as well as tools. I had no means of baking cakes, but I discovered that placing cakes on the body of the deceased allowed one to absorb the qualities and virtues of the deceased.

I learned that it was important to place an effigy of a rotting corpse on the stone. I was told by these writers that I should have removed the heart and intestines, and buried them somewhere else. I discovered that I should repeat these words over the body: "Eternal rest grant unto him, O Lord; and let perpetual light shine upon him."

It went on and on. I could find no agreement among men as to what was proper, and so the idea of all of this somehow seemed senseless. The words I had chosen seemed to be the only ones that spoke the truth. I felt compelled to put these words on the stone. I secured a chisel and hammer and began my work. By and by, I finally finished my task. The inscription was not as well formed as the lettering on the other stones, but it was readable. As I was finishing my work it became more and more obvious to me that men refused to accept death as a final end.

By engraving in stone the name of the creature beneath it, one gave some measure of immortality. I myself had no name and no date of birth, for only Frankenstein knew my birthday and he is now unable to speak. The thought of having no name made me angry. I dropped the chisel which made a ghostly cold clink, and before I knew it I was at the burial mound, full of a fury that had grown as I moved.

"On this mound I swear that your memory will be wiped off the face of the earth. I will have my revenge on you, on all of you!" In a fit of rage I seized the shovel and exhumed Frankenstein's body so that his head was visible. I reached down into the grave and opened his mouth. I raised the stone tablet and slammed it down into his face. I used my hands, and in a frenzy pushed all of the dirt back over his body. When I had finished, the stone was buried with him.

"You are truly destroyed, Frankenstein! No one will ever know you are here. I will tell no one of you, and even though you were given a name I have taken it away! I have denied you as you have denied me! Cursed be this day and all of the days after! I seek vengeance forever, to obliterate all, living and dead, until this scourge called man is destroyed!"

With rage in my heart I ran from the site and began toppling as many gravestones as possible. The larger ones I toppled with the use of my shovel, digging on one side until the structure was unstable, then shoving the gravestone over. With a large hammer I broke many tombs in half, shearing them off at ground level. I went in a fierce frenzy of fury from grave to grave until dusk began to approach.

I continued in this way for hours until I was tired, cold, and hungry. Then finally I headed toward my stone haven. At the entrance to the door I looked back on my work. I could see toppled and broken stones in the direction of my creator's grave like a procession of chaos. As the sun set, clouds began rolling in and with them a cold wind which blew my hair and howled across the frozen landscape of tombs. I stood at the threshold of my home and surveyed the stones that still stood, looking out across the panorama of death in every direction. Now, as I surveyed the scene, a thought moved slowly across my mind. I thought of my past and of Frankenstein's grave. There was nothing. There was no past. My time was now! My time was in the present. My future was now represented by all of the stones still standing

I cried out through the cold darkened cemetery, "There is a void within me, a wellspring of empty space, a part missing that fixes my being to oblivion. I have no name or purpose for my existence! I have nothing!"

After men are born, unlike myself they continue to receive protection, security, and shelter. In addition, they are shown affection and love which is demonstrated by the ever-attendant watchful eye of the mother and father. They are given food which produces physical strength, and when the threat of harm becomes imminent the parents do whatever they can to protect their offspring.

I have noticed this even among the animals in the forests of the countryside and moors. The larger creatures continue this caring for longer periods of time resulting in a strong animal. When it is time to leave the protection of the parents they do so with confidence. The wild bears, the cats, and the larger hoofed animals provide their young with those necessary ingredients that ensure calmness of mind, strength, and all of the manifestations or outcomes that love generates. The creatures grow and leave the protective world of their parents, and they do well. It is only a matter of a few years before they too are participating in this cycle; they then are loving, feeding, and protecting their offspring.

It was not so with me. Instead of loving parents I was rejected by my creator! I was not given food, but left to starve and sustain my life any way I could. I was subjected to cold and denied warmth and affection. I was hunted and had to rely upon my own strength for survival. My strength was an asset, as humans are not so endowed as myself. I slept in the forests and on mountains, unprotected from the elements. I had no one to touch me, or to demonstrate affection, or to even recognize my existence!

The frightful darkness that I was born into would not allow me the comfort of thoughts that humans experience. I lack the exquisite knowledge of existence of self! I do not know who I am! This void in the depth of my soul rips at my heart.

Long periods of sobbing racked my body, and death seemed a blissful alternative to extinguish my pain. If it were not for exquisite revenge, I would not have had the strength or will to carry on. Without revenge to sustain my life all would be hopeless. I would be like a dead fish floating on the surface of a vast ocean. Oh, how exquisite the thought of vengeance! It fills the void. When I am about to be engulfed by extinction, by the lonely hell within me, I find meaning and substance to my existence through revenge. Yet, I am still at a loss. When I look ahead there is nothing! When I try to feel there is a stabbing nothingness! Yes, vengeance is exquisite, but it has one flaw; I must sustain it or the void returns and engulfs me in a stream that tends toward death.

The funeral pyre that I had once thought to celebrate my extinction, that would extinguish the void and the remorse of my soul, now appeared an unpleasant proposition to end my suffering and the misery of life. For a moment I thought of perishing at the grave of my creator, but as with all the other times revenge soon snuffed out the desire for death. During these moments of great despair revenge is always uplifting. It sucks the life out of my despondency. My dreams have often been filled with swirling clouds of smoky nothingness. These horrible dreams only subsided when revenge became my constant companion, and revenge is a far better state of mind.

The furious anger within me did not cripple my being or numb me. Revenge did not allow me to think of death. It gave me life and raised my spirits! This powerful force dried my tears and controlled my sobbing. When gloom weakened my whole body, revenge uplifted me! When I relaxed my will, the overwhelming pain of loneliness would not subside. I once thought, foolishly so, that I could be a man, a human being. I wanted to tread the wide earth and be like them; but there was a constant reminder, my face, my horrid features, which haunted my every move. This prevented me from being normal. Even when I awoke into life with the warmth provided only rarely, the void was always there, menacing me, wanting to destroy me.

It is here among the dead that revenge will have its fulfillment. I will range through this city of the dead consumed by my friend Revenge.

My creator has deserted me! He would not comply with my wish for a mate. This would have been my salvation. Frankenstein would not conduct himself as the animals of the forest do. He would not provide for his offspring. For this he is cursed! The curse will be consuming. I will make sure of it! Frankenstein's name and existence have been extinguished from this earth. The secret of his death and burial will perish with me.

Men will ask about Victor Frankenstein and the whereabouts of his remains, but they will be hidden forever. They will be here, unknown to all but me. Soon, after some years, all memory of his existence will cease to be. Revenge will consume all! The void that men wrought in me will be theirs!

Being here in this cemetery, amongst the dead, has given me insight. It is here that immortality can be gained. It is in these inscriptions and stones. It is here in the vast land of death that I will seek to accomplish my goal. My gloom and misery will be no more! My wretched condition will no longer draw me to seek death. All I have is my life!

While corpses decay in this place season after season, I shall flourish. My revenge shall flourish! I am exhilarated beyond any point I have reached before! My spirits are now elevated by my new nature; the past is forgotten, the present is determined, and the future is guided. I will destroy mankind until I perish! My path is clear. My goals are clear; vengeance is mine!

Hamel's Diary
December 1848

Upon my return to England my first impulse was to see my beloved Jane. I pondered the strange circumstances by which we had met. My heart longed for her presence. I could only think of her beautiful eyes as I rushed to her home. The many letters I had written to her were kept close to my heart in my coat pocket. I clutched them often during my voyage to the Arctic.

As we arrived at her home, I opened the carriage door before it had come to a complete stop and jumped out. My heart beat rapidly as I waited for a response to my knock at the door. The door quickly opened and there she stood. My beloved Jane was as beautiful as ever.

"Joshua! My God! You are here before me!" she said.

My eyes could not look upon a more glorious sight. Jane's eyes watered and my heart was moved. Before I knew it my arms were around her and our eyes mingled with each flowing thought. Our lips moved closer with each moment. As we were about to kiss, suddenly Jane stepped back and said, "Why have you not written? Surely there were opportunities to convey messages to me on your way north . . .?"

I did not allow her to finish but gently placed my hushing finger on her lips and whispered, "Hush, hush. My love for you has been recorded in the numerous letters that I wrote and kept clutched to my bosom inside my coat. Here," I said.

I reached into my coat pocket and produced the bundle of letters which fell from my hands. "Each letter was as warm as a fire. These letters provided warmth against the coldness of this life. Though I wanted you to receive them they only reminded me of you. I could not then part with my treasure and they became my hope as a whole. I could not part with my feelings in pieces, but present them to you as a whole."

I tried to go on but Jane interrupted. "Give me all of your heart. I will read each one as a piece of your soul. I long to hear your love for me. I love you, my beloved."

She moved forward and in that moment my dreams rushed forward. We kissed and embraced one another for what seemed an eternity. Finally we moved inside the house and the door closed behind us.

BOOK III

THE REVELATION

The Creature's Notes

December 1848

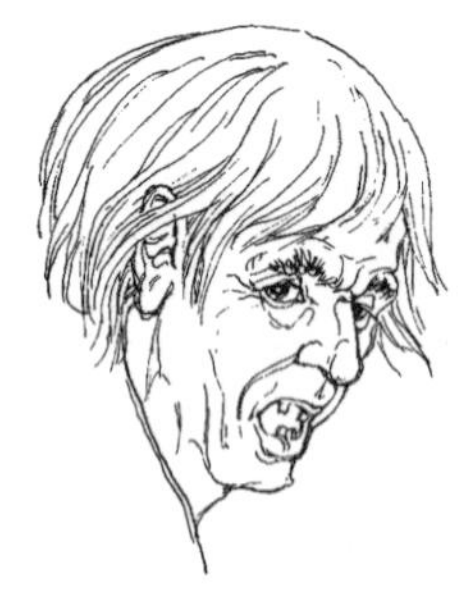

From time to time my mind faltered. I could not sustain the vengeful thoughts. When this happened the haunting music returned. A sad song played in my ears, a wailing dirge of wind whose notes welled up in me with a gloom that was frightful. I could not tell if it was the wind playing with my mind or my mind with the wind, but each note danced a sorrowful waltz across the stones of death. I expected to see some mournful ghost appear before my eyes. The music had a mysterious significance which froze the landscape like a drawing on a canvas. The bare trees no longer shook from the wind; the twigs and bushes stood still and quiet, as a black and white painting on a large easel. I shut my eyes to rid my mind of this haunting picture, but it lingered. I moved backwards, slowly, to shut the door, and imagined that what I had envisioned was still being seen by unknown eyes, still being heard by unknown ears, and still being felt by a sorrowful heart. The last rays of light were closed out of my tomb as I retired to my vault. I no longer wished to know the mystery of the music. I accepted it.

The following night I experienced a strange occurrence. It was a dark clear night and the moon was down. I decided to leave my tomb and sit out under the stars to ponder their meaning, and mine. As I sat at the entrance to the vault I saw a light a considerable distance away but heading in my direction.

As it came closer I heard the hoofs of horses and the roll of wheels. It was a wagon being drawn by two horses. As it approached, I positioned myself behind a gravestone to obtain a protected view. The wagon came to within a short distance of my vault and two men began talking and unloading items from the rear of the wagon. I moved closer to observe what they were doing at such a late hour.

When I was within hearing range I stopped and looked in the direction of the light, which came from a lantern, and watched the men leap from the rear of the dray. They were now removing shovels, ropes, and other tools. I thought their activity strange for I was not familiar with burials at night. The relatives of Frankenstein were buried during the day so these happenings were very strange. I moved a little closer and saw that the men had a unique lantern. It was covered on three sides, thus directing the light in only one direction. They pulled a large roll of cloth out and laid their tools upon it. These tools consisted of crowbars, files, awls, and chisels. They were also equipped with shovels that were totally made of wood. There was a covering which they began to assemble into a makeshift tent. Within a few minutes the tent was erected over a grave, and I began to hear the muffled sounds from the wooden shovels as they turned over dirt. I crept to the side of the tent until I could see within.

One man referred to his accomplice as "Limbo" while the other was called "Finny Price." Limbo shoveled into the area above the grave and placed the dirt on a large cloth next to the burial site. He worked quickly, and it was not long before I heard his digging instrument strike what sounded like wood. I was astonished that they were burying someone so late at night and on top of an existing grave.

My deductions soon proved to be incorrect. They were stealing a body! The men used the crowbars to pry open the side of the coffin. Then one man jumped into the hole and tied a rope around the corpse's neck. When he climbed up from the tomb, they tugged together and pulled up the corpse. I was horrified at what I saw. This corpse was being exhumed from its resting place!

I watched them remove the clothes from the corpse, and then a most ghastly event occurred. One of the men opened the corpse's mouth and with an awl punched each and every tooth out of its gaping jaws, laughing as he did so! After removing the teeth they threw his clothes back into the grave. Each tooth, still bloody, was dropped into a small sack which Limbo carried around his waist.

After this I watched them bury the empty coffin with the utmost care. They replaced the dirt and gravestone along with the flowers.

In a very precise manner everything was replaced in the same exact position that they were in before the excavation began. With this accomplished, they folded the corpse with the head touching the knees and the feet folded back to the rear. They tied the corpse in this position and crammed it into a bag which was sacked up and thrown into the wagon. The men disassembled the tent, loaded the tools on board, climbed atop the wagon, and then hastily departed.

When they were out of sight I reflected on what I had seen. While the digging was taking place the dirt was thrown onto a canvas sheet so that the grass would not show signs of being disturbed. I noticed that the clacking noise produced by the wooden shovel was quiet compared with that of iron, which they occasionally used when a large rock was encountered. Their procedures were methodical and professional, and I realized they were grave robbers who made their living in this manner. With a shock I realized that I had witnessed the mechanics of my own creation!

I followed the wagon for a considerable distance until they came to a barn. Unloading the corpse from the wagon, they took it inside. They pulled the corpse out of the sack, untied it, leaving the noose around the neck, and stretched it out on a wooden table. It was here that another barbaric crime was committed. They inspected the body and noticed various identifying marks. They pulled out very sharp knives and sliced these marks off of the body, then put the corpse back in the sack and returned it to the wagon.

From their talk I learned that this cemetery was very close to London. They began a discussion, and I turned my ears toward their conversation. I remember they spoke these words: "We have made an agreement about the price of these things with Golem," said the one called Limbo. "He does not want to pay a fair price! Perhaps we should begin selling our goods elsewhere! I have spoken to our fellow resurrectionists and have an agreement that we will all raise the price together! I have persuaded them to follow my leadership,"

"I think we should take what we can," Price replied. "Times are changing and our occupation grows more perilous by the day. Riots have broken out in various parts of the country."

Limbo was reticent as they boarded the dray. As they pulled off, I heard Limbo say; "Still, we might raise our price and be successful. If we mention to Golem that Inspector Glennon would be interested in the sick man we took to his laboratory . . ." I could hear no more as they drove on. I decided to follow them.

Was I created thus? Why do they not respect the end of a life? This poor man, having been exhumed, was being denied his resting place. The wagon proceeded along the dark deserted lanes until it reached the cobblestone streets of London. Slowly it moved ahead, like a funeral wagon, with the two men looking warily about. Finally they arrived at an abode which appeared to be the mansion of a wealthy businessman.

They drove around the garden and unloaded the sack beside the rear entrance. Limbo rapped on the door and soon a light appeared in the window. A servant answered the door and a discussion took place which I could not hear. The servant left for a short time and returned with a small bag. The man called Finny opened it and began counting the money that it contained. The two men thanked the servant and placed the sack into a hamper by the door. They went on, with fiendish grins on their faces, into the night.

I stayed behind to see what would transpire. While I waited I noticed the name of the resident engraved on the door. It read: "Sir Jeffrey Wolf - Member of Parliament." Before daybreak, two servants appeared and loaded the hamper into a carriage. It was still dark with few people around. When they departed I followed them by leaping onto the back of the wagon.

We soon passed St. Mary's Axe Street, on to Leadenhall Street, and then across the river Thames into Southwark. When the carriage began to slow I leaped and hid behind a row of hedges. The carriage stopped at a building, which, according to its sign, was called St. Thomas Anatomy School. Below this name was written two other names; "Astley Golem, M.R.C.S. - Surgeon, Joshua Hamel - Assistant Surgeon."

Within a short time two young men came out the front door and unloaded the hamper. They looked about warily and took it inside. The carriage then quickly left. I went around the side of the school building and found a window through which to spy. I saw the two young men at the hamper, removing the sack and pulling out the body. They untied the ropes and lifted the corpse onto a table, where they stretched it out.

Daylight was now approaching. I was unable to see what would happen next for I knew that the townspeople would soon be walking about, and my ability to conceal myself would be greatly hampered. I retreated to the cemetery to weigh the horrible things I had witnessed.

In my haven I pondered with a heavy mind the events of the day. Two men had removed a corpse from its grave. Instead of burying the body they resurrected it and carried it to a wealthy man's house where they received payment for it. Again I felt sure that I had witnessed the same horrid crime that brought me into existence! This poor soul was to be delivered to yet another crime which was to forever change the course of my mind.

* * *

I wanted to see what was to become of the poor creature that had been so unceremoniously snatched from its resting place. I waited until dark to return to town and went back to the school to see what had become of the corpse. It was fortunate that upon arrival I was able to use the same vantage point. The body was still there and a group of men were gathered around it. Two of the men were the same ones I had seen the night before. Their voices came to me faintly through the window.

There was one gentleman whom the others referred to as Dr. Golem. He looked familiar to me. Dr. Astley Golem seemed energetic and attentive. His mannerisms were graceful. He was introduced by a fellow physician who talked about his position in various professional societies. This physician went on to say that Golem had great influence in political circles in London with Members of Parliament, and was one of the most highly respected surgeons in London.

As I peered through the window I watched Golem lead a discussion on the medical importance of dissections, and the possibility of immortality for mankind if disease could be conquered. After his speech he picked up a knife and with great skill began to dissect the corpse. As he cut, he explained the function of various organs and the extensive accomplishments that science had made over the years.

As he excised the rotting flesh, he remarked that, "If putrefaction could be controlled then man could live forever." He threw the rotted flesh into a pan on the floor. Making a large incision in the chest cavity, he removed the heart which he held up as a pagan priest would hold an offering, to the pleasure of those gathered around.

I discerned that of those gathered, some were students, some were doctors, and others merely spectators. The students were there to learn anatomical science through dissection, the doctors were there to teach, and the spectators just to satisfy a macabre curiosity.

Dr. Golem emphasized that in order to operate on the living, the dead must be used to acquaint the student with the names, likeness, and location of the organs. Another surgeon, whom I subsequently came to know as Joshua Hamel, questioned Golem about the necessity of using corpses for such work. He remarked that models made from casts or paper could be used just as effectively.

Golem responded to his questions with bloated sobriety. "Blood is what you will encounter on a living being, and tissue, real tissue! Perhaps red dye and clay would be more to your liking!" he said. The audience erupted in laughter and Hamel's apparent protest was turned to mockery.

Golem continued his oratory as he mutilated the corpse, pointing out that there were not enough resurrected bodies to meet the demand. He then, with great insincerity, denounced the men who resurrected the dead which he called the "lowest dregs of society." He promised those gathered that he and Sir Jeffrey Wolf would support reform of the laws, which, in their present form, "allowed for this sort of grave robbery to occur." In the same breath he pointed out that cadavers were being sold for as much as fourteen guineas, and that any act making resurrection illegal would raise the price, something with which he was greatly concerned.

Playing to his audience, Golem began to tell anecdotes from his practice. It seemed that the more gruesome the story, the more his listeners laughed and enjoyed him. Their laughter struck a chord of anger in my heart.

"Once, at Newgate Prison," he related, "a prisoner had died of a rare disease. His corpse was therefore quite valuable, for we surgeons would pay a good price for such a body. The corpse had to be as fresh as possible, however, and so the vile resurrectionists devised a plot. With intelligence obtained from inside the prison, they learned that the deceased prisoner had no known relatives, so one of the resurrectionists dressed as a clergyman, another as a mournful sister, and the final one as the bereaved brother. It was with tearful eyes that they convinced the authorities to release the body. They were followed to the cemetery where two others, dressed as gravediggers, joined in. Seeing the coffin lowered into the ground the prison officials left, after which the body was quickly exhumed and dropped off at Guy's Hospital."

The laughter was now sickening to my ears. I closed my eyes so that my anger would be restrained. When I looked again, I saw body parts splattered into the pan under the table. Soon the pan was full, and a student came over and unceremoniously dumped it out of the rear window. My revulsion for them increased. I began to thoroughly loathe these men of science; they are animals, less than animals. These fiends were of the same ilk who educated my creator.

The thought now occurred to me that my creator had come from such a school. Tears rolled from my eyes as I now imagined the laughter made over the scraps of bodies that made up my existence.

I thought of my creator hearing and laughing at the time of my creation, and even extracting some laughter himself while participating in the demonic act of my creation. He created me from the mutilated bodies of these wretched men! I was able to compose myself and attend to more of these grotesque tales. I needed the notes of Captain Walton. The story of my creation is in those pages. If he lives I will find him.

Soon Hamel took over some of the cutting as Dr. Golem spoke about each part removed. Golem explained the classic sequence of dissection as done by Vesalius, which started with the abdomen, the pelvis, the chest, the face, the surrounding muscle tissue, the head, and finally the extremities. As he continued to mutilate the corpse, he spoke of the almshouses in the eastern end of the city and the cemeteries for poor people. He pointed out that several pauper cemeteries were the favorite target of Sir Jeffrey Wolf's men. Wolf personally ordered the men in his pay to work the eastern sector; he had a dislike for the destitute and found it particularly pleasing to ravage the cemeteries in this part of London.

Golem went on to tell his filthy audience that once Wolf, in his early years, attempted a resurrection himself. Finny Price, a sycophant for Wolf, misled him about how easy it was to rob the eastern cemeteries. Price found the poorhouses in the eastern sector of London easy targets. There were ferrymen at most of these institutions; these were men who worked at the poorhouse who could ferry a body for a price. Wolf, thinking that he could economize, tried to do without the services of Price by going directly to the ferrymen. On one particular occasion the corpse was identified as friendless by the ferryman, and soon thereafter Wolf appeared masked as a relative. He was tardy, however, and the corpse had already been taken for burial, so Wolf was forced to go to the cemetery alone to exhume the body.

Being inexperienced in resurrections he did not wait for a moonless night, nor did he take along the proper equipment; his lantern was not shaded on three sides, and his shovels were steel instead of wood. As a result of the noise from his shovel hitting rocks, the townspeople in the nearby area were alerted. Soon a small mob gathered on the road. One in the mob was armed with a horse whip. This man proceeded to charge down the road, surprising Wolf, and whipped him quite severely before he managed to escape. Wolf was not recognized and he was able to escape with his life.

After this baleful tale, Golem grew serious and took the lecture into another direction, while beside him Mr. Hamel continued with the final chores of the dissection. Golem explained, "Water is the matrix of life, gentlemen. Without its presence no life would be viable. We are essentially aquatic creatures despite the fact that all of our lives are spent walking the earth. We have dissected the human body, and have seen that fluids inhabit most parts of the human organism. Cells, tissues, and organs, as well as skin, live in a watery environment. This wasted body before us was once able to maintain internal temperature; from icy extremes to excessive heat, our body can survive because of its watery structure. When a body is frozen at very low temperatures, we have discovered that the water between the cells and surrounding tissue crystallizes and destroys those cells, making it impossible to revitalize life or limb." He paused for a time, looking up to the heavens in a preposterous show of intellect.

"Anatomical knowledge is not yet complete," he continued. "We have discovered the way blood is distributed, the names of bone attachments, and have knowledge of muscle structures. We have studied the works of other surgeons, in typhus fever cases, and the different forms of the fever as explained by various physicians. Through anatomical research we have discovered lesions in the brain, and as a result have made some progress in understanding fever, including the massive deaths that occurred in 1812 among Napoleon's troops. We have a greater understanding of the brain, and of the fever that struck in the period from 1816 to 1819. In Ireland thousands died from it. Smallpox devastated the children of Chester from 1772 to 1777, even though inoculation was introduced in 1721.

"To understand this disease better we have had the benefit of cadavers. We have seen the liver and spleen enlarged, and are able to deduce the outcome of such happenings. If not for our friend here, we would not have made this progress!"

Golem's voice grew in intensity and seriousness as he continued. "We will one day be able to defeat these diseases and find a way to extend life! We may even find a way to prevent the blood from freezing, which, in my opinion, would usher in a new era in medical science. When we can find a way to stop the water in the body from turning into ice we may be able to freeze a body after death and resuscitate it later. Death will be eventually conquered! There will be breakthroughs, and when that happens we may awaken the patient, cure him, and restore him to life!"

My desire for revenge was heightened when I heard the fiend say, "We have found that at -320 degrees Fahrenheit, no decomposition of the body takes place. We could, gentlemen, freeze a subject with the hope that our science will revive him in the future. With the advances being made I am confident that this will be a possibility. Perhaps sooner than you think!"

To continue this filthy race? I cannot allow it!

The students listened attentively. It was apparent their curiosity had been aroused. As Mr. Hamel finished with the cadaver and threw the last pound of flesh into the pail on the floor, he walked over to the window just above me. I was almost discovered. Hamel looked directly at me but did not seem to see me. He appeared to be lost in contemplation. I was ready for whatever was to happen, but Hamel turned and began cleaning the medical instruments.

After the students had disassembled and left for the night, Golem invited Hamel to his laboratory. Mr. Hamel's spirit was somewhere else but he went along. The two hailed a coach and were off to their destination. I ran behind them for a distance, and when opportunity presented itself, leaped onto the rear of the vehicle.

When the coach began to slow I jumped from it and secured a hiding place from which to spy on these ghouls. They paid the coachman and entered through a side door. I ran from my hiding place and crept to the rear of the structure, where I found no windows from which to spy but discovered a ladder positioned against the side of the building. I scurried up to the roof where I was able to peer down into the laboratory through a glass skylight. As I looked down I could see the two surgeons had approached a coffin-like box. It was equipped with wires and tubes on the outside which projected into the interior of the structure. The container resembled a coffin in that it was the approximate length of a body, though somewhat longer, and was hinged with a lid. The lid had a glass covering at one end through which one could look inside.

I heard Golem say to Hamel, "This will be for us. I have another that I am constructing."

"What are these devices?" Hamel asked.

"They are cold units. A simple enough name for a complicated device, my dear friend," he responded.

"And their purpose is no doubt linked to the fantastic lecture I heard tonight?" said Hamel.

"Quite right, but not so fantastic, Hamel. These precious devices will change the course of history. When I have boarded this vessel I will have obtained bliss! I offer bliss to you if your trust can be assured!"

Hamel looked strangely at Golem. He turned for a moment facing the window. Abruptly, he turned once again and spoke. "My trust? I have listened to your lectures and to the complaints about them. I have heard your tales of resurrection and have only just returned from the icy regions with you, attempting to bring back the corpse of a demon. 'Trust,' you ask?"

Now I recognized the fiends! I had seen them through the ice, in my half-conscious state aboard the ship. Their faces I now recognized! They were the ones that brought me back from the ice.

Golem spoke again. "Well, then I see you are just a contrary fellow, opposing me in private, but reticent in public. Yet your soft heart offers no solution to the problems of men. You can offer no ultimate solutions to the problems of disease and aging. Well, let me offer you a solution. I have almost gone insane from being unable to talk to anyone about the details of my experiments. For over three years I have worked on my project and have kept the details a secret between me and the walls herein. I had hoped to retrieve the corpses of Frankenstein and his creation for the purpose of study. I had hoped to analyze the creature, not in the way it was animated, or created from cadavers, but in the way the blood and body reacted to prolonged cold. I would have been able to study the frozen organs, limbs, blood, and tissue, from which I might have been able to deduce the necessary data for my own experimentation. Unlike Frankenstein, I am not concerned with creation but with preservation, with preventing the corruption of the body and the loss of the essence of life, or what makes us who we are. Why bother with scraps of dead bodies as Frankenstein did, to create a fiend? We can do without such reanimation if we can cheat the grim reaper. I want to deny heaven and hell their populations!"

Golem was now pacing the room, gesturing with both hands.

"For what ultimate purpose could the reanimation of lifeless matter serve, you ask. And I tell you that lifeless matter could be reanimated in the womb. We can then train these children as our own and not leave chance to develop the mind of our creation, as did Frankenstein. Our offspring can be born into a world from which they will never have to depart. The gravedigger will be put out of business! Let us no longer trouble ourselves with wills and preparations at the cemetery, or with the construction of catacombs and vaults!"

Golem was raving as a man possessed. "I have heard your protests about resurrections! They will no longer be necessary. Death will not have to occur! Who shall be the recipient of such a precious gift? That will be for us to decide, Hamel! The greatest minds will be worth preserving! The men of our profession can decide who lives forever! Our decisions must be geared to save the most productive of our society. Let the men who make the discoveries be saved, as well as those whose expertise allows for the operation of government. All the others can have their heaven or their hell if they so believe!

"I have thrown myself into this endeavor with pleasure. I was alone, but now I have you. You will help to carry out this project and we both will journey into man's future, each with full credit. This I offer you!"

Hamel said nothing. I saw him turn and look blankly ahead.

Golem continued. "I would have liked to have had the benefit of examining the corpse of Frankenstein and his creation, even of taking them with us, so that at some future date they might be revived. But I am now sure that the journey was not in vain. The blood sample that I took from the creature has proven my hypothesis about glycerol! We can prepare the human frame to defeat the ravages of death. I have discovered how to do this! I have discovered how to lower the temperature to -373 degrees Fahrenheit! At this extreme the waste and degradation are defeated."

Suddenly Golem lowered his voice, leaned toward Hamel and grasped his arm. His tone was persuasive, beseeching, as he said, "Listen to me, Hamel. I have found a way to cheat the grave. It will no longer matter if there is a heaven or a hell for us. We will never enter the gates of heaven, or be vanquished to the fires of hell and into the jaws of Satan! Nor will we be eaten by worms, or tormented by devils as Dante claimed. The flames of hell from this day forth are meaningless! There will be a continual dawn in which the poets will no longer view sleep as a taste of death, but of life! There will be no passing.

"If you join with me, Hamel, we will literally be friends forever! The poets will no longer be able to write of autumn decay as a symbol of man's demise. Oh, I know you may argue that men may be changed for the worst, but listen, will not love and hate take on new meaning? What of youth and age, man and nature, and mortality and imagination? You will ask these questions! I have the answers.

"I have imagined you arguing that if men did not die then imagination would suffer; that the great works of art would never have acquired the imagination and beauty needed for their creation. You would argue that we would not feel the desire to create things that endure time. I have heard you argue that once the threat of death is taken away imagination will cease. Look there, Hamel! At Hogarth's painting! It is a horrid drawing, but it reveals a truth. Time itself will cease to exist!

"Well, I say let the earth devour the artistic works that fill London's museums! Let the earth have back the fine engravings and paintings, and let us soar off, not into heaven, or into hell, but into eternity! Let us experience timelessness and allow our imaginations to offer other works, works unknown at this time, but no less great and imaginative. Yes, I can say with certitude that man's imagination will not falter with immortality, but will grow to understand nature and science and all that needs conquering. Imagination can never be fully developed with death knocking at its door!

"You cannot be a sworn lover of gloom, of falling leaves, of autumn, of cemeteries, of Dante's poems, of suffering now, of eternal death! You see . . . yes, I see at this moment that I am at the beginning of a creed unknown to other men! You can help me shape the tenets of that creed! With an eternity ahead of us we can find the cures! We can explore the entire earth and solve its mysteries! This beautiful precious dream can be ours to share with those who deserve it! The hourglass of time will have run through its course. The year and date, and the hour and second will no longer matter!"

Hamel seemed stunned and indecisive. He attempted to say something but was cut off.

"That is not all," Golem said. "The seed of man could be preserved so that his line could continue with the mate of his choice. Women could enjoy the gift of intelligent offspring by choosing the frozen sperm of men of their choice. At some time in the future the world can be populated with the offspring of the greatest minds; the exact details of which, though difficult, could be worked out in the beginning, by *us*!

"We stand to be the greatest scientists in the world of forever. How can you refuse? Let the poor die and keep their kind in the cemeteries, and let us live forever! The places of the dead will become museums, places for us to visit and muse over, of those who did not have the opportunity to experience the joy of everlasting life. We can laugh together at the fact that they never knew of the reality that we now live!

"We will not have to worry about literature being lost or destroyed. We can simply freeze the mind that created it. We will not have to ponder the meanings of nightmares, of worms eating our flesh, and of greatness being denied. The end result of our experiments can be borne out before our eyes. If my understanding of typhus or smallpox is not correct, then I will have all the time in the world to find its solution!

"Why this fate should fall to me is unknown. I will have an eternity to ponder it; precious life will be extended! Civilizations will not sink, and strife will not permanently destroy our treasures. The murdered can be fixed and restored at a future date while the criminal will be denied immortality and sent to a cemetery. Those who are guilty of hideous crimes shall be denied everlasting life! Do not think of me as mad, Hamel. I have discovered many things which I am now only beginning to share with you.

"The quantity and quality of ideas will increase with the passing of each day. I have thought of the great works of literature and how many of them would no longer be applicable to the immortal. *Paradise Lost* would soon become a meaningless allegory. Men will no longer have regard for the warring between heaven and hell, between Satan and God. It will no longer be necessary for us to ponder, for we would be between these two worlds, not in either. To reign in hell, or serve in heaven is now irrelevant!"

Golem turned and walked with Hamel into an adjoining room still raving about his obsession.

I had heard enough. These were the fiends who brought me back from the ice! They did not know that even in my frozen state I had seen their distorted faces. I heard and thought of their goal. I learned of the trip to retrieve my body for experimentation. I have heard their sermons, of pretended love for the human condition, of the hypocritical cry for the advancement of science and the welfare of mankind; it is only a guise to hide the true character of men who have turned their trade into a horror. Golem's spirit of benevolence, which he would bestow on the wealthy but not on the destitute — unless it were on a dissection table — was transformed into the most horrid wretchedness. His dissection room — a warehouse of cruelty from which men, who only the day before lay in an almshouse bed, friendless and luckless — was to me a symbol of all that was evil. Men who were carted away from Tyburn Road, dead by hanging, mostly poor, were stretched out at the intersection of his science and morality.

The world of forever is not his to possess! Who bestowed upon him the right to put upon the world his ideas! Who gave him license to resurrect me from my icy tomb, his purpose being now quite clear, to dissect my body! Well, it is of no consequence, for no one will remember if he was an evil man or a good man. It will not matter what he did, or why he died! His life will be forfeited! His existence will be terminated, and his filthy assistant will die also!

My existence has been denied even though I walk among the living. Even now, though the red fluid flows through me, I reside in the depths of darkness. I shall live there no more, but work my vengeance in the brightest spirit of enlightenment. Revenge has once again lightened my path!

As I began my descent from the rooftop I looked down and saw two men. One of them had a sack at his side. He knocked at the door, and when Golem answered the knock, he recognized the gentlemen. With a great show of politeness he invited them inside. I overheard the caller naming the other man Limbo and I knew these were the men I had seen at the cemetery. Limbo instructed his partner to carry the cadaverous sack inside.

I have decided to put my pen down now. I can write no more of the events of this day. If by chance I encounter Price or Limbo again . . . they will die!

Hamel's Diary
December 30th, 1848

I write these things today to record that Golem is quite mad. After his diatribe I said to him, "I must be going now, Dr. Golem."

He grabbed me by the shoulder and urged, "Ponder what I have said, Hamel, and remember that what you have seen must be kept secret."

I quickly left the lab. As I was going to the front door there was a knock at the rear entrance. I looked back and saw two men entering, both of them criminal in their appearance and mannerisms. I walked away from Skinner Street with a heavy heart and mind. Golem's proposals were dangerous and I could not agree with his ideas. Feeling bewildered and tired I returned to my apartment. All was quiet and the dampness of the air made me naturally sleepy.

I fell into my bed totally exhausted, and within a short time I succumbed to fatigue. I awoke in a state of confusion from a horrible dream. In my dream I was standing face to face with an evil woman. I did not recognize her. She taunted me. She attacked my sense of being and dignity. She stood before me and berated me until she was ready to convert her argument to violence. I saw her floating, hung by strings it seemed, like a puppet, floating from side to side around my body. I was unable to move, and as I tried to struggle free, my legs were paralyzed! I grew extremely fearful. I screamed and agonized in a state of terror.

Just when the horror was at its height two daggers suddenly appeared in front of me. I looked down at them, grasped them firmly in both hands, and without thought I struck at the evil figure. I penetrated her body several times but there was no blood. As she came closer to me I managed to thrust one knife into her face. Again there was no blood, and to my horror she just laughed. She laughed hysterically and then said, "You cannot kill me, I am immortal." I stabbed again furiously, and when she swung low at my knee level I stabbed her in the back with all of my strength. I saw her swing backward, suspended on strings, into the dark recesses of the void ahead. She swung back at me, right up to my face, frozen, with a horrid grin. "You cannot kill me, I am immortal!" she screamed.

I looked into her eyes. I did not see existence but a dark void, darker than the void just behind her, and in front of me. With my fist I pounded her in the face. "You can die and will die, or I will beat you for an eternity!" I screamed. I hit and struck at her violently and screamed, "You will die!" The creature stood her position despite my ferocious attack. She floated there and grinned a horrible smile of hatred. I stood firm and never stopped beating the fiend until I awoke in a dreadful sweat.

I sat up in bed for a while, trying to shake the terror from my soul. I forced myself up and looked into the mirror. It then came to me, in a spontaneous moment of insight, that I was never attached to anyone. My father would not look me in the eye, and my mother was completely detached from all around her. In fact, my father was distant with our relatives, as well as with my mother. They were both alone and isolated in the world. My mother tried to find comfort for herself by letting me sleep with her every night. I did this until I was five or six years of age.

My mother never communicated her love. She slept in her bed, quiet, in a state of depression, with only me to hug. I did not play with other children at this time, as I was kept inside and never taken anywhere by either parent. I remember feeling isolated and extremely detached when I was old enough to be given my sister's room. She had long since departed, leaving us without any explanation. My mother's condition grew worse. I attempted to find a brighter perspective, but I continually felt as if I would become insane or die from loneliness. I grew into a voiceless creature.

It has taken me years to come to grips with my past. Still I am not sure of all the manifestations of how my mind has been affected. It is quite clear to me that I am floating through life. Things come and go.

People and events pass by me, leaving no mark. There must be others — people who live unaware of who they are, lost, without hope, survivors with missing parts and links. It is my hope that I can fill the void and the blackness that dwell within. I think of this emptiness as The Void.

I left my apartment after washing. I was soon to understand the omen of my nightmare.

* * *

December 31st, 1848

I remember seeing a cloud in the sky that was as black as I had ever seen. There was not a single other cloud in view on this day, and its forlorn aspect grew into a great representation of isolation. This was the day that I learned of my mother's coma, and owing to my state of mind, the cloud took on forms of her desolate existence. She was alone in the world. She had no loving relations or family. No one in the world could have been as stoic as she. My father was no better. He never told her of his love, if he felt any. He could not help her. She was like the isolated dark cloud that I now beheld on the western horizon.

The sun was beginning to set, thrusting behind the cloud which made it all the more dark. The cloud had no particular shape, though my eye searched for an unconscious design. It was thick in the center, but around its edges, tangential to the sky, it had the appearance of a paintbrush smear, a stroke beaten into the sky.

At the hospital I looked into the face of someone I did not know. I whispered into her ears that I would be with her daily, and that in death she would not be forsaken as in life. I knew not if she could hear me. I tried to feel for her as a son would, but I did not know how. I only felt the same emotions that one would feel for a stranger.

I was overwhelmed and began to sob uncontrollably. I was totally isolated and separated from all. My detached state of mind has hindered me throughout life. I am not sure I ever experienced love, for all relationships now seemed but a desire to be part of something. I need companionship more than anything else in the world. I have an emptiness which lives and undulates on its own. I cannot believe anyone has ever been as familiar with oblivion or knows it as well as I.

As I stood at her deathbed, I could not feel what I was suppose to. She had taught me well. I could not feel the normal pain that a son feels for his mother's final illness. I did not know the poor wretch that I stood beside. When friends and colleagues discovered that my mother lay on her deathbed there would be great sympathy — but the kind of sympathy that normal people feel. They could not possibly know that what I felt was the pain of her life, not the pain of her death.

As I stood before her the full force of it struck me. My mother was insane! Her father left before she knew him, and her mother felt extreme hatred for her. As a result she had no one to care for her. When my father abandoned their relationship she fell into utter despair. She went insane. To my knowledge she was always a misanthrope. It grew worse after the divorce. She hated and distrusted people so much that she shut herself off from the rest of the world. She would not receive callers or see anyone and consumed herself in despair. She began to take laudanum in such great amounts that she often fell into unconsciousness. She was adrift in a sea of madness. Her constant companion was laudanum. My parents were doomed from the beginning.

My father committed suicide. The precise reasons remain unknown to me. He had been a heavy drinker most of his life, and as a result suffered an injury which required the amputation of a leg. He could not show emotion except when dominated by gin. He did not know himself. He was afraid of closeness and was extremely reticent for my entire childhood. I sought his love and often became dispirited when he denied what I needed most.

I tried with all of my heart to be as he was. If I saw him reading, I read. If he conducted experiments, I tried them. My attempts to reach him always ended in failure. I could not break the coldness of his heart. I am so much like him that I hate myself! He had the same cold routine for over twenty years. I do not think my father ever hugged or kissed my mother in my presence, or told her of his love. In fact, he was hardly ever present in our household. His presence became known to me by his drunken returns, and his denial of my attempts to communicate. He was a man running away from intimacy. He was fearful of direct expression.

He was pained by his past, a past I knew little of. I know that his mother often sobbed for no apparent reason, and he scorned her for this. When she died I was not told of it. All of the circumstances of her death were kept secret. My father said nothing. I will never know what happened to my grandmother, nor even the circumstances of my grandfather's death, or where he was buried. The most ordinary knowledge of family relations was hidden from me. I know almost nothing of my relatives.

My mother drank excessively also, and soon I began to stay in the garden to avoid seeing her. I have only now realized that the garden was where rejection soaked my mind with emptiness. I often went there just to weep. I had no desire to see my mother lying in her dark chamber. I left her for my own little world. Fortunately, I was given a childhood friend. His name was Trevor, the child of a neighbor. He was the only one allowed to visit me behind the locked garden gate. My mother once told me that she and my father agreed to keep me sheltered, away from all outside influences. They believed that the mind could be cultivated in solitude, through reading the great works of literature, yet they gave me little guidance. They thought that interaction with too many people made one foolish. There was a lock on the gate which was always kept secured. Only Trevor was allowed in.

I often spent the night by my mother's bed trying to comprehend what was wrong. My mind was left to wander on its own, to drift, as if on a raft in an icy sea. I think the dreams that haunt me come from there, but I cannot confirm it with any certitude. I cannot comprehend with any exactness their meaning. I have tried to find the reasons for the night terrors. I have searched the literature for an answer, but all the words of centuries cannot end my suffering. I feel that I must learn to live with the darkness. Trying to fill The Void will only lead to disaster. I suppose it can never be filled. I am not sure. Those who believe strongly in God can fill the emptiness, I am sure of that. But for me, who has little faith in the interpretations of men, I find it more difficult to give myself completely to God, whom nobody really knows despite all the religious writings.

I often retreated to the garden with my friend to enjoy his companionship. It was a brief joyous time to forget the terrible oblivion. When my friend had to return to his abode I simply went to sleep. I forced sleep upon myself to avoid seeing my mother in a state of utter hopelessness. I no longer looked forward to seeing her or my father. My friend was the only contact I had with the real world. My childhood years floated away from me in that garden. All day, during the summer months, I enjoyed the florescence and tranquility of the peaceful garden. It saved me from utter self-destruction.

After my father left, my mother's reticence grew darker and the cupboard grew bare. I ate whatever I could get. There was never enough to eat and so I became quite gaunt. After a time I no longer wanted to eat. Despite the outward richness of our home I was starving. It was only Trevor's companionship that sustained me. I was so attached to him that I considered him my brother. By all accounts we were brothers! We became kindred spirits. If Trevor had ever ceased to come during that time, to provide companionship, I would have perished. His daily visits saved me from unknown horrors. I have not seen him in years. I wonder whatever became of him.

I think it a miracle that I have lived this long. It is indeed a miracle that I was able to attend medical school. Somehow I survived the horror of my early years, enduring rejection and bitterness. I began to love the world and its forsaken people as I would have liked to be loved. My heart felt the strongest pity and sorrow for the wretched of the earth, and it was through this opening that I was able to channel my frustrations in a positive manner. When I saw the downtrodden being abused I raged within and vowed to vanquish their enemies.

Whenever possible, I tried my best to politically destroy those individuals who would harm innocent people. I have not understood the motivation for this until now. I continue to be in the service of mankind for one reason: to satisfy the stomach of The Void. The destruction of Golem would be a most positive action toward that end!

I have felt a strong need to be careful as to the road chosen, for the wrong choice will starve The Void. This will make it want to devour my peaceful thoughts. I know what happens when I try to satisfy it incorrectly — it grows and troubles my thoughts with melancholy, and drives me to self-pity or remembrances of horrors. Nevertheless, I will either destroy The Void or reduce it to a state where it is powerless. The death of Golem would be the first step in my healing. My fortunes have been cursed, yet I continue to defy fate. I do feel good about it all when I take stock of what I have done. But still it is not enough. Every accomplishment withers away within my unfulfilled soul. Perhaps once I have destroyed Golem . . .

* * *

I could not see my mother over the years, the pain was too great. To see her now in a coma was more than my feeble heart could bear. At the moment of her death, I could only feel commiseration and sorrow for the hell visited upon her in life. She had no one! Even I was a stranger to her.

I could tell no one of her condition, for it would mean trying to explain why I had not spoken to her in years. I could not bring myself to see her until now. People would question why I did not communicate with her. People would say that my behavior was strange for a son. No one would be able to comprehend the depth of despair that she had bred within me, or the oblivion that ate at my heart. She once told me that a funeral would not be necessary when death came. To ensure her wish she left a will that instructed the surgeons to deliver her body to the dissectors immediately upon death.

I did not know if this wish was a calculated affront toward religion — for she was an atheist — or if she was mindful that she had no one to care for her funeral arrangements. I had lived in terror that one day I would have to care for the details of her death. We were so separated and distant that she probably never thought of my feelings. I will respect her wish.

I could not tell a soul, not even my beloved Jane, my real feelings about my mother. I had to bear my sorrows fully and alone. My friends had tried throughout the years to console me. Some tried to convince me to talk to my mother, to visit her before her death, but I could not. To look into her face, to hear her voice only made me tremble inside, for I did not know her. I now stood before her a stranger, yet her son. Who in all of the wide world would understand? I was utterly lost. I had tried to reconcile my feelings with her. I communicated to her once by letter how much I had despised her, and how from a distance I had forgiven her. I did not have the courage to face her and convey my true feelings. The Bible had given me the strength to realize that forgiveness was necessary for my own sanity. But I could not forget. Even now as I write these words hatred holds on. It will not release me.

I could hardly bear to face this alone but there was nothing else I could do. I did not have the strength to explain my fears, my emptiness, or the darkness that lay within to anyone, nor did I want to be perceived as strange. I had visited her only once in all the years since I left home.

Sometimes she would send me birthday greetings, or a letter, or some article clipped from a London newspaper concerning medicine. My thoughts raced back to that ghastly visit to her some years before. It was a horrid affair. She was in a drunken stupor. She lived in the house I grew up in but it was different. The hovel that she inhabited was littered with papers, books, and discarded items. There were large stacks of rotting papers on the floor next to her bed. Newspapers layered the floor, making it extremely difficult to walk. Cats were everywhere and filled the air with a terrible smell from their urine and feces. The air was saturated with the vile hairs from the filthy creatures.

As I entered her hovel I was sickened by the odor. The ceiling was partially torn out and there was a chill in the house that smelled of death. I thought I had died and gone to hell when I entered her room. She had been separated from my father for a long time now, and it was upon hearing of his death that I overcame my fear of her situation long enough to convey to her the news of his suicide.

I was so overcome with shock upon seeing her in this condition that I immediately began throwing the rotting papers into a corner of the house somehow left uncovered by the filth. I tried frantically to dig through the layers of paper to find the floor. I was in a frenzy trying to reach the floor just to know if one existed. In my agitation I did not notice the vapors that belched from the pile. These fumes filled my nose until I began to choke. My hands were blackened by the filth, but still I struggled on until I found solid boards.

I stood up and looked around in disbelief. This was the home I grew up in. Extreme sorrow tore at my heart at the wretched conditions in which my mother lived. Cats were in the rafters. They pranced around as if in bliss, for it was apparent that they were better fed than my mother. The cursed creatures bounced from pile to pile spewing their filthy hair throughout the house.

As I made my way through the mountains of filth, and down a corridor toward the bedroom, I saw my mother lying on a bed of rotting paper and rotting clothes. She was not conscious, and the bottle of rum that lay by her side was empty. Her companion, who lay beside her, awoke and tried to explain their sad condition. He told me that she would not let him throw away a single thing, and that every time he made such an attempt she would scold him into submission. She would not even allow him to remove the spiderwebs that littered the house. His words seemed insincere.

My eyes were filled with tears and my whole body trembled. I screamed and ran as fast as I could. I could not control the despair that now filled my entire being. I fell on my way out, over cats and papers, choking from the vapors. Terror gripped me as I struggled to free myself from the paper that tangled my feet.

My heart pounded as I struggled to regain my balance. I finally saw the half-broken door which was barely on its hinges. I made it to the entrance and flung the door open, hurling myself out into the street. I was screaming in agony at the horror I had witnessed. I ran past derelicts and half-humans who now populated these regions. My heart was broken. I vowed to never visit my mother again.

The incidence of her coming to the hospital caused yet another pain. She was taken to Guy's Hospital by a stranger. I discovered that she had been there for two days, but it was not until the third day that a nurse became aware that she was suffering from a severe blow to the head. A policeman asked me if I thought my mother had been struck. He was suspicious that perhaps the man she was seeing had murdered her. I had no way of knowing one way or the other. I dismissed the accusation, but the thought lingers that she may have been murdered.

It was the horror of these thoughts that now revisited me as I stood looking into her unfamiliar face. I turned away, shaken to my depths with sobs. The hospital attendant tried to console me as if I were just another grieving son. Though it was well-intended he could never have guessed that I was crying for a mother that I did not know, or ever had known.

* * *

January 1st, 1849

After my mother died I returned to her home. As I looked through the piles of rubbish, which had grown since my last visit, I discovered that there were letters buried within the filth. Most were correspondence between my mother and my grandmother. As I sifted through the rotting paper the stench was unbearable. I now became aware of the importance of finding any evidence from my past. There had to be, buried within the rotting heaps of paper, playthings from my childhood as well as daguerreotypes that could help me to find the substance of my past.

The letters proved to be even more important than I initially realized. The first was a total shock. As I read the following letter the tears rolled from my eyes.

January 26th, 1819

Dear Mrs. Hamel:

I am writing to you in regard to your daughter, Mary. She has recently been admitted to this London sanitarium. At this time she is with child, confused, and very disturbed. Her physician, Dr. Somerset, feels that she is unable to care for herself or the child, and has requested the court to appoint a conservator for Mary. A conservator is much like a guardian and if appointed would be responsible for seeing that Mary is provided food, clothing, shelter, and treatment if possible, as needed. I am Dr. Somerset's assistant and have been appointed by the court to evaluate Mary's past and present condition and to make a recommendation as to the best way to help her. In order for this to be accomplished I need some information which Mary is unable to provide. You are the only relative for whom we have a name and location, and I am writing to you in the hope that you can provide me with some of the information.

I need names, ages, and location of Mary's father, husband, children, and brothers and sisters. I need information on her past physical and emotional health. Has she been in other sanitariums? I would appreciate it if you could give me a description of her past life, her education and family relationships.

I assure you that we are concerned and are trying how best to help her.

Yours truly,
Alexander Creda, M.D.

My mother never told me of the letter. I do not know if she ever replied. I was shocked! The sanitarium where Captain Walton was incarcerated was where my sister had been, and may still have been there when we made our visit! She may be there even now! I had heard rumors and slight remarks about my beloved sister's location, but I had always thought she was living in Scotland. I was engulfed in sadness. I cried this day more than I ever had.

My sister was sick. My mother had the same disease, as did her mother, and as my great grandmother had. The disease has been passed on from generation to generation. Being a man of science I could not accept the idea of a family curse, but a curse it was, affecting only the female members.

April 6th, 1819

Dearest Dorothy,

I was saddened to hear about my granddaughter. She attempted to convince me to keep the child she was expecting, but under the circumstances I could not. She seemed quite incoherent and often wailed about being the queen. It is quite obvious that she suffers from some disease of the mind.

I received your correspondence about the cats. I still have at least twenty. I have no time for anything else but the creatures. I have named them all. One has not been feeling very well and as a result has been irritable lately. Two of them come to wake me every morning. They are such a delight. One of my favorites likes her solitude, she will not come to me until all of the others have gone. I do not know what I am going to do about her, as she likes to rub against my leg at the same time another comes around.

Well, there is not much more to discuss except the gossip! I hope the people around here do not find out about Mary. Well,

I have been telling people that Mary lives in Scotland, is married, and that she lives a normal life with family and friends. No one must find out about the child being born in a sanitarium. Has Julia been adopted yet? Please keep our secret about Mary. News travels fast in these small towns. Some of the residents often go to London and read the papers. They then carry the news back with them. These people talk a lot and can make life difficult for me. How are the cats? Are you sensitive to each one's likes and dislikes? It takes a while to acquaint yourself with each one. Do not fail to return a reply.

Love,
Mother

My mother gave birth to Mary, my sister, one year prior to their marriage. Five years later I was born. I never really knew my sister, she ran away at the age of seventeen and I never saw her again. I remember her being a bright and promising student. She desired so much, but her dreams were cut short. She became involved with a bearded fellow, who used opium often, and not being quite the man he pretended to be, left her pregnant. She departed London for the western part of the country where, being of heavy heart and pregnant, she went completely insane. It seemed from the letters that she had a girl child that was adopted! I was extremely saddened when I realized that somewhere in the world I had a niece who would now be a young adult, unknown to me. Where she was, or who had adopted her I did not know, nor could I find any other documents that would reveal her present location.

I was surprised to find one letter referring to my activity in the medical school protests against the resurrectionists when I was a student. Her only concern was that people would find out I was related to her.

July 30th, 1828

Dearest Dorothy,

Received the favor of your letter. Your father was named Charles. Your son Joshua looks very much like him. You look like him also. Did Joshua get out of trouble with the authorities for opposing resurrections? I think it is appalling that the youth of today are so rebellious. Windows being broken out — how awful! I am sorry to hear that Joshua is getting himself involved in that type of rebellious activity.

It is my hope that you will not tell a soul where I live. People get into trouble sometimes and notes are found on them. It can become troublesome for an innocent person. There is nothing I hate more than any kind of gossip, good or bad. I loathe it! Imagine, a medical student opposing resurrections! How could he have done such a thing!

Did Joshua's name appear in the London papers? There are a lot of people who come through here, who read the papers in London or send them back home. I am always afraid there will be leaks about things I would not want advertised.

My mother cried and constantly worried herself, and my father was very strict. Father imprisoned me in the clothes closet all day while he was gone. My mother would surreptitiously release me and sob all day. When it was time for Father to return she would carry me to the closet and swear to him that I had been locked up all day. I did not benefit from the release, being free of the closet in the day, for my mother worried about everything and cried about everything. Father would return and I would stay locked up in the closet, sometimes all night. There was a sword in the closet that I became deathly afraid of. Father often talked about the men he killed with it.

Well, some of my beloved animals have passed away. Two of them died a few weeks ago. I buried them in the garden next to the others. There are large markers in the garden for fifteen now. They will be missed. Well, you have your task ahead of you with six new kittens. It is very difficult to care for so many!

Love,
Mother

Cats! That constant obsession with cats! These filthy creatures, I despise them all! As I was reading, one of the nasty beasts approached me, and without a thought I hurled a pile of rubbish at it. It looked surprised. I saw fear in its eye. I felt no pity for it. It slithered away and withdrew to the recesses of the dwelling.

I could not believe that my great grandfather was so cruel. My maternal grandmother was cruel as well. I remember once my mother saying, that as a child, her mother berated her for any fault or mistake committed. She was punished with vicious remarks, scolding her in a most violent manner. She degraded her in every way imaginable. My grandmother was far from virtue. She had several suitors and word of it was soon spread around to the schoolchildren who would mock and taunt my mother to tears.

At an early age my mother ran away to London with an older man. They soon separated and it was under these circumstances that she met my father. Being without support she was forced to provide dance in a pub for patrons. My father, who often went there, escorted her home one night, protecting her from the pleadings of her former lover.

One letter after another revealed things I never knew. The pain was almost unbearable. I was learning about my past and my family in this pile of rot! As I continued to dig, hoping to find more letters, my mother's companion came to the foot of the heap. He said his name was William. This was the same man I had encountered on my previous visit, a few years ago. My eyes came into contact with his, and some strange cold feeling rushed through me. He looked familiar somehow.

He told me that he had lived in this condition with her for years and never once left. I could not fathom why he endured living in such squalor. I did not want to believe that he had struck my mother as the police had suspected. He had been coughing the whole of the time that I became aware of his presence.

He spoke to me again. "I tried to throw away these things," he said, "but she would not let me. She would purchase food for the cats when we had no stores for ourselves. She spent a large sum providing care for them. She loved these animals more than anything." He seemed detached as he spoke and hung his head, avoiding eye contact with me.

"I hate these filthy creatures!" I lashed out. "The air is filled with their hair. I have coughed ever since being in this house, and you are coughing now. They have spread their filth around this house, and you are now ill partly from their hair and defecation, and partly from the filth of rotting paper. This is insanity!" Since I had first seen him he never looked me directly in the eyes. He did not seem to understand.

"You must leave these premises or you will die," I said. "How could you have lived like this? How could you have let her do this to herself, and to you? What in God's name has happened here?"

He continued to look off and said nothing. I tried to be angry with him but thought him insane. I could only shake my head in utter disbelief.

"May I continue to search for the things that were mine as a child?" I asked.

"Yes, go ahead," he replied. I detected some irritation in his voice but I did not dwell on the matter.

I did not know if he stood there or retreated to the dark recesses. I became oblivious of him as I continued to dig in the piles and piles or rotting paper. There was at least twenty years of layered papers on the floor. As I tore at them with my bare hands I soon realized that the oldest newspapers and books were at the bottom, and that the oldest items would be in the rooms that were abandoned. I knew that what I sought must be in these rooms.

I worked well into the night until, almost ready to give up, I found several boxes tied shut with string. I was coughing regularly from the cat hair and the filth and had to hold a handkerchief to my face to withstand the stench. When I blew my nose a black substance consisting of small black particles exited my nostrils. I blew my nose time and time again, and was beginning to become exhausted when I found the boxes at the foot of a rotted-out bed. When they first appeared I was perched on the top of the crater of rubbish that had formed. The rim of this hell was constructed by my digging in one spot for a time. It was very cold in the hovel as there was no heat. Yet I perspired profusely.

I looked down into the grave of filth, and there before my eyes lay the treasures I sought. As I looked at the topmost box I recognized its design. It was from a shop in London long since closed. I had been to this shop with my mother as a child. I realized that this box was the one my mother kept in her chest of personal papers. I had found a piece of my past! I could not wait to open it. Each moment was like an eternity.

I clutched at the strings binding the boxes to reach the one I recalled so well. I grew anxious, fearing that it would be filled with unrelated items. I did not have to suffer long, for I tore at the strings that bound the box in a frenzy. There lying before me was a toy clown and a wooden horse, daguerreotypes, and portraits of myself and my sister as children. I heaved a sigh of relief. There were portraits of my mother and grandmother as children, and more letters from my grandmother to my mother.

As I continued to peruse the letters I noticed a thin sliver of light entering the dark and gloomy room. The windows were all but completely covered except for a small crack. Morning was approaching. I was exhausted but could not pull myself away. I glanced ahead into the distant ruins of the house. I bent my head and cried in utter agony. I wanted to die!

I lost track of the time. All day and all night and into the next day I searched in the rubble for my past and my future. I prayed to God, and in the darkness of these filthy mounds I said these words: "God,

I have hardly ever asked for anything. I have prayed more for others than for myself. No one will remember, when the matter is decided, except for you, if we were good men or evil men. All will be unimportant except for your kingdom. So I pray to you to grant me this request: Grant that my mother receive eternal life, free from the ravages of the curse. Grant that my offspring and other family members do not suffer the same fate. Please grant that the world be free from stoicism and from the tyrants of science — from Golem!"

Just then, as I was about to quit praying, I heard the rustling of papers. I peered into the dark and from the shadows William appeared.

"I heard you in here," he said. "You have been here all night." I looked into his eyes and felt anger, but it dissipated when I thought about the fact that his mind was as diseased as my mother. I spoke to him, telling him to go back to sleep, I was almost finished. I told him that I was sorry that his wife had died. William left me again.

I stared at the letters still unopened. I could not draw myself away. There was a letter, undelivered, which my mother had written. Never was there a human being that learned about his loved ones in this way! Surely no one else has gained insight into the lives of their relatives from a pile of filthy rot! Before reading these letters I had no idea that these things happened. I was completely alone. Through the tears I read yet another.

Jan. 5th, 1822

Dear Mr. Golem,

I obtained a mortgage loan to build a tenant house in July. I fulfilled my first financial installment in September. In October I became ill and now am three months in arrears. I do have someone who is able to take up my note. He has done business with you before. Since two dwellings are involved, he would prefer to make it in two separate notes. If this arrangement is satisfactory please contact us.

Sincerely,
Dorothy Hamel

Golem? *Astley* Golem? I had no knowledge of his involvement in my family affairs while I was still a youth. I remember well when we were thrown off of our family property. My father had left us without any explanation that I was aware of. He had sent large sums of money which my mother used to build a tenant house. She was then under an obligation to manage a double mortgage. After a time

Father cut off the funds. My mother was now without a means to pay the mortgage notes. I was even more terribly shocked when I found the next letter:

Jan. 20th, 1822

Dear Mrs. Hamel,

The matter of your delinquency in the payment of the note has been referred to this legal firm from Sir Astley Golem for attention. Your payment record shows that you are delinquent in your payments. Unless satisfactory arrangements are made by the 10th of February next, this firm is instructed to initiate proceedings to remove you from the premises.

Sincerely yours,
Maver and Tyn
Solicitors

I was stunned. Golem owned our home! He had hired solicitors to evict us! I remember well when we were evicted and thrown out into the streets of London. My mother found another house. I was fifteen years old at the time, and the streets of London became my home. My mother never discussed with me where I would live. We loaded our belongings onto a dray. After we arrived at our new home and our things were unloaded, I was not invited inside. My mother stood at the door and said "Go, live with your father."

It was many years later that my mother was able to return to our home as a renter. She had written me that a friend was able to enter into some sort of business arrangement with the landlord. The payments on the mortgage were dropped and they returned to my childhood home as renters.

I struggled to find more shreds of my past within the debris that lay around me. I felt hopeless as I looked around at the massive piles of paper. I tugged at the refuse, tossing aside filthy, dusty, rotting books and newspapers that smelled of excrement. There were the torn shreds of Hawthorne, Bunyan, Shakespeare, Milton, Zeno, and others, all lying in a heap of maggot-infested rot, with a stench that was unbearable.

I was exhausted. I placed the letters I had found into the box. This area of the house was finished and I resolved to return to try to learn more. I carried the box into the room where William was sleeping. I was filthy. My clothes were soiled, and my face darkened with dirt. William was asleep on a pile of rubbish. I walked past him and pulled the door closed. I stepped out into the alleyway and walked for a while until I came to my apartment. I went upstairs and had my bath drawn and safely put my treasure away. Soon, with my bath complete, I lay down and fell into a deep sleep.

The next day I gathered the letters I had discovered. It suddenly came to me like a blow to the head. My mother had been quite successful in bestowing upon me the seed of oblivion. She often remarked that all was futile, and that once dead that was the end of it. Why did she spend so much time trying to convince me that being stoic was good? I had night terrors often, and even now I feel as if I am drifting to oblivion. If oblivion is the ultimate end for all, and indeed for the earth, then why live? Hence, when sorrow and fear overcame me, death loomed like a sweet dream.

I never accepted oblivion. Things do matter. I cannot shake the thought from my mind that there is nothing after death but oblivion! I have often tried to be hopeful. To live under the darkness of stoicism was as wasteful as death itself.

Oblivion taunts me. Perhaps Golem is correct. If there is nothing else we must attempt to cheat death. Now it is clear. I reject oblivion! I refuse to accept it. I understand why Golem's ideas have appealed to me. I will join Golem's quest for immortality, but not for the same reasons. If there is a God I pray that he will forgive me. I will find the will to destroy Golem!

* * *

January 2nd, 1849

The next night, more forgotten events surfaced. As I sat on the edge of my bed there was the recollection of strange men coming to my mother's house for wild gatherings. They would drink and drink until they became riotous in behavior. I was depressed by those parties, and detested the crowd who came. I tried to shut myself up in my room so that I could sleep, but it was of little help. I can remember these gatherings from the age of six until I was thirteen.

The singing and laughing became a nightmare. Once, I peeped into the chamber and saw my mother sitting in the lap of a strange man. She was in a drunken stupor and the man had a grin on his face. Though the event was joyous my mother's face reflected a profound sorrow she could not hide.

I cannot remember the details of what I did during these times. Huge parts of my memory are missing. I do know that my spirit rapidly collapsed after my father abandoned us. My mother's life was equally destroyed. What sanity she had left slowly disintegrated into a drunken craze. The reality of being totally alone sank in.

The great Void that engulfs my innermost being has left me despondent and filled with gloom. Hard as I try I cannot remember the moment at which the gloom overtook me, or the sequence of events that led to my blocking out of time. I must live long enough to discover the secrets that haunt my soul.

Sometimes I imagine that there was one specific incident, but I cannot lay my hands on it. I have imagined men holding me down and assaulting me. I remember the feeling of helplessness, but cannot mark an exact event. Deep breaths of doom mark my soul.

I remember the swirling milky clouds that filled my thoughts in night terrors, and how much the clouds resembled the design of the rugs on the floor. I cannot understand what meanings these terrors have in relation to the floor. It is all so strange. On many a night my fingers gripped my pillow like the frantic grasp of a man fighting death.

Having just completed these words in my diary, the thought occurs to me that perhaps someone had attacked me. I see an image in my mind of a man staring into my eyes. His look strikes fear into my heart. Then I see my mother chasing him away. Whether this incident occurred or not I do not know. It may be that I imagined it so. My memories are like phantoms. I want desperately to remember. It may be many things producing the gloom. One thing I am quite sure of is the fact that this emptiness is killing me. This Void is tugging at my self-conception and my ability to think. I am tired of it. I desire to fill the empty spaces with the truth, if I can find it.

This limbo that I am in forces me into fits of gloom. My mother spent a great deal of time crying and drinking to ease her own pains and never any time with me. I have portraits of myself ranging from two years to fifteen years of age and yet can remember nothing of who drew them. Years of my life are blank and empty. I still have not started to live. It is all quite confusing. There are times when I want to end it all. I cannot comprehend the emptiness. I am at a loss to explain my lapse of memory. Why is it that knowledge does not answer my questions? Knowledge is often worthless.

My father often spoke to relatives in a foreign tongue. It was French. I never learned any other language as my mother only spoke English. He lived in a world other than mine, and never did he attempt to bring me into his. When I tried to speak with him at night he would only go to sleep, saying little or nothing to me. There was never any indication that he even liked me except when he was intoxicated.

On the days he was free from his duties at the hospital he would frequent the shops and theatres of London. He never spoke a word during these excursions. I followed beside him like a lost soul. Often he left me at the theatre and went to an unknown place. He never said where he was going, nor did I dare to ask.

He began to stay away all night, only returning the following day. Often I would awake and find him ill sitting by the side of his bed, and vomiting from drinking the night before. His absence from the home affected me greatly, and his frequent sickness prompted me to plead for him to discontinue drinking. Worse was the violent response of my mother. Often she waited up all night to confront Father with violence.

On one particular night Father arrived home late staggering drunk and was physically attacked by my mother. She took plates from the cupboard and stacked them up on the table. When Father came in he sat at the table. He was hardly coherent. My sleep was often shattered and I was awakened this night in terror at the sound of crashing china.

I jumped from my bed and saw Father sitting at the table. Mother was pounding him with dishes and cursing him. Her tirade was unbroken as she threw plate after plate at him. Some of them hit his head and blood spewed onto the floor. I never saw anyone bleed like that before. I was frozen in fear. I cried and pleaded for my mother to stop, tugging at her dress and crying in agony. After Father was a bloody mess and the supply of dishes exhausted, she finally retired to her room in the recesses of the house and I went to comfort my father. He only looked at himself and sobbed. He cried uncontrollably. I searched for towels to bandage his wounds, and after wrapping his head and arm I tried to wipe up the blood from the rug and the floor. I prayed that the blood would disappear. It never did.

He sobbed and sobbed, and mumbled some pitiful words which I could not understand. After this event I never slept soundly again. Each and every time Father was late I stayed up, hoping to persuade my mother against violence. Once my mother waited for him to return and did nothing immediately but waited for him to fall asleep. She waited patiently. I surreptitiously watched her secure a knife from a drawer. She ran to Father's room and pounced upon him. She was screaming at the top of her lungs, and threatening to dispose of him.

Father awoke in a panic and pushed her from him, but not before she managed to cut him. He survived the attack, but I don't think I did.

Often, Father put me in his bed, and when my mother attacked him I too was aroused in a state of terror. I was fearful that my father would be killed before my eyes.

I often cried for hours before sleep extinguished the agony. I could not attend school regularly, for in addition to the horrors of my household, I was a sickly child. All of this acted together to darken my world. My parents left me little to remember except pain and neglect. I never fully awakened from the floating shock that ruled my mind. Agony was my only guide.

During the long hours of Father's frequent absences, my mother at first bore the deprivation. As time went on, however, she grew more withdrawn. Her loss of motivation and concentration sucked away her rational judgment. Soon she began to drink. Her cats became an obsession with her. She drew pictures of them. She let them climb over her. She talked to them. She brushed their hair. She loved them more than she loved me.

Soon her personal hygiene and looks deteriorated. She withdrew from friends and became anxious when visitors came. In fact, she grew fearful at the knock on the door. Finally, the persistent use of liquor and laudanum drained her soul and body. The final blow came when Father left and never returned.

She retired to the dark seclusion of her bedroom, from which all entreaties for love from a suffering boy went unheard. Now I spent much time outside in the garden looking at the flowers and animals and learning to love them. I traveled the length of the yard, becoming familiar with the shrubs and trees along the perimeter of the wall. To the front of our home, which faced the south, was greenery that shielded me from the outside world. These trees that grew along the wall painted my thoughts with nothingness.

I have rambled on in the leaves of this diary. I do not want to forget what I have discovered.

* * *

January 10th, 1849

When mother died she had signed papers for her body to be given to science. What remained she wanted to be cremated. I did not want anyone to know that this poor wretch was my mother. I knew that no one but I would see to her funeral arrangements. She did not want a grave marker. She wanted only total oblivion as if she were a meaningless creature. I respected only part of her last wish. I made provisions for an acquaintance to conduct the dissection. I wanted her spared from the clutches of Golem. Though she did not want a gravestone I had one constructed which read:

Here lies Dorothy Hamel, under a
peaceful cerulean sky, released from
the cycle of desolation and sorrow that
has been passed on from one generation to
the next; vindicated by her son - Joshua Hamel.

Thou art my hope, O Lord GOD: thou art
my trust from my youth - Psalm 71:5

When the ashes were collected, I arranged for a memorial service. Though her remains were cremated I chose to bury them in a full coffin. I had the coffin transported to the cemetery and buried. I told no one except a local minister who met me at the grave. As the last shovels of dirt hit the coffin I sobbed terribly. It was at her grave that I vowed to return once again to her hovel. I had to return to search for objects that would force memories into my consciousness. The coachman carried me back to my apartment.

That night I returned to the house of horrors, but to my dismay William was gone and the hovel was burned to the ground. I fell to my knees at the sight, for it was now impossible to retrieve any other items. A constable at the scene said that the cause of the fire was suspicious and under investigation. He would not elaborate but he told me that the authorities had a suspect in mind. It was William! I slumped down on the roadside and cried until the coachman raised me and helped me back into the carriage.

* * *

I could not even tell Jane of the misery that haunted my soul. She of all people would surely understand, but it was too late. I told her nothing of my mother for I could not find the words to express the horror and emptiness that gnawed at me.

Even before my mother died I lied to Jane. I told her that my mother died years earlier. She therefore knew nothing of my mother or my past. She was unaware of the memorial service and the pain that I could find no answer for. She accepted my absence as being due to my work, which had a negative unintended consequence. She thought I was spending too much of my life with Golem. I lied to her. I feel extremely troubled that I did so.

* * *

January 11th, 1849

I returned to the laboratory today and as I entered, Golem was writing notes and looking at the skulls that lined the shelves of the laboratory.

I interrupted his thoughts with a prepared speech. Though I tried to remain calm I lashed out at him. "Look at the skulls around our laboratory, Golem! Once they were men and women just like ourselves. I am sure they thought that when they died they would find peace, but look what we do without even a second thought. We have what is left of them on shelves! They are as curios for guests or medical students! Should not these bones be interred and left in peace?"

As I spoke these words to Golem he looked at me, but I could see quite clearly that he had not heard. I did not know why I continued, but I did. "A true and proper right of the dead is to be left alone and in peace," I said. "The remains of the dead are not objects to which we have rights, nor must we disturb them. I am as guilty as you in this regard. We could at least agree that after we have completed our experiments the bones should be returned to the grave!"

I said these words with such force that Golem looked at me, temporarily stunned. He did not know that I had already labeled and stored many body parts for the purpose of returning them to the grave.

Golem then went into a raging diatribe about his work. He revealed to me many secrets that I was not aware of — secrets that he had discovered while dissecting cadavers and various living organisms. He said that there was now hope against oblivion. This gave me pause, since I have fought with emptiness all of my life.

* * *

Golem had constructed a clock that displayed the hours that remained in his life. He had deduced that his death would occur at age seventy. He said that of course this was an arbitrary number for one never can predict the hour of their demise. Aside from any accidental or unnatural death, Golem thought that seventy was a fair estimate. His mother had died at that age and both of his parents died of natural causes; Golem's grandfather and grandmother had also died of natural causes close to the mark of seventy. Golem's clock had only 175,200 hours left, which he had calculated after having spent fifty years so far.

He constantly watched the numbers. After seeing the hours click away he would rush off to begin a new experiment. He once offered to make a clock for me, but I declined his offer. In fact, each and every time I saw the clock I turned away and would not even glance at it. When he first brought the horrid device to the laboratory I often turned it away from my sight or draped some cloth over it when he was not present. The device did not tick as a normal clock but made a clacking sound. With the roll of each hour the clacking sounds were like those of brutal metal gears, rolling over one another. The clock was quite large and its sound was terribly loud at times.

It did not take long for Golem to become dissatisfied with the clock. He often said that 175,200 hours seemed too dreadfully short a time, so one day he replaced the hour device with another which displayed the estimated seconds that remained in his life. It displayed millions of seconds. For a time Golem was satisfied. However, this satisfaction also dissipated. The speed of the seconds flashing by became worrisome for him. I noticed that as he worked he constantly looked at the device and seemed to pace himself to the rhythm of the palpitating time. By the end of the day he was quite exhausted, but it did not deter him from working at a feverish pace day after day.

His appearance soon grew haggard and his attire became filthy. His hair was all about his head and there were wrinkles in his forehead that had not been there before. Even in the most casual conversations he spoke in a more arrogant manner.

I never looked at the device. It frightened me. I tried to remain at a laboratory table away from the timer. The device made me all the more aware of the fact that I most probably would die before I ever discovered the reasons for my night terrors and the total emptiness of my soul.

BOOK IV

THE REVENGE

The Creature's Notes
December 1848

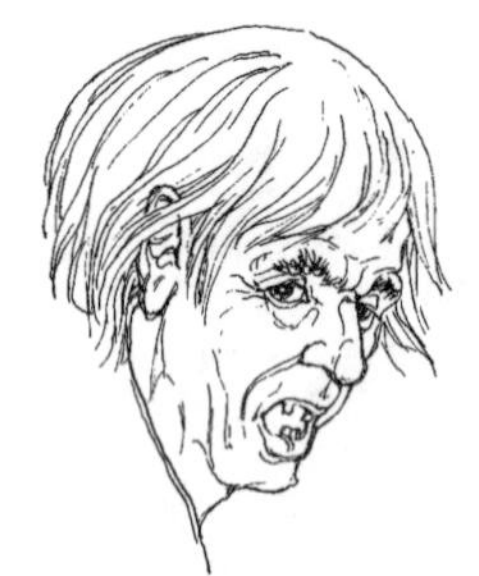

Every night I observed Golem's activities. I set to work memorizing every detail of the order of events to freeze a body. My first task was to commit to memory the details of setting the timers for the kyro-units. I had to set it to the time, by the date and number of years, that I wanted to be awakened. The next step was to set the secondary timer which allowed enough time for one to climb into the receptacle and to hook up the needles to your veins for withdrawal of blood and the infusion of the special fluid. The top of the receptacle would close after a short time and engage the pulley system which would lower the frozen tomb into the vault, sealing itself for the trip to the future.

Mr. Hamel would on various occasions go to his left upper coat pocket and pull a paper out. He never did this in the presence of Golem. If by chance Golem arrived while Hamel read, Hamel quickly folded the paper and replaced it surreptitiously. I could not see the details of the paper from my vantage point, but thought that by and by I would become knowledgeable of its content. I eventually discovered that some of these papers were newspaper articles. These articles were stories about past riots. Hamel was once a participant. He was once a sympathizer with the wretched of the earth.

One night as I listened to their discussion, they talked of their plans for the third unit.

"We will need three kryo-units," Golem said. "Two will be utilized for ourselves, and one for a cadaver. We will need a body of the right type that will journey with us. We will need the body parts at some point. We will have to compensate a resurrectionist for the cadaver, but that will not be a problem since there is a profusion of them available. All we need do is frequent Cock Lane and Giltspur Street at the tavern. A resurrectionist will be there for hire. I hear that a man by the name of Geary has raised over five hundred bodies."

Hamel looked off and responded, "Stealing bodies has become quite a problem lately. The cost has gone up. Worse than that, this wave of anger that has swept across London makes our work continually chancy. I am not so certain that Geary, owing to his reputation, will be the best man for the job. It is rumored that he has killed to obtain cadavers for St. Bartholomew's and Guy's hospitals. I have heard that he has been arrested or detained on occasion for stealing the property associated with the corpses. To employ him would be extremely risky, Dr. Golem."

"Geary, from what I hear, can provide us with the type of body we need," said Golem. "We will be able to cure idiopathic fever in the near future, I am sure! We need a corpse that has succumbed to the fever. Geary may charge as much as forty pounds, but we can negotiate the price. We will need the body to be as fresh as possible. If the subject is in great misery, Geary's methods of alleviating pain would be humanitarian, in my opinion. There are such patients at Guy's which . . ."

"In Carlisle, near the border, men have killed surgeons!" Hamel interrupted. "Some of these people have friends. On one occasion one of our colleagues was shot in the face while another was murdered and thrown over the bridge. Haven't you heard of this? Who has the right to decide if the pain is great enough to justify killing? Geary? We are treading on unstable ground, and for what? If we postpone our actions and wait for the Anatomy Bill to pass the House of Lords, we will not need to hire the likes of Geary! What of Limbo and his cooperation with the inspector? I am sure that there are resurrectionists who want us killed. You have opposed them!"

"Why wait, my dear friend? The sooner we start, the sooner we awaken. It will be like the blink of an eye. We will not feel the time pass. Do not worry, Hamel. Geary will provide us with a body. I will choose . . ."

"But when do we estimate that a particular cure will be found?"

"Let us go way ahead, Hamel. See the rate of dissection and the advances being made; there were 592 dissections completed a few years ago. Students from all over England will soon have all the bodies they need. While we sleep, a cure for idiopathic fever will be found. Science is already on the brink of a cure!"

"But Geary has been associated with murder! There is even talk that he has abducted children for dissection! I do not want to end up with a rope around my neck, nor be dissected in full public view. Besides, it seems quite horrid to me that Geary has even been accused of putting people to sleep. He has done his job on people who were not even close to death! I am not so sure that Geary is a humanitarian!"

"Come, come, Joshua. You cannot be so naive as to not know that mercy killings are a fact of the medical profession! Though we deny it, mercy killings have been practiced for years. Geary has been falsely accused . . . as have I. The ignorant rabble that question science have resorted to lies! Come, Hamel, let us go to the tavern and engage our man. We need a corpse that has succumbed to fever and that has been dead less than a few hours. Let us engage the resurrectionist Geary for a job which will make even him famous. In another time his work may not seem so horrid. This snatch will undoubtedly be classified as of historical significance. This event will be to save the world for new life rather than for a dissection! What of your moral doubts if it means everlasting life?"

Hamel said nothing immediately. He looked up and past me as I spied upon them. Then he spoke in a pleading voice. "I have dissected cadavers before," he said, "but they were prison inmates executed for horrible crimes. Their bodies atoned for their crime by enabling us to educate another generation of physicians. While at Guy's and at St. Thomas we did not have the problem of shortage of cadavers like the independent anatomy schools now have. I tried my best to inquire before each dissection if the body was obtained through moral means. Often, I could not procure a body as quickly as my classmates. I had to wait and would suffer the ridicule of my fellows for a time, but I maintained my distance from stolen bodies. I wanted nothing to do with bodies that arrived under suspicious circumstances!"

Golem was a master liar. He could persuade in a most evil manner. He approached and placed his arm on Hamel's shoulder.

"Well, well, now, Joshua, listen to me. Anatomical schools have closed because of a lack of cadavers. Science has been hindered! The human race has suffered longer because of your sanctity of the grave and your morals! You know very well that some of the most skilled doctors have been trained as a result of the mutual understanding between the schools and the resurrectionists! The police have worked with us and continue to do so, as well as the Lord Mayor of London. Be practical, man!"

Golem calmed Hamel's spirit and he relaxed.

"I am being thoughtful and cautious, Dr. Golem. Do you not remember the Edinburgh incident? That a woman was murdered? Here, I saved the horrid account as it appeared in the *Edinburgh News*."

Hamel went to his desk and produced a copy of the account. It was dated October 16, 1848. He read it to Golem:

> A most extraordinary event took place on Friday last, in a house in Edinburgh, where an old woman of the name of Campbell has been murdered. Her body was sold to a medical doctor. Witnesses have given various accounts of the horrid occurrence. There is no doubt that the body of the woman was seen at the house of Tom Geary. We received the following information on the subject. It read:
>
> "A woman named Campbell came to Edinburgh from Ireland some days ago, in search of work, which she found. She took up her lodgings in the house of a man named Geary. It appears that there was merrymaking at Geary's that night. The noise of music and dancing was heard. The woman, it is said, joined in the mirth, partook of the liquor, and went to sleep on the floor. During the night terrible shrieks were heard. Neighbors paid no attention for such sounds were not unusual in Geary's house. In the morning, however, it was reported that the woman was lying on the floor as if dead. The witness said that circumstances transpired which led to a belief that all was not right.
>
> "Two known resurrection men came and removed her, pretending that she was a friend who often drank too much. The body was removed from the house, and it was suspected to have been sold to an anatomy school. By the time the event was conveyed to the local authorities Geary had left the area. The next day the body was found in the lecture room of a respectable surgeon, who, being confronted by the constable, released the body and provided all information in his power. The body was left at the school. It will be examined by experts within a short time.
>
> "There is strong evidence that the victim was murdered. A warrant has been issued by a magistrate for Geary's arrest."
>
> This was the event as reported by credible persons.

Having read the report, Hamel continued. "Geary may be executed and publicly dissected. After this, it was reported that other resurrectionists barely escaped a rioting crowd. In any event we will be in danger ourselves."

"Not true, Hamel. The *Edinburgh News* routinely exaggerates to sell its papers. The surgeon in this case had no idea that the cadaver was murdered. If anything, he would only be guilty of not paying closer attention to their condition at the time of delivery."

Hamel was quiet for a time but soon spoke these words: "I do not know, Golem. Despite the erroneous reporting, the public blames us for the actions of resurrection men. Science has come a long way but humanity suffers. Because one is without relatives or lives in the poorhouse he is forbidden the sanctity of the grave, and his peace in death is violated! What have we come to, Golem? There have been thousands of dissections and a circus show made of the human frame and still there is no cure for idiopathic fever. Perhaps it is our curse for what we are doing. The number of fallen colleagues has risen. We have become victims of the disease-ridden corpses we so fondly display at public places."

Golem continued his lies. "Why, Hamel, you speak as a superstitious man instead of a surgeon. Geary is paid well and fell into crime as a result of his resurrectionist activities. It is a most hideous business. I have said publicly that they are rascals and of the lowest dregs of society. There is no crime that is beneath them!"

"But, Dr. Golem, we still accept their goods without question, and have put our profession below its standing. We have made a mockery of human dignity by using the bodies that are delivered by these men. And now we are about to use Geary, or whomever, to conduct an experiment which defies death itself. What moral ground do we stand on? You have paid a villain to steal a corpse and smother a man! Unknown to our new victim is the fact that we will ferry him away to cheat death. Will he be awakened in a future that he will not know or understand? Are you going to use the corpse you have? Is the third kryo-unit for him? What moral ground do we stand on, Dr. Golem? What have you done?"

"You believe in the sanctity of the grave. Well, why not believe in the sanctity of science, in the goal to free men of disease and suffering and death! He was a beggar, a thief. He was of no consequence!"

Hamel was now in a rage. "No consequence! . . . And what price do . . ."

Golem shouted back, "We pay whatever price is necessary! For the good of mankind, and . . . "

"Then, sir, to accomplish this ultimate dream we are to use all necessary means, even if we lose what morals we have and what dignity is left?"

"I admit the price is great but the reward is greater. The . . ."

"I do not think we can agree on this matter. Let us stop this talking in circles, Golem."

"Perhaps we should. If the medical society discovered that you participated in the riots . . . Hamel."

"How did you know? . . . You have read my notes! You have violated my privacy!"

"Come, Hamel . . . you know about the man I smothered. I know about your part in the riots!"

There was quiet between them. Their arguments made me aware that the poor were despised as I was, though not to the same degree. These men had transgressed the very rules and morals that they professed to live by. They have robbed from the grave to satisfy their lust. Hamel knew of the murder of the poor man but did nothing. Hamel raves about injustice but has made no effort to prevent it since his participation in the London riots.

The machine of ice drew my attention away. I looked at its tubes and small containers which cascaded through the inner structure. I studied its coffin-like structure and the mechanism for exchange of fluids. I looked down at them and saw the future.

It was time!

I crashed through the glass structure and landed at the side of a dissection table.

"You will grant me immortality!" I demanded.

"My God, my eyes deceive me! The monster lives, Hamel!"

"We are cursed . . . Golem, we are cursed! My God!"

It was then that I spoke my plans.

"You are not cursed yet! You will be destroyed if the mechanism of life is not put to my disposal. Look at me! Look at my hideousness! Your science has done this to me! You can repair me! You have said that the future holds promise for the cure of disease, of age, and of suffering. This is what your science has done to me! Look at my face, look at me! This hideous face can be fixed. You will fix me and awaken me in your future which will be *my* future!"

"What you ask is possible," Golem said. He turned and tried to whisper to Hamel. "We can avoid doing business with Geary. Mr. Hamel, we have a subject! A perfect subject!"

"We need to discuss this . . ."

Golem pulled Hamel away to discuss my proposal. I kept a wary eye on them and resolved to kill them if they tried to escape. I heard their whispers, my ears being more sensitive than they knew.

"Listen, Hamel," said Golem, "We can avoid your concerns. We can depart for the future with a perfect specimen, a creation that is sure to make us famous, perhaps a way to better the creature, and human life, but in any case the opportunity presents itself!"

"Shh! The creature may hear us," said Hamel. "If we proceed, how can we be assured that it will not destroy us when we wake?"

"The timer, we can set it for our awakening first and sedate the creature before he can fully recover," Golem said.

Hamel looked worried and frightened. "What if the future world thinks us fiends, and destroys us upon learning we have transported such a horrid creature to their time?"

"He will only be a legend by then. It will be only a tale of a deformity which led to fantastic stories! Well, would you rather hire Geary?" said Golem.

"I had rather take my chances with a cadaver than this! This creature is capable of unbelievable acts of terror," said Hamel.

"How would you know that? Walton told us very little. He only raved like a superstitious fool! Let us delay response to the creature until we are one on this matter." He had once again silenced Hamel's protests. They moved toward me with deceitful eyes.

"We need time to ponder your proposal. We would need to refit the length and size of the kryo-unit to accommodate your frame, to review the calculations and . . . ."

"This you will do or the cursed nature of your work will be made known!" I shouted at them in fury. "You will repair my face and give me immortality! *If I don't have your agreement within two days the embodiment of what you do will be found at your doorstep!"*

I flew from the room using the table as a springboard to leap up through the ceiling. I left with an idea, with a plan, and a time limit on my demand. They did not suspect that I stayed within earshot of their conniving. From the roof I heard them converse once more.

"Thank God he has left. How did he survive the seas, the icy waters? He moved with ease from the table to the roof!" said Hamel.

"The icy waters, Hamel — the icy waters — that shows we are on the right track. Cold! Cold! The icy cold holds the secret of life! He survived because of his strength and the glycerol in his veins! I have analyzed his blood. It has a high level of glycerol! Now that the creature is here we can study his organs and the chemical mechanisms at work in his blood. We now have a live specimen! I am sure that an analysis of his body will yield many secrets! We can give the world new life!"

"This is wrong!" Hamel protested. "The creature must not go with us. We should not take a cadaver either. Let us suffer whatever befalls us alone. You know enough of this science to do what must be done. You can transport us to the future without any more bodies. We do not need the creature! Let us not complicate the venture. Let us only condemn ourselves!"

"We will not be condemned!" Golem began one of his sweet sermons. "The world of forever awaits us . . ."

Hamel would not listen this time. He said, "I will not do this. I had rather go to Geary. I had rather commit a murder myself than to take this demon with us. It is a demon, and remember what we know of its actions. I will not help you destroy yourself or me. I will not!"

"Very well." Golem seemed to be acquiescing. "But we must hurry to see Geary. We must depart before the monster returns."

Just then someone knocked at the rear door. Golem quickly told Hamel to get ready to leave for the tavern and went himself to the rear. I heard him greet the man as William. He had returned demanding more money for delivering a body which he had stolen from another anatomical school. Golem became angry with him. He was turned away and left in a fury.

I had heard enough. I now begin my plot.

* * *

January 1849

My plan was simple. I was going to divert the authorities to Golem and Hamel. I traveled to Bone Hill Cemetery and to the newly-opened Kensal Green Cemetery. My watchful eye had provided me with the experience to dig into graves from an angle. I had procured ropes which I used to extract bodies from their graves. After a time I decided to exhume entire coffins, scattering them throughout the cemetery, so as to create an atmosphere of terror.

I used a dray to help me carry as many of the bodies into London as possible. I exhumed several corpses from Bone Hill and folded their bodies so that they fit into sacks, then went to the other cemeteries and continued my efforts. I soon ran out of sacks and so heaved the remaining corpses into the wagon until it was completely full. With the moon down I was able to carry out my business under starlight and finally to deposit these corpses throughout the townships and at the laboratory of Sir Astley Golem.

As I went about my work I thought on the fact that some gravestones were much larger than others. These hideous statues of death filled the cemeteries of the rich. The placement of them was done with more precision in some sections of the cemetery. I saw large fantastic stone markers in the shape of angels. There were gateways with arches of stones at small entrances and small figurines. There were bronze plaques laid down in stone over the deceased and busts of the deceased. Some of them were completely covered in stone which made it difficult to excavate, for I had to start digging on the outer perimeter and shovel my way toward the grave. These were the tombs of the very wealthy.

While engaged in my task I saw on a lone hill the grave of Bunyan. He went to prison and wrote *The Pilgrims Progress*, in which the destiny of man was laid out. He had died in 1688 and had heard a voice which said, "Will thou leave thy sins and go to heaven or have thy sins and go to hell?" He left the City of Destruction and the Slough of Despond as I will do. His plight was not unlike my own. My path to revenge lies in my journey in the icy coffin. I will not compromise my revenge. I will have immortality until the world is destroyed! Perhaps I will write a book some day from all of these notes which I have, for now, kept in this journal.

Bunyan gave up all earthly desires for one goal — everlasting life! I too seek everlasting life, and revenge is the vehicle that will carry me there. I have lived in hell already! My heaven shall be immortality and revenge the chariot to carry me there. While in my vault I read of the ghastly Black Plague that strewed death everywhere. The disease will return. I will unearth the newly interred at the rate of a hundred a day until these rotting corpses disease mankind. These diseases will aid me in the destruction of man. I am immune to earthly diseases.

Man is a worthless creature. All of his high-sounding morality means nothing. He talks of going to heaven, but all of his actions are hellish. These hellish actions are sobbed and prayed over, and he then thinks the gates of heaven are opened for him. With a kryo-unit I will be able to wreak destruction upon man from century to century. I can outlast them! I will kill them as they pray for everlasting life, which they will not have! I will obliterate their stones with the speed of a demon. I will carry out my work faster than the stones can be worked by the masons.

If I cannot obliterate them completely then I will change their names, adding a letter here or there or removing one. The dates of birth and death will be changed: 1741 can be changed to 1747 or 7747.

Their horrid statues with their wings of angels will be clipped, and the legs of stone chairs removed and toppled over.

I will carry their gravestones to other places. I will throw them into the Thames or line them along London Bridge! This will create such a terror that crowds will kill the resurrectionists and the surgeons and each other. As armies attempt to quell the riots, friend will turn against friend. The corpses of their small daughters will be exhumed and left at a neighbor's house. I will make stones for the living — stones with the names of men who have not died yet. These gravestones will be planted at their doorstep! Their predicted date of death will be kept accurate!

Thinking they have been cursed, some will kill themselves or go mad. The most murderous prisoners at Newgate I will release, and aid them in the plunder and murder of the upper classes. There will be fratricide on each side, thereby creating upheaval and civil war. I will not limit these machinations to London, but with my great speed go to Edinburgh and Glasgow. I will fly to Ireland, France, Italy, and other parts of the European continent. Eventually, my plans will take me to America where hypocrisy rules supreme.

Rotting corpses can be shipped at Jamaica Street. Boat loads of dead bodies will be steered into their ports, hidden in food crates, and unloaded with the fever, onto the shores of other countries. They will count their dead all over the world while I sleep. If, when I awaken, the toll is not near enough to extinction, I will commit the same acts of vengeance again until the toll rises. I will be aided by them, for they will destroy themselves daily.

Where I am able to destroy waterways, I will do so. I will live only for the pleasure of destruction. I will devise a way to divert the Thames onto precious crops. I have forever to contemplate my designs and the methods needed for such a major catastrophe. Dikes and dams shall be sabotaged. The most precious things will be reduced to despair. Despair will be reduced to utter hopelessness and gloom!

Hamel's Diary
January 13th, 1849

The creature has sought revenge because we refused his demand and in a wild tempest of rage committed the most horrible of murders. The hair of several female victims, well-to-do Londoners, was torn from their scalps, braided into rope, and then used to hang their corpses by the neck from lampposts. The bodies of several graduate students were found in different parts of the city with shovels stabbed through their chests, and one with a stone mason's chisel through an eye. A young medical student, caught in the clutches of the creature, was literally torn apart and left sitting down next to a lamppost. His arms and legs were ripped from his body and neatly placed in what was left of his lap.

The horror did not end. Freshly buried bodies were exhumed and corpses placed at the doorstep of the anatomy school at which Golem and I worked. Often the cadavers would be mutilated in various ways; pages of torn books were stuffed into their mouths. The most ghastly thing of all was the finding of six corpses by the inspector and his men. They were dangling by the neck from a stolen chandelier, apparently taken from the home of some wealthy person. These corpses were suspended by ropes from a lamppost in front of Guy's Hospital. The bodies rotated slowly as the wind blew this carousel of death. The corpses were those of recently deceased politicians.

The people of the city were horrified. Shutters were closed, doors and windows that normally stayed open where shut. People who usually went about alone were now always seen accompanied by a friend or acquaintance. People went home earlier as the air became thick and foul with the stench of murder and mutilation. Constables doubled up on patrol and heavily armed themselves. Detachments of soldiers were seen more often in the streets at night, and everywhere there was talk of the "mad doctors" who must somehow be connected to the tragedy that was overwhelming the city. There were reports of a gigantic man seen in the cemetery. Others reported seeing the creature throwing gravestones into the Thames.

Citizens looked and pointed to the building that housed the laboratory of Dr. Golem. Small groups of people would sometimes gather across the street, or down the block, to discuss why the constable had not investigated the laboratory. Indeed, the suspicions ran ahead of the official investigation. When Golem and I arrived at the laboratory in the mornings there were often small groups of silent onlookers who watched our every move. The way our legs carried our bodies forward became familiar to the stares of the onlookers. After a short time the crowds became testy. On one such occasion they jostled us after we disembarked from the coach. The angry crowd accused us of carrying out ghoulish experiments and of being responsible for the murders.

It was on one such morning that the police paid us a visit. The inspector greeted us. "Good morning, gentlemen. I am Inspector Glennon from the Union Street Police Station and I wonder if we might come in to ask you a few questions?"

The inspector was accompanied by a fellow officer. I was relieved when Golem responded. "Yes, you may, Inspector. I will answer any questions you may have."

Glennon eyed the laboratory very carefully. He went from one end of the room to the other. I feared that he would see something that would increase his suspicions. He spoke with authority. "No cadavers around, I take it?" he asked.

"No, we are not experimenting with cadavers," said Golem firmly.

Anticipating this answer, Inspector Glennon almost interrupted Golem with this retort. "Then I would ask, sir, what are you experimenting on? For what ungodly reason are you conducting this business? What do you know of the corpses at your doorstep?"

Golem eyed him up and down as he did with everyone, and retorted, "Ungodly! Hardly, Inspector. We are working on the effects of cold on the human body. As you may know, or probably do not know, the far north is being explored with regularity. As our men venture out to these remote regions of the earth we will need to know how their bodies will be affected by such extreme temperatures, temperatures well below the freezing point. I know nothing of the horrid crimes. It is probably the work of resurrection men."

"I dare say, good sir, that it is well known to us, or most of us, that if you do not dress well you freeze. What more could these experiments tell us about the cold? A school child knows the effects of extreme temperatures!" His tone changed from sarcasm to accusation. "What can you tell us of the giant that has been lurking in the cemeteries?" He looked at his colleague with a smirk on his face. His colleague reciprocated with a shift in his stance and a short cocky nod.

"I know nothing of such fairy tales!" Golem replied. "And as to your questions, what a school child knows is quite elementary, my kind sir. Of course the school child knows that exposure can be detrimental. But at what point does it become so, and what internal changes take place that cause the heart and pulse to slow? What signals are sent for such a response to take place and what chemical reaction produces the response? What happens to the human body after long periods of freezing? Does the school child know? If so, Inspector, kindly direct me to this child prodigy, for I will need to discuss with him his findings!"

The inspector inched closer to me. He may have noticed the nervous look on my face, though I tried to disguise it. Golem treated the inspector with condescension as if he possessed no deductive skills that would enable him to draw conclusions.

"I would say further, Inspector, that the rate of exchange of heat between the body and the outside air plays a direct role in the transmission of signals, by chemical activity, that ultimately leads to hypothermia. It is this rate of exchange, or rate of loss of heat, with which I am particularly concerned."

The inspector was not moved. "Very impressive, sir. But let me ask you if you know a man by the name of Limbo? He seems to know you!"

"I do not recall that name, Inspector Glennon. Is he a surgeon?"

"I suppose he might be considered a surgeon of sorts. He is a resurrectionist, and he was last seen escorting a fever-ridden man to your school. This man was named Shadwick. He was alive when he was escorted to your door, Dr. Golem! It turns out that the fellow had a relative who has obtained a warrant from the Marlborough Street magistrate to search St. Thomas. Mr. Limbo claims he was quite alive when he was taken to see you."

Golem stormed off quickly, but just as suddenly turned to exclaim, "I see many patients, Inspector Glennon. You cannot possibly expect me to remember the name of all of them, or the people who bring them in. I . . . "

The inspector was growing irritated by Golem's air of authority. He interrupted. "Not all, Dr. Golem, just one! Limbo has not told all yet. Perhaps when we find him again he will have more to say. Quite strange, you know! He usually has plenty to say — though most of it meaningless to us at the police station. We have not seen him of late. You must have paid him a handsome fee for his trouble. Well, time will open his mouth. In the meantime, I just wanted to know if you have seen Shadwick, or can tell us his location — his body, I mean. I can see you have no bodies here."

"I do not know of Limbo or of Shadwick, Inspector!"

"I suppose not, although most of the poor chaps cut up on your bloody table are brought here by resurrection men."

With a great show of snobbery, Golem put his hands to his hips and bent forward a little. "Now, now, Inspector, that sounds like an accusation! You know that I loathe those dregs of society, as you no doubt have heard me say in the House of Commons. In fact, Inspector, you have brought me most of my business by way of Newgate Prison. You have made the arrests of criminals, and they being lawfully convicted and executed their bodies have been brought here. All were legally obtained!"

"Perhaps, Golem, but putting a soaked cloth over someone's mouth is murder. Limbo has made the accusation that you have committed a crime. Though I can see no obvious evidence, I will talk with Limbo a little more, and by and by you may remember him. I will return if I need to, Dr. Golem. In the meantime, please let me know if you hear about the location of this man or his body. Be careful, sir! Good day, Doctor."

The inspector turned, and as he opened the door he added, "Oh, by the way, sir, let me report that from December second to January second, St. Giles reported twenty-five graves were dug up and the bodies were missing. From January third to the ninth, a period of only six days, St. James' Parish as well as St. Andrew's, St. Bride's, St. Sepulchre, Bishopgate, Aldgate, Whitechapel, and Shoreditch reported twenty-seven bodies were torn away from their graves. What have you to say about this occurrence, Dr. Golem?"

Golem said nothing and I walked away. The inspector looked at the floor for a moment but soon continued. "Though I think you know something of these incidents, I do not believe you will tell me anything. I believe I can locate someone who might. I ran into a sailor just now who claims that you and your assistant sailed to the north and returned with two bodies. That sailor is across the street now. Before you speak, my friend, let me tell you that London has become a most dreadful place. Resurrectionists in the pay of surgeons to desecrate the graves of the dead, that is what we have! I have given this account to the magistrate who has given me assurances that the culprit or culprits will hang for this!" The inspector added, "There is more, Golem. I have seen with my own eyes that some of these corpses have been terribly mutilated. In fact, fifteen mutilations were reported to the Lord Mayor's office. From Hadrian's Wall and north there have been reports of similar deeds, seemingly all connected. And moreover, since January ninth, Celestial City Cemetery has been robbed of twenty-three corpses, while St. James reports seven. St. Leonard's and Cripplegate report over sixty-two.

"It was because of this that the Lord Mayor has ordered watchmen at the cemeteries, and shortly after his first order, a watchman at Celestial City Cemetery reported a strange incident. On or near Lamar Walkway, in the northeastern sector of the cemetery, he reported a gigantic figure moving through the cemetery toppling gravestones. This gigantic man has been seen here, at your laboratory, after being followed by watchmen! I need not say that the watchmen employed at this cemetery are above reproach. They reported the incident to the Lord Mayor.

"Many other stories abound about this resurrectionist, who, because of his frame, will be easy to identify. One such report placed him on the road from Glasgow, driving a death cart with dozens of his victims in it. One watchman reported to me that a gigantic figure was seen lurking here one morning, and when he gave chase, the fiend ran with the speed of a demon. What do you know of this giant, Dr. Golem?"

Golem was now sarcastic, attempting to dismiss the question. "Nothing, Inspector, nothing. I know nothing about such fantastic stories."

Again the inspector rejoined. "Well, Dr. Golem, I will leave you, but beware! I am going to question the sailor at the police station. Remember, Ecclesiastes 9:12 says: 'For man also knoweth not his time: as the fishes that are taken in an evil net, and as the birds that are caught in the snare; so are the sons of men snared in an evil time, when it falleth suddenly upon them.'" The inspector paused for a moment and left us with these words, "The sailor from the *Loshkin* reported that you have traveled to the pole, that a giant was returned to English waters and buried at sea. The sailor informed me that the creature was not dead when it was dropped into the water! We shall see . . . yes, we shall see. I am on my way to discuss the incident with the captain of the *Loshkin*. Thank you."

As the inspector stepped out the door, I moved over to close and bolt it behind him. I turned to Golem and said, "We are lost, Dr. Golem! We must leave this place. We are being put in a position where our lives are at stake. And what about this Limbo and Shadwick? What does he know of them?" I asked.

"Inspector Glennon is being led by the nose," Golem responded. "The sailor and the captain can only report their perceptions. Two men, one of them a freak, were buried at sea. That is all! Apparently the monster has carried out his threat. We must now revise our plans and move with deliberation. The creature must be killed and I will do it."

Golem moved quickly to his desk and gathered his notes. It was now that I learned that the doctor had perfected the timing device. It could be set for hours, months, and even years. He had perfected the mechanism so that many years could pass before the device shut off and began the process of draining and filling the body with fluid.

Dr. Golem told me that he was ready to leave this world and board a kryo-unit. "I am leaving for immortality," he said. He would put himself into the device and awaken at a time in the future when science would prevail over disease, sickness, and aging. With this device we could live to see such things.

Golem argued that if we were successful, men could extend their lives indefinitely, and deny God his vengeance. If this were possible then God would no longer have the power to condemn. "Man could decide the parameters of God's power," he said. I thought this was wrong and disagreed. I saw the need for men to experiment and to make life better, but a line had to be drawn. Though Golem often spoke of God I did not think him a believer.

"What if we are found out?" I asked. "We are almost done for now! Is this not the devil's work? Will the church and religious bodies not conspire against us? The good citizens of London will have our heads if they discover what we were doing. Can we expect it better in the future?"

Golem sighed with irritation. "I think we can, Hamel," he said. "Science has shown a capacity to educate. Superstitions fall before the march of science. Men will change! The path of science and of human thought is toward progress! What was inexplicable and mysterious in the past is now explainable. The world will change, Hamel, and we can see that change ourselves! These experiments and these devices are more precious than all of the hitherto discoveries of man. We can be immortal and have a chance to change the future!"

I made my objections once more. "What if, when we awaken, we are judged to be heretics," I said, "and after our long icy sleep we are then burned at the stake, without even being given the opportunity to explain ourselves?"

"We will not be awakening a short time from now, my friend," Golem rejoined. "I have perfected the timing device to allow us to sleep for five hundred years! There will be plenty of time for the world to evolve beyond many of its barbaric ways."

* * *

He did not convince me. But despite my objections, my fascination with the project would not let me withdraw from it. It was a chance to rid myself of the oblivion that I feared. Now, night after night I engaged in the workings of freezing and reanimation with animals. I became totally attached to the experiments, but my mind never drifted from what I knew I must do. I thought that Golem might try an experiment using himself as the subject. I then would be able to kill him in his own machine, with his own invention. But my disagreement with the ethics of the project were not as strong as my desire to continue. I kept thinking of Jane and her protests about my relationship with Sir Astley.

The debate never ended, however, and on one particular night it renewed itself with vigor. Golem spoke to me thus: "In places where there is famine because of no rain, could men not mass produce our devices and put entire populations to sleep until better times came along? Could not men who died of disease sleep until a cure was found and then be revived and treated? Your objections go against the grain of our training, Mr. Hamel. We want to extend life and build a better world. What objections do you have this night?"

Again I tried to make the argument by speaking thus: "If we travel five hundred years into the future, who will provide protected storage of our bodies? Who will hinder those wishing to condemn our activities on religious grounds or otherwise? Can these forces not disrupt our sleep? If the timer is tampered with we might awake too early, or worse still, if the fluid lines are cut the device will fail. We have not yet tried the device on a human!"

Golem looked intently into my eyes. His irritation grew. He spoke once more. "Have you no faith in my genius! I have contracted with local men to build a vault, a walled structure of concrete and brick, like a crypt, to be constructed beneath these chambers. At the proper moment we will board our vessels and journey to the future. Here, at this place, in the floor, our vessels will sink into the vault where we will sleep, protected from the barbaric thinking of the time, into immortality! What have you to say now, my friend?" He leaned toward me and lowered his voice to a fiendish whisper. "And I *have* awakened a subject! It was Shadwick."

Golem had murdered the poor wretch! I was horrified.

I turned away, too stunned to utter a word.

* * *

The weeks began to pass quite rapidly and it was not long before the workmen began to construct the vault. Dr. Golem paid them handsomely for their work. These men did not know the reasons for the construction, for it was explained to them that a basement was needed for our work. I never said another word to Golem about Shadwick, but from his notes I discovered that Shadwick was murdered twice. He was put to sleep and killed upon arrival. He was then frozen and revived only to be killed once again. Golem now had this body in a rear chamber.

It was many weeks before the construction was completed. Golem had the workmen build three openings into which the icy coffins could be lowered by means of pulleys. After the work had been completed, Golem and I set the pulleys to lower the kryo-units. We tested them, sealing ourselves into the basement during this time. No one would be able to find us. The pulleys were then set to the timer, and the following night was set as a practice for the real event. The creature did not return but continued his crimes. We were like prisoners in our own laboratory. The creature had created an atmosphere of terror to which we were attached.

During this time my mind once again fixed itself, ever more firmly, toward the destruction of Golem. He helped to ruin my family and my friend! I would gain my revenge!

I learned how to operate the device and became completely familiar with Golem's notes, with an eye on murdering the cursèd man. Golem will pay dearly for all of his crimes! What ultimate revenge! To obliterate the wretch and then take credit for the science. I will destroy Golem's future as he has destroyed mine.

* * *

How would I tell Jane about my goals? How could she travel with me? There was room for her in a kryo-unit, since they are quite large. A unit only needs to be fitted with extra fluid lines and valves.

I would adapt my unit to accommodate her.

But how could I face her? She had warned me about Golem, but still I followed him. Doctor Golem has provided me with esteem and a way to realize success. His intelligence is beyond any I have ever known.

Lord, what am I to do? I needed to find Trevor and reach Jane. I was hampered. I could not move about the city as before. The creature had seen to that. I needed to tell my beloved what I had learned of her past.

I was totally distraught when I discovered that Jane and her uncle had gone to Edinburgh to visit relatives. Mr. Singleton's servant told me that they would be stopping along the way at various villages to visit friends. I could only send a letter to her at Edinburgh explaining that I needed to speak with her immediately. I prayed that she would return soon for time was runing out.

The Creature's Notes
January 14th, 1849

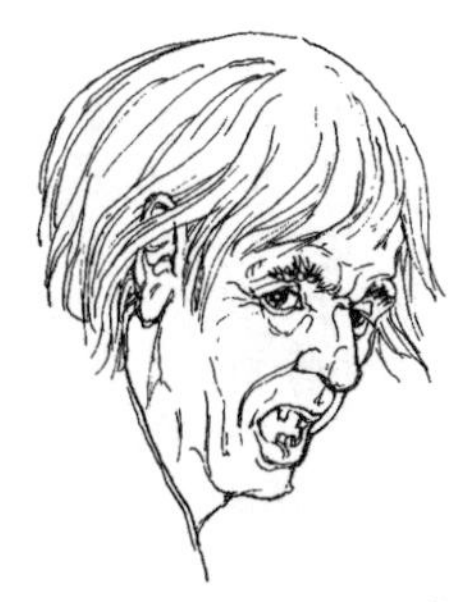

I have written these notes with enthusiasm. I shall not call these writings a diary. It is more of a journal. I visited the laboratory but found that my men were absent. I have searched the streets and the anatomy laboratories, concealing myself outside of the premises, trying to find and confront them. I was unsuccessful. They have escaped me for now. I went on through the alley ways of Vine Yard Street, Saffron Hill, Bleeding Heart Lane, Lambeth Street, Windmill Street, Great Marlborough Street, Crabtree Row, Cock Lane, and Giltspur Street. I crossed the South Bridge looking and hunting for them. I traveled to Scotland's university cities of Glasgow and Aberdeen and their anatomical theatres. When I returned to London it happened that I came upon a large building. It was a medical facility in which physicians dissected bodies and it was under siege by a mob of people. I learned from the rumblings of the crowd what events precipitated the riot.

The bad weather, which produced rain the night before, had unearthed human arms in great abundance. The remains were sticking out of the ground in the rear of the building. These human body parts, discarded by the doctors, littered the dark wasteland. I was there as the crowd gathered, a witness to see the dirt slip from the protruding fingers in the landscape. As it was still raining, drops of rain revealed them, slowly at first, and then quickly underneath the flashing of lightning in the ominous thundering sky. Far out ahead of me, hands and stumps pointed to the heavens. This macabre scene, fantastic to the eye, confirmed to me that these "men of science" were mad and did not deserve to live. Townspeople, strolling about their tasks, happened upon the scene. In a frenzy they organized thousands and marched toward the medical school. Their anger was soothing to me. Their scorn of these doctors was just!

As the sky began to clear, I watched the crowd with enthusiasm as they totally pulverized the building. I saw the dissection tables ripped from the floor and their tools of carving broken and bent. The mob put a torch to parts of the building and carried out furniture for a bonfire. Twenty or more corpses, scheduled for dissection, were removed from the butcher's table and hoisted up by the crowd. The bodies were held high as men are held aloft in a victory celebration. The corpses were later dressed in the best of clothes — some of which were stripped from the doctors — and buried.

Several surgeons were lynched on the spot. Their bodies were cut down within minutes, some of them still alive, and viciously hacked on the tables and on the ground with axes. At the Churchyard of St. Nicholas, several doctors who had tried to hide behind tombstones were captured and buried alive in the tombs where they stood.

As this riotous procession marched on, I followed. I found a discarded shawl on the side of the churchyard road and pulled it over my head and joined the mob. There had been a circus in town that day with a giant man. Many in the mob thought my height was because I was the "freak" from the circus. For the first time since I killed Victor Frankenstein's loved ones, I was a satisfied creature. Revenge by the mob against the surgeons was blessed. I was jubilant! I accepted an axe being passed around by the mob.

We made our way up the main street and headed into the town looking for anatomical schools. We marched on, looking for doctors, laboratories, and known resurrectionists. We headed for College Street where there was a dissecting room, which was well known for accepting bodies stolen from a nearby cemetery and the local churchyard.

At the College Street room, the crowd found several bodies on dissection tables. They removed them and carried them off as before. One doctor who tried to prevent their removal was seized. The crowd wanted to know if a man named Tom Geary had been seen in the town. The doctor, pleading for mercy, said he had not heard the name before. He was held and beaten until he confessed that Geary was last seen near a certain tavern. Word was dispatched by messenger that Geary was to be killed by those who were sick of this business.

I walked along shoulder to shoulder and closely packed with the mob. Many of them were peasants who were hollow-eyed from destitution. I kept my scarf raised and the shawl wrapped about my head to avoid detection. The crowd was humming with threats, curses, and ideas for vengeance as we moved ahead. I had never been so close to humans before and felt warm inside as we slowly moved ahead.

At times the crowd surged, and as it did, I felt the heartbeat of its anger; these men were consumed with it. Their faces boiled and were flushed with the fluid of revenge. It drove them on. Their eyes were determined. Everyone's head moved violently, jerking in a searching pattern here and there, looking for more of the fiends. Because of my stature I could see well ahead of the mob.

They had taken some students and medical men and were thrashing them to the ground. Others were lighting torches and throwing them into the schools after the doors were battered down. Smoke filled the air quickly and was soon in our nostrils and throats. The smoke was sweet to my senses. I took in a deep breath of its pleasurable vapors.

The crowd marched on to the next anatomical school. Thousands had now joined our ranks. Just as we turned onto the next street, bringing the structure into view, I could see an armed detachment of soldiers loading and fixing bayonets. The commander was giving orders. The detachment of men were well dressed in stiff uniforms. As my eyes surveyed their faces, I knew they were going to fire into us.

The detachment could be seen forming rows, getting ready for multiple firings. The people in the front of the surging mob saw this but it did not alter their will. They had the most satisfying look of determination in their eyes despite the fact that many would die this day. As my row turned the corner I saw the side of their faces and eyes. They seemed oblivious to the death that faced them.

Then a strange thing occurred. The shouts of the mob were deafening. My ears had grown accustomed to the quiet of the graveyard and my solitude. This panorama of noise, of bravery, of anger, of vengeance, was all ecstasy. What my eye could not see — the size of the mob, the complete picture of the people, and the city in flames — my mind provided. I could grasp the whole picture — of the marchers, of the city in flames, of individuals fleeing from the flanks of the crowd and others joining, of detachments of soldiers, of police, students huddled in fear, and surgeons being beaten. It was a glorious scene filled with the noise of anger.

I could see in my mind's eye the smoke rising above the city and climbing to the heights of the surrounding hills. I saw a bird in the sky as I looked up through the smoke. My marvelous vision continued. I could see the whole scene backing away, as a bird would see it as it rose higher in flight. I saw the whole city, the cemeteries, my vault, the hills, the sea, and the countries beyond. I knew what my mind demanded at that precise moment.

This sea of people moved me forward. I was crushed side by side by its power. My footsteps were shortened and behind me the crowd pushed me forward. My flanks were guided ahead by the shoulders that brushed me. We moved ahead, sometimes a little faster, sometimes a little slower. As the panoramic view began to fade the sounds of the crowd came back to my ears. I marvelled that such a vision had come to me.

I saw stones fly over my head mixed with farm tools and sod. The sky darkened with them as they arched in the direction of the troops. Some fell short while others found their mark. One soldier fell to the ground as his face was struck by a stone. Another crumpled to his knees after a large board hit him in the leg. The soldiers began to fall a few at a time.

The commander of the company took heart as he saw another detachment of troops, reinforcements, marching in his direction from the other end of the street. He quickly organized his men for firing. As they knelt in position, the crowd surged ahead. The guns vomited their loads and the first volley went into the crowd. A wall of lead cut them down. They fell in great heaps, the first row, mortally wounded, falling onto the street.

The next row walked over the dead and injured, and they too fell with the second volley. The blood ran along the street in small streams, then in rivers, deep red and thick, through the grating and into the sewers. Another row of men lurched at the soldiers and were struck down. By this time the second detachment had positioned itself. They let go a volley into the next row. More of the mob fell dead and wounded. Their bodies crumpled to the ground with a thud.

The mob began to lose its courage and deserters fled from the flanks. The disintegration of the crowd now began to take place as fear set in. Many ran from the flanks and as a result a hole was left in between a deserting row and the next bulk of people. One more volley plunged into this bulk causing those in front to panic. This row of men retreated into the rows behind them.

Those fleeing from the flanks streamed past the remaining bulk full of terror. Their retreat swept through us like a hot knife through butter. The once brave vengeful force turned into a frightened rabble of fleeing rabbits. I tried to stand my ground but was pushed backward by the pulsating terrorized mass horrified at the prospect of losing their lives.

They could have overcome the troops despite the disadvantage in arms, but instead chose to flee. Why did these destitute and miserable beings not take advantage of their numbers? What was left for them except a potter's field! They had no chance of being laid to rest with bronze covers, or gigantic marble angels over them, nor vaults of marble supplied with books. Their end would be a wooden cross, an old wrapping cloth, or a small stone of such poor quality that nature would obliterate its shallow inscription before their corpses rotted. The bodies left behind were already being looked at by resurrection men who had run behind the wall of troops for protection.

The mob ran in every direction, licking their wounds, defeated. I felt pity for them and resolved never to disturb their tombs. Bully's Acre and the potter's fields would never be desecrated by my hand. I vowed to kill any resurrectionist I caught in their graveyards.

I ran to the nearest flank, and then along the walkway, moving against the tide of people. It was no use. The fight was over. I ran out past the town and into an open field, saddened and disgusted at the same moment. I could only think of revenge against the hypocrisy and poverty of filthy England. Children roam the streets begging for food, doing whatever they can for daily subsistence, while their mothers sell themselves to the prosperous. In this maelstrom of poverty, the lame, the blind, and those ruined by liquor wander the streets of precious London.

The surgeons, who readily dissect the poor after waiting like buzzards in the alleyways and lanes, are invisible to the masses. They make themselves available when a patient is about to die. This is how they help these hopelessly incapacitated citizens. The sick are taken care of at St.Thomas and St. Bartholomew's Hospital under the vulturous eyes of surgeons. Those who can find room, sleep in the poorhouse. Often women give birth to children there, only to lose them to disease. Starvation is rampant. This hallowed city for amusement imprisons the poor who must steal to eat. Those who owe London a debt can be gaoled as well, leaving their wives and children to suffer in the unsanitary streets.

The destitute who are Tyburn-bound — that is, to the gallows — provide macabre pleasure to the respectable Londoners. This filthy hypocritical city, by a river that stinks with human waste and degradation, is a mockery to life. These same well-to-do Londoners who stroll in their gardens and squares after fattening themselves on food made available by the labor of the poor find it appalling that so many destitute are on the welfare rolls, although these petty sums are not even enough to remove the peril of starvation!

When those who are poor rise up, they are executed. Those who live on, relegated to the workhouse, must eat food that contains animal and human remains — these remains often being from their own brethren! The workhouse poor are beaten, starved, and then dissected at the anatomy schools in this wonderful city on the river.

The police are part of this cadaverous festival. They have been known to murder men, feigning self-defense, and then turn the cadavers over to the resurrectionists for compensation. I have seen this barbarism with my own eyes. Where they have not committed the evil itself they have turned their head, after receiving payment, at corpses found in coaches and in wagons on the road to London, and on London Bridge itself.

The politicians, like Sir Jeffrey Wolf, have received funds and political promises from those wishing to use the body bank of the poor. In the House of Commons itself, one of its former members, Francois Walker, who has a mistress with resurrectionist connections, talked about the good and wonderful surgeons, and how he would not excuse himself from voting even though he had a relationship with his mistress and resurrection men. This is public knowledge! These hypocritical representatives are then lauded in the financial districts, among the wealthy, as fine gentlemen! Walker has even had his name placed on a building for others to gape at. Walker, as a member of Parliament, represented a district in which police corruption and grave desecration were rampant. The police and the resurrectionists knew that they could commit their heinous crimes because Mr. Walker was there to protect them. The social elite were quite impressed by this sycophant, so much so that after his term had expired he was whisked away by a social superior to oversee the poorhouses. This pitiful excuse for a human being continues in his abominable profession and fancies himself a man of integrity. He writes editorials for the local paper in which he discusses the merits of the surgeons in a most hypocritical manner.

London, filthy London, a city enveloped by the smoke of coal fires which obscures the view from a river seething in sewage, is but a city of death and hatred. From this sinful city, the rich somehow are inspired to a practical benevolence of charitable impulse. They have provided finances for St. George's Hospital, a hospital for the poor and for the sick of Soho and Middlesex Infirmary. Their filthy money eases their conscience. Their philanthropy is tainted with easy kills, on hospital beds, for the waste of human bodies. Oh, you are a despicable race! Not fit to inherit the earth!

Then there are the demagogues among them, a race of evil-doers, whose most famous bunch north and south of Hadrian's Wall seems to be skilled in finding out what people's ears are willing to hear. A Mr. R. Limbo is the most notorious. I have seen him at work in Glasgow. After the people had become infuriated, he led them into enemy fire, encouraging them all the way, but when time dictated, he departed from the mob only to be seen collecting corpses that had been mowed down in the streets by musket fire. I have seen him being paid. He has become quite wealthy. Lesser men in the employ of Limbo helped him to carry out his evil work. They were so efficient in their work that the local police were often angered when their booty was loaded onto wagons before the bodies could be identified. These ruthless despicable men are but representations of the whole of the precious ilk that Golem wants to immortalize.

Golem's form is different from these men, but not his essence. The essence of his fellow brethren is no less evil. In the journey from Newgate Prison to the gallows, never have I witnessed such a mockery of justice. I can still see quite vividly in my mind the procession of a condemned prisoner to St. Sepulchre's Church. Along the way a great bell would toll, and a chaplain would board the wagon at the church to exhort the prisoner to repent. The wagon also carried the executioner who wore a black hood. He stood next to a coffin for the condemned man. This wagon of injustice and hypocrisy angered me.

From a hiding place I have watched the chaplain, a paid accomplice of the resurrection men. I have seen the executioner deliver intelligence to the grave robbers, and to the authorities who strode in front of this cruel parade of justice. The local constable denied that there was police collaboration with the resurrectionists. His duty was to exonerate those who were guilty. As for the crowd, they were but macabre onlookers, all alike, standing by to watch a man die. All are but guilty men who kill guilty men. They shall never inherit the earth! The rich are evil and the poor are cowards. I vow to end this madness! Dr. Golem, and the filth that inspired my creation, will be disposed of! I am full of revenge . . . but room remains!

* * *

I rested in the countryside and soon it was early morning. The sun was barely visible but the wild rage of my heart fervently burned. I felt total rage for Golem and Hamel. The intensity of my fury could only be satisfied by what I now must do. I walked toward town, toward the location of the riot which had taken place the day before, and just on the outskirts of the city I found a newspaper lying on the ground. A story on the front page described the riot as though it were a minor occurrence, with only two people killed. Londoners were urged to "remain calm as reports of heinous crimes are greatly exaggerated. We have talked with experts from across Europe who say that mass hysteria is common in these circumstances." I became numb with rage that the local newspaper had printed these lies.

Despite the lies of the paper, word soon spread that Golem and Hamel were dissecting murdered bodies. Crowds of people read the distortion in the paper but knew that many killings had taken place. I could not find the medical monsters, but I was sure that the crowds would. The police and crowds were searching for them.

Hamel's Diary
January 14th, 1849

A sad and strange thing happened to me which I must record. Often, when leaving the anatomy school or returning from an afternoon stroll, I encountered a beggar. He would be standing a short distance from the entrance to the school, begging for money. He seemed extremely sad. It was with a feeling of pity that I always gave him a few pence. He was a small fellow, with long white hair and a wrinkled face hewn by the blows of time.

His eyes, though they expressed sadness, were extremely kind. His voice expressed this kindness when he asked for money. I was taken by his pleasant attitude despite his penurious state. He looked somehow familiar to me.

One afternoon I decided to engage him in conversation. He proved quite intelligent and his loquacity and faculty impressed me. He conveyed to me a great deal of information about himself which I found quite sad. He had seen better times working as a stone mason for several funeral parlors, but had fallen into debt. The state of his poverty led to the confiscation of his home. This was the result of an unpaid mortgage. He was forced to move from his clean little cottage and take up residence in a run-down dwelling. His wife died from the fever, and both of his children had succumbed a short time later.

"My wife was a loving woman," he said. "She gave me strength throughout the years. When she died I could no longer manage my own affairs. I depended on her as a child depends on its mother. Soon, because of carelessness, uncleanliness, and neglect, my children fell to the disease. I could not afford a proper funeral and so buried them myself at the potter's field. I carved the small stones that now mark their resting place. I went into an extreme melancholy which has walked with me every day. I lost most of my belongings when I was evicted from our cottage, and I began to drink more and more."

I listened intently at the recounting of the dire events leading to his present state. As he spoke I reflected upon my own life, and how fate had delivered me to a different reality. My life had also been shattered, but, unlike my acquaintance, circumstance and the Will of God delivered me from a similar situation.

I paused for a moment, feeling kinship with his plight. He never used a container in which coins could be tossed, but kept his hands in his trousers until he was sure of receiving something. This I did not take with any ill intent, but thought of it as some small measure by which he could retain his dignity. Many of London's beggars went about with tin cups and pans from which the sounds of dropping coins could be heard. He had more dignity than that. In fact, I never heard him actually beg for money, but simply and nicely make a request. "May I trouble you for a few pence," he would always say. He never pitifully besieged pedestrians with the usual laments that often annoy Londoners.

Another day, as I stood before him, I remarked, "It is a cold day, sir. Not a good day for the elderly. I have found that many old people die during the months and days such as we have been experiencing lately. It seems that the cold has a way with our bodies, especially when we become quite old. The cold temperatures allow disease to invade and wreak havoc upon a weakened frame."

The beggar replied, "The cold makes one shiver and grow weak. The body in a weakened state will invite whatever host that wishes to feed on it. One is then easy prey to be taken to death's gate. My wife was chilled before she became ill. She had been in the field tending to the cow when out of the north a cold wind rose up. It came upon her quickly and grew quite cold before she was able to bring the cow in.

"She became ill that night and within a week was dead. In a few short weeks my children contracted the fever. Being in low spirits I had gone to a tavern. When I returned home I found the hearth empty of wood and my dwelling frozen. There were so many cracks in my hovel that unless a fire was kept going it would become extremely cold within a short time. My children lay in bed, coughing and trying their best to stay warm, but it was too late. I gathered some wood from outside and started the fire once more, but still I could not drive their chills away. They died from fever."

"So you believe that the cold invited the fever?" I asked.

"I do," he said in a low voice. "My landlord is a monster. I lost my little cottage for missing one mortgage note. He put me up in a small, dilapidated shed which I rented because there was no other place I could afford. When my wife and children died, Doctor Golem evicted me from there as well."

Golem again! His evil touch tainted every human relationship of my life! If I believed in Satan I would see Golem as the personification of the Devil!

I could say nothing. My heart felt anger and sorrow at the same time.

"I am a surgeon at the school," I responded finally.

"Yes, I have seen you come and go to St. Thomas and at Guy's," the beggar said. "I must go now. It was good to talk with you." He lifted his head to stare hard into my eyes. "I have heard the arguments before. They lay the blame on blankets from infected people or on animals, but if it were not for the cold my family might have lived. The winter months and the cold northern winds bring death. Cold death will come to London soon."

It was then that I blurted out these words: "My life is empty as well. At least you know the reason for your emptiness. I do not know the reason why I am so filled with emptiness. The Void in me is a phantom." He said nothing, but looked me over, seeming to understand some of what I said.

Suddenly, without explanation, he said, "There is a gigantic creature that lives in the cemetery, in the Lamar Tomb. He will bring death. Yes, I have had one disaster after another wreak havoc in my life. I had a younger sister who was lost along with my father. Father was traveling to Scotland, by carriage, to visit relatives, taking little Emily with him. They never returned, nor were we able to discover their whereabouts. Their carriage and horses were never found either. They just vanished. I often think about what little Emily might have been." He paused and rubbed his eyes. "There is yet more to come, with the creature about. I must witness more sorrow."

He said nothing else as he walked away. His last words struck me. He knew about the creature. There was something strange in his look, in his eyes, which pierced my soul and frightened me, yet took my mind to the past.

"What is your name?" I called out.

"Trevor. Trevor," he said timidly, looking back over his shoulder.

I was shocked! This was my childhood friend! It hit me hard. It was Trevor Wallace and Jane was his little sister. My beloved Jane Singleton was Emily Wallace! I had not thought of it before now, but her beautiful eyes were the same ones I had seen when she was a child. She was some eight years younger than Trevor and I only saw her once or twice during my childhood friendship with Trevor.

I tried to stop Trevor and screamed out his name, but he had disappeared into the crowded streets of London.

I ran through the avenues and alleys shouting his name, looking everywhere, to no avail. I must have been lost in time, for when I finally decided to stop I was far from where we had been.

* * *

January 20th 1849

I searched for Trevor every day for a week without success. There was still no word from Jane and my heart grew anxious. The events unfolding required my attention.

We went out in search of Geary. Golem pretended that he did not know where he was, but I had looked at his notes secretly and knew that he had met with Geary before.

We proceeded by coach and after a time Golem spoke. "I think this is the tavern where we might find Tom Geary, Mr. Hamel."

"Yes, it is the Fortune of War," I responded. The pub was a large solid building, and through its big windows I could see many patrons.

"Hurry, let us go in," I said.

Inside the tavern Golem and I looked around cautiously and presented ourselves to the barkeep. We asked for ale and when the barkeep returned with our potables we asked where we might find Geary. As it was a Saturday we were fortunate, for the barkeep informed us that Geary always sat in the back of the tavern on this day, near the rear alley door. Golem quickly spied the man and we approached his table.

Geary sat with another fellow and had several slips of paper in front of him. I could not make out what he was scribbling. He looked up before we reached his table, and Golem addressed him.

"How do you do, sir. I am Dr. Golem and this is Mr. Hamel. May we sit for a conversation?"

Geary was tall and hardy looking. He had no expression on his face which was as stoic as a corpse. He was wearing a smock and was in conversation with the other man about where he might purchase a dirt-resistant piece of clothing. We did not learn the other fellow's name; as we started to sit, Geary looked at his accomplice and waved him off with a slight tilt of his head.

"Well, sir, we understand that you may be able to obtain what we need."

"A thing, no doubt!" Geary responded. His voice was heavy and coarse.

"Yes, a fresh one and one specific to our needs," said Dr. Golem. Having said this, Golem reached into his coat pocket and produced a quantity of money which he kept in his hand.

"Specific needs, gentlemen, may cost you!" Geary said "Is it a head, arms, eyes, or a very, very fresh one? Perhaps teeth, or a specific disease?"

"Yes, yes, a specific disease — idiopathic fever." Golem looked directly at Geary, measuring him. The man seemed to pay no attention as Golem's eye wandered up and down his face.

"A dangerous task indeed. First, you want a fresh one and then it must have succumbed to fever! Hm! Let us say fifty pounds? That is not asking for too much."

"I am afraid it is, Geary," said Golem. "I can get what we need for twelve guineas!"

Geary looked off and sneered. He twisted the necklace that hung from his neck for a moment, looking at it and rubbing the strange ornament.

"Well, gentlemen, what are you doing at my table? There are some twelve-guinea men at the other tables!"

"We heard you were one of the best," Golem said sympathetically.

"Aye, that I am."

"Hamel and I have only twenty pounds between the two of us. We can give you twenty pounds," Golem said.

"I will need forty, and that is my final offer, or otherwise you can take your chances with those twelve-guinea men sitting over there. Of course, there may be among those men one who is willing to tell the local constable of the whereabouts of a Dr. Golem, and some fellow named Hamel!" Geary pushed his chair back and relaxed. He had a grin on his face.

"Thirty-five pounds is our top price," Golem said and pushed some money over to Geary's side of the table.

"Sorry, gents. It's forty or nothing. Twenty now and twenty on delivery to your place."

Golem demurred. "I hope you will reconsider," he said, rising, and stalked off. I followed.

Outside, Golem stopped and said to me, "Perhaps I was hasty. We probably had better deal with Geary, much as I dislike to. Would you go back and give him this twenty pounds as a down payment and promise him the rest on delivery? Give him the instructions for time and place. I'll wait for you here."

He handed me the money and I reentered the tavern. Geary was about to leave by the back door when I reached him and was talking with another man who quickly departed. I concluded the deal and paid the money, giving him the address of our laboratory, which I suspect he knew well enough already. I told him to use the rear entrance since crowds would be about at sunrise. He assured me he would have no trouble procuring the cadaver because the poorhouses were full of fever, and said to expect him within two to three days.

When I rejoined Golem, I asked him if he had become unnerved at meeting the famous Tom Geary, but got no reply. "He bore resemblance to a demon," I said. "He had a cross around his neck with a skeleton being crucified. I have never seen such an ornament before."

Golem spoke in a mild tone. "He has been impressive. He and his men know their trade, would you not say, Mr. Hamel?"

"They know it well — quite well, Dr. Golem." I perceived a distant look in Golem's eye, the stoicism that I hated. Soon we were at Cock Lane. We noticed a crowd of people gathering at the other end of the street. At first we paid no attention to them, but as we drew closer one of the men looked familiar. It was Limbo. As soon as he recognized us he screamed, "The surgeons! Get them!"

The crowd moved slowly at first, walking toward us. Some of them began picking up stones and boards from drays nearby. We looked at each other and knew that there was nothing else to do but flee.

We ran, with the crowd at our heels. We were most fortunate that the arbitrary path chosen took us back past the Fortune of War, for some of the crowd recognized it as a resurrectionist gathering place, and someone in the crowd diverted their attention to the tavern. As we turned onto another street I could hear shouting and windows being smashed. We were able to lose the remaining men by hiding behind some barrels in an alley.

When I had caught my breath, I spoke with fear. "My God, Golem, we were almost killed!"

My chest heaved as I tried to catch my breath. The cold air burned my lungs.

"Geary left just in time, Mr. Hamel! He probably received some intelligence. We had better return to the laboratory. We can lower ourselves into the basement until the resurrectionist arrives in a day or so. It has served us well. It is a good hiding place."

When we arrived at the laboratory, there was a crowd of people milling around outside, besides a constable with a sizable detachment of police officers. They were shoving a crowd back away from our front door. I could not see what was going on and so Golem and I climbed onto the roof of a shop across the way.

When we gained a vantage point we saw, to our horror, corpses of mutilated bodies at our doorstep. The police were investigating. One corpse, which had apparently been cut down from the lamppost, had the rope still dangling from it.

At that moment I thought of London, its people, its surgeons — and Dr. Golem. How shall I stop him? There is no public support within our profession to stop the dissections. From whence will my help come? The poor and destitute can be of no assistance. They have no standing in this wretched society. They are only destined for poverty and disease, or for the gallows.

If I just kill him . . . but who will champion my cause? Will I not just simply become a murderer? Yet the longer I wait, the more I see of desecrations . . . and he has murdered! What can I do that would expose the horrors of Golem and his accomplices? Perhaps I could murder Tom Geary and the others, as well as Golem, and readily admit to the crime, in protest to their vile deeds. My trip to the gallows would be worth it to accomplish this task. If I could attach the crimes to Golem perhaps public sentiment would swing in favor of my cause. The current reform bill, better than any so far proposed, would have a better chance of being enacted to stop these fiends, to put an end to body-snatching.

My mind falters. It is like soft clay. It is not yet burning with fire, not yet stone. Those pieces of flesh that Golem so brutally throws into the pan beneath the dissection table once were a man who could talk, love, and enlighten others. These victims are just waste to be thrown in the yard behind the school for the dogs to devour. I need to expose this filthy business to future generations.

Worst of all is the intelligence that I came upon which confirmed my growing suspicions. When I returned to Geary in the tavern to conclude our arrangement for the cadaver, I had overheard him tell the other man that Golem had "put the poor devil out of his misery." By offering him more money, I persuaded Geary to tell me what I had already suspected — that Golem had placed a cloth over the mouth of a Mr. Cooper, who, having fever, had come to St. Thomas for treatment. Golem had murdered another man, and had used his body for dissection. The man had come from one of the poorhouses and was referred to Golem by the ferryman there. Golem had Mr. Limbo deliver the sickly man to his laboratory but then he refused to pay the price being demanded.

Geary went on to say that Golem seduced the poor man to his death. "Golem received the sickly man at his laboratory," he told me. "I had only just deposited some cadavers in the hamper next to the back door when I saw the doctor receiving a patient brought to him by Limbo. I watched from a rear window as Golem escorted the man to a table to examine him. The fellow was in terrible pain. Golem gave him a potion which quieted him and soon began to speak to him. 'It is like a pleasant field,' Golem told him in a soothing voice. 'A beautiful scene, a meadow, gently rolling, floating, blurred at first, but gently rolling, moving to crystal clarity. The picture clears, and at that moment the sound of a babbling brook comes into your mind. The water gently flows across polished rounded rocks, which glisten in the wonderful sun, gently striking the incline of each rock, and then rolling in a continuous stream over the sparkling stones situated in the stream.'"

It was uncanny to hear Geary speaking in so clear an imitation of Golem's voice. It put chills down my spine.

Geary continued, "Golem preached his sermon of death like none I have ever heard before. I remember it well! He said this: 'There is only peace. Sweet calmness rolls through your body as you look upon the scene. Think of the most pleasant dream. Think of floating on soft clouds. You are there, seeing the trees, the brook, the meadow; the soft clear brook is rolling through the great green meadow. The wind blows your hair, with rising cool eddies of air created by the cool waters. You can rise above the scene and see all, above and below the horizon. You can descend from these lofty heights and sit by the brook in the cool air, completely at peace.'"

Geary went on to say that Dr. Golem prepared an ether-soaked cloth which he used after saying these words: "Your pain is gone. You can see yourself as two people, one at peace and one in terrible pain. Your painless self communicates peace to your other self. You feel bliss! Close your eyes to feel bliss! The pain is leaving you now. Your ears hear the babbling water. Your nose smells the delightful fragrance of spring blossoms, so sweet that you can taste its joy on your lips. You are floating to happiness, to calm, down, down, to the stream, toward the eternal horizon."

Geary pulled away from me and left me with these words: "Your colleague is truly an evil man!"

There must be something I can do. Is this my sentence, my punishment for my complicity , that I must endure the sight of Golem, knowing full well that he has murdered? Knowing that he helped to destroy my mother and Trevor! How can I rid myself of the pain I feel? Would it not have been easy enough to assassinate the man at a public dissection? Would this not be a way to create public outrage if I were sacrificed after the act?

Could I expose the filthy crimes of my fellow surgeons before paying the price at the Tyburn Road gallows? Is this what I must do? Surely I could kill Geary? He is truly a mercenary! When I looked into Geary's face I could feel how easy it would be for me to kill him. Geary never knew that I almost shot him then. My gun remains loaded for a better time when the act may be done in such a way as to gain the maximum effect.

God will support me in the struggle with this devil! I have no doubt that God Almighty will absolve me for what I am about to do to Golem, Geary, and all the others. They deserve to die! I will pray for guidance as to when the right moment shall be.

I pray that Jane received my message and will return to me before it is too late.

The Creature's Notes
January 21st, 1849

I have learned from my readings that I must leave the City of Destruction andDeath. The marble, stone, alabaster, purbeck, wood, and metal will not prevent a body from turning to dust. The workers and craftsmen of these materials, variously known as carvers, image makers, tomb men, stone-cutters, lapidary men, masons, sculptors, coppersmiths, marblers, and others, will all be dust themselves!

I learned that the origin of these names, for the materials to build graves, stemmed from the area in which the material was found. Alabaster could be found in Staffordshire, Yorkshire, and elsewhere. Darkish blue-gray marble came from the Bethersden quarries in Kent, and purbeck marble was used in the older tombs. All of these facts were meaningless! These cold hard stones were cut, and designs of trees with apples, with Eve and the serpent engraved onto its surface. In my journey I have seen horrid stones which read:

Life is the Road to Death
And Death awaits us all.
All must pass alone the
Unknown Road.

Nothing was a comfort for me, for I was but an abomination. I read one inscription which said, "O Friends and Earth Refrain from Tears," but I had no earthly friends to know of my fate. It was from The *Sorrows of Young Werther* that I remember these words, which, in my previous state, I once applied to myself, but now imagined as Golem's words. Before I kill him I will force these words from his lips:

> *It is as if a curtain has been*
> *drawn from before my eyes,*
> *and, instead of prospects of*
> *eternal life, the abyss of an*
> *ever-open grave yawned before me.*

My mind's eye vividly saw Golem speak these words to me as I struck him down. As I imagined him dead the pain in my heart was momentarily released. Though I am alone in this valley of death, forlorn and filled with rage, I am warmed by the thoughts of revenge. I am the prize Golem seeks, for in my body the magic fluid flows. In my body the glycerol flows, the fluid that allowed me to survive the cold. Golem would prefer me alive, but he now must kill me and dissect my body to discover the function of the magic fluid. The quest of his life is now mingled with my existence.

As I thought these things my mind wandered toward the potter's field. In contrast to the eloquent tombs of the rich, the potter's field was marked with small stones whose inscriptions were faded and almost gone. Far from the fantastic tombs were those despised creatures that were mowed down by life. I lifted not a single corpse from there. These despised creatures were robbed even in death of their stones of immortality, for their design and workmanship would not endure the ravages of time. I felt a pity for them and could not disturb their resting place.

I drove a wagon that I stole from a nearby barn and quickly went along the lonely road past Bully's Acre. I saw a resurrectionist nearby digging close to the roadside. He heard my wagon but was unable to avoid detection for I was rapidly upon him. I pulled up and he noticed the bodies in the rear of my wagon.

He spoke these words to me. "Well, I see you have devised a new way to transport them! A full load I take it?" he asked.

His smile did not hide the evil of his deeds. My desire to kill heightened. I reached into the wagon and quickly threw a spade at him. It penetrated his heart. It stuck in his bosom and he fell to his knees holding it with both hands. For a moment it appeared as if he were praying — as if he were sorry for what he had done. His knees buckled, and his body slumped back onto his haunches as his head fell forward. He was frozen there.

I bore his body onto the wagon and noticed he looked familiar, but I could not remember where I had seen him before. It might have been at Golem's laboratory. This might have been Limbo, but I did not dwell on the matter. I raised my whip from the holder and cracked it over the head of my steeds, rushing on with my pallid cargo toward my destination.

When I arrived at Golem's laboratory the streets were deserted. I placed another corpse at the front door and then hung one from the lamppost in front. Perhaps the mobs would burn them out. Having completed this I drove on to the other anatomical schools and unloaded my things at each stop. The deposit of corpses at various places took some time, and I was not finished until three days later.

I returned to Golem's laboratory one last time and while searching for resurrectionists I stumbled upon a female who was in the rear of the laboratory. As she left the building I approached her from behind. I had seen her with Hamel previously and watched them spend their days together. It was unjust that Hamel should be the recipient of such affection while I still had no hope for any such relationship. She would be a great prize in my demand for the creation of a mate. I squeezed her until she was unconscious and placed her next to me on the wagon. Having accomplished this I went to my hovel to rest, to await my destiny, and for Golem and Hamel to fall into my clutches. They had no choice. They were now forced to seek the destroyer of their dreams. Golem could not do without me.

And So It Came to Be

Now and then the old man appeared, walking the streets of London, begging, in all types of weather. He often went to the cemetery at night for it was the only place he could find refuge. Sometimes he would sleep in the caretaker's shed, which was abandoned at night. At other times he would have to sleep on the streets of London, or in some run-down abandoned structure.

He remained on the streets of London, familiar with the pathways of its well-to-do residents. He never said much to anyone, nor did anyone say much to him, except for one. He often ate on the streets, using his hands for a table.

On one cold afternoon, with the wind howling out of the north, Trevor was allowed in a tavern. It was not easy to frequent such establishments, for the barkeepers were generally watchful for beggars, making sure they were able to make a purchase before allowing them access. Trevor sat at the first available table and ordered some victuals whose quantity was governed by his purse.

Trevor was indeed pitiful. Even when he smiled, the sadness in his eyes never left. The most stone-hearted person could not help but feel, if only for a moment, true sorrow at the sight of him. Trevor sat and consumed the watery food. His mind was on the evil that was surely at work in London.

On many occasions he witnessed resurrectionists at work, both at the cemeteries and at the anatomy schools. He saw the gigantic creature living at the Lamar Tomb. Though he was preoccupied with begging, Trevor never missed a moment to reflect upon what he saw and the people he met and talked to. He watched the very wealthy scorn and berate the poor and ignore the hundreds that littered the alleys and streets of London. He watched the surgeons ignore the dregs of society, the rail-thin bodies of cold and half-starved human beings. He knew of the coldness that lay ahead.

He stood often at the entrance to St. Thomas Anatomy School. He knew that many of those who graced its doors were of wealth. He was observant, a quality which provides insight, at the contrast between his own predicament and those who pitied or hated him. Though his condition was wretched he was keenly aware of the emptiness of wealth — of the people who because of their social standing thought themselves knowledgeable and wise.

Sometimes he walked past the inns and restaurants, not to beg but to watch the thick cluster of wealthy Londoners as they ate. They filled themselves with delights. They were wise in the use of proper etiquette. They knew how to sip their tea. "I would rather live as I do now than to be like them," he said to himself. He often thought of them as passing wisps of air, too fragile and unwise to inherit the earth.

He heard them speak of the "thrilling times" for science and the future ahead. Trevor saw no future in their faces, and indeed his stare was reflective of their doom. He was often chased away from the windows he peered through.

"What is that beggar staring at?" they would ask.

"Why is he looking at me like that?" others would say.

His eyes touched all who happened upon his gaze. Trevor witnessed many events and knew many things. From his place on the streets of London he peeped into the anatomy schools and heard the exasperating discussions of the surgeons. He listened to Golem's public lectures and knew what kind of man he was.

Once, when Golem was arriving at the school, he felt the need to berate the beggar. Golem simply approached Trevor and began scolding him. Having satisfied himself, he then stormed off. Trevor said nothing as the doctor walked away triumphantly. Golem's feeling of success, however, did not last long. He had taken but a few steps when he realized that the force of his contempt had fluttered away.

He did not know why he felt the need to return and begin scolding the old man once more. The eyes of Trevor were unrelenting during the entire excoriation. Trevor did not blink but looked deeply into

Golem's being. Having concluded his diatribe the doctor again turned to walk away. Still he could not shake the feeling that what he had said and done was empty and without substance. Trevor's stare was piercing. It was a stare of knowledge . . . a look that declared he knew Golem better than he knew himself.

Golem could not understand why such a look would cause these feelings. When he had again walked but a few paces he felt a disequilibrium that undid the effects of his attack on the beggar. It was as if his statements were strewn about their mark. He did not force himself to return for he no longer felt powerful. The effect followed him. He was not the same afterwards. Unknown to him, he was now in possession of a subtle insecurity which softened his hard core of arrogance.

When Trevor was young he had overheard a servant telling a relative that Hamel's mother was seeing a resurrectionist by the name of William. He was not around much as he worked the poorhouses in the day and the graveyards at night. This man did not like young Hamel and had attempted to smother him. William's desire was Dorothy Hamel but without the bother of a young child. Trevor overheard the servant say that Dorothy Hamel had gone out late one night to drink at a pub. She had left William there to watch the young boy, who was sleeping.

William was in a drunken stupor when he tried to smother Joshua Hamel with a pillow. William had also figured on selling young Hamel's corpse to an anatomy school. Hamel's mother arrived just in time to prevent the deed from being accomplished. Though she clearly saw the crime her drunken stupor prevented her from the realization of it. She accepted William's excuse that he was only removing the pillow from Joshua's face which he claimed was in that position as a result of the boy's tossing and turning. William was still with Dorothy Hamel at the time of her death.

After Dorothy Hamel was evicted from her house, Trevor thought that he would never see Joshua again, but after recent encounters on the street, he gradually came to recognize Joshua's face and eyes in the friendly surgeon. Trevor now knew that he had found his childhood friend. However, he could not bring himself to tell Hamel. Trevor's fear was that of the unknown—of not knowing how Hamel would feel when he realized that his childhood friend was reduced to this miserable creature that lived on London's streets.

Returning to the caretaker's shed where he often slept, Trevor resolved to find Joshua the next day to tell him these truths and renew their friendship. His words would free Joshua Hamel from the emptiness of his heart. He would learn of his near murder as a child and know that his childhood friend still loved him.

* * *

Hamel's Diary, January 1849

I finally received word that my love and her uncle had returned, but upon my arrival at their home Mr. Singleton informed me that she had gone to the anatomy school.. He explained that she was distraught upon hearing that Golem was being charged with receiving cadavers that had expired under questionable circumstances. Mr. Singleton said that Jane had insisted on going to speak with Sir Astley so that she might make the demand that he sever his relationship with me.

I explained to Mr. Singleton that I had discovered Jane was really Emily Wallace and that I had located her brother. He was shocked, and so weakened by the news that I left my driver there to attend to him. I rushed to the laboratory and questioned some students lingering by the door. They had indeed seen a beautiful woman with dark auburn hair, but to my horror they told me that a huge, hideous creature had killed my beloved Emily and carried her away.

I fell to the ground in utter grief. The medical students tried to rouse me and persuade me to go inside but I could not move and waved them away.

I was finally about to rise from the ground when I became aware of a pair of ragged shoes before me. It was Trevor!

"My God! Trevor! It is my lifelong friend!" I said.

He raised me from my knees and we held one another in a tight embrace.

"There is something I must tell you," I rushed to say. "I have found your beloved sister. She is my Jane Singleton, my love!" Trevor held me close so that our faces almost touched. "But I am afraid she is dead — murdered by the fiend we brought back from the Arctic," I sobbed.

"Where is her body?" Trevor demanded.

"They say the monster took her away," I replied.

Without another word Trevor released me and said, "I have more to tell you. I will return to your laboratory soon. Please go there and wait."

Before I could utter a word, Trevor left, walking away at a swift pace. I could do nothing. I was ruined.

BOOK V

THE CHASE OF THE DEAD

The Creature's Notes
January 31st, 1849

I must fight Golem. Golem is but Satan in the flesh. I am on the King's highway! I once thought — wrongfully so — that my condition was likened to Satan. My study of men was yet incomplete. I know that the way to the Celestial City is in the destruction of despair. Despair has driven me to the edge, and has almost succeeded in overcoming my spirit. I swear that Golem will perish this night!

My choice to live allows me to pass sentence upon all the workers of iniquity. I will escape Doubting Castle, ruled by despair, even though I reside in the bowels of death. As I lay in my tomb night after night, reading, sometimes by candle, sometimes by moonlight, in the shadow of death, I knew my pilgrimage was about to commence. I was about to begin my journey to the Celestial City.

My only companion has been the howl of the wind and the patter of raindrops. The wind often whistled through me. Its serpentine wail awakened in me a calmness, a disposition toward self-reflection. I hear the howl of winds even when no air stirs. Often during a rain storm I would listen to the blowing, bellowing wind batter the hard surface of my hovel. It was during this time that I became most reflective. The wailing notes of gloom led me to remember when, owing to my misery at the loss of my creator, I had once contemplated self-destruction. As fate would have it there was no fuel from which to build my funeral pyre on the ice. I lay with my creator in icy gloom, becoming frozen with my maker; I am here.

My true spirit lies in this sepulchre. The builders of this tomb have left the literature that has severed me from *Paradise Lost*. My dead host and his family have been more helpful than any living creature. Somehow I have been provided with shelter and the works that shall provide salvation. These notes I commit to paper.

Hamel's Diary
February 1st, 1849

Trevor never returned. I waited and waited and even instructed my coachman to search the city for him. My life is saddened. My Jane is dead and her body has not been found. I have been through hell. Nothing matters now but killing Golem and the murderer of Jane. It is now a matter of following through with Golem's plot and my own.

Golem's plan was to separate. Each would walk along the outer perimeter, finally meeting at the western edge of the cemetery. We were both armed with pistols and Golem carried a musket as well. If either of us sighted the monster, we were to fire shots at the creature. The sound of gunfire was the signal by which the other would join, surreptitiously, in the hunt, waiting for an opportune time for the creature to be chased into an ambush. Golem's plan seemed sound . . . but it did not matter.

The entrance arch to Celestial City Cemetery was a haunting structure. The words engraved on the arch were focused in my eye: Abandon All Hope Ye Who Enter Here. At the foot of the arch was a stone tablet which said: Here you will die, Golem. Hamel will not be spared. The engraving was obviously done by the fiend, whose threatening taunts did not waver Golem's resolve to destroy him. He appeared to ignore the terrible omen, but within a short time I detected in the mists of his eyes a strain of terror.

When he entered the cemetery gate with Hamel, Dr. Golem was tense and eager. His mind was keyed to his purpose and his thoughts determined.

"There is nothing left for us to do but find and kill the monster," he thought. "With crowds of angry people searching for us, and the police suspicious, we could only clear our names by silencing the monster. He will surely implicate us further if he is not hunted down and destroyed. In his twisted mind, improperly shaped by his poor education, we are his enemies, as are all men of science. Perhaps after I have destroyed him I can return his corpse to the laboratory, to study and to take into the future."

As he gazed at the words above the gate, Golem could see the fear in the air. He looked away quickly, thinking that fear could cross through the air on unspoken currents. The arch at the front of the cemetery looked like a deadly rainbow crossing the threshold of a doomed city. Our fate and that of countless others would be decided here.

"If the monster destroys us," he thought, "he may have seen enough of the workings of the cold units to be able to operate the machine by himself. I saw him once looking through the glass on the roof as I descended into the vault. I know he was aware of it. He did not attack because he was hatching his plan. He could set the timing device, board the vessel, begin the fluid exchange, and then be lowered into the time vault. Even if the laboratory was burnt to the ground, the crypt would survive and he would be transported to the future, to commit horrid and ghastly acts upon the world. We would be left to explain the murdered corpses to an angry court that would represent an angry population. While we hung from the gallows the monster would cheat death. Our only hope is to kill him."

I addressed him thus. "I have walked through this place before, as a child, and know that it is quite large. Howlton Walkway is the center. Here, at this arch, looking northward, it extends about one mile to the northern edge which is bounded by hedges and large shrubs. It then extends westward to Lamar Walkway, in the neighborhood of a potter's field. To our south lies Commerce Walkway, and away then into a westerly direction it extends some four and one half miles. Its western edge is called Flowers Path. In front of us lies a vast city, a city of the dead. We may be able to apprehend the creature, but it will be difficult, Dr. Golem. There are narrow lanes and catacombs, places that provide many recesses to hide away."

Golem was confident. He spoke these words with the confidence of an experienced hunter. "From the resurrection men I have discovered that they have seen the creature on Lamar Walkway, in or near the large vaults between the mausoleums of Lockhart and Givers. Others have seen the creature near Thorns Tomb, in the southern section."

Being the practical man that Golem was, he accepted my suggestion, based on my familiarity with the place. "You take the north end," I said, "and I will search the southern sectors. We will both head west to the edge of the cemetery, turn in, and meet again at Howlton Walkway. This walkway is very narrow. Catacombs line the path; they are set close together. It would be best to proceed there together. We must guard against trickery."

Golem spoke with readiness. "Good. Our weapons will serve as warning to one another that the creature is within grasp. Then it is settled. Only this task remains, Hamel, between us and eternity!"

As I turned to proceed I could not help but smile as I contemplated the road ahead for Golem. If the creature surprised one of us, our shots might indicate that we had tried to protect ourself; if our shots missed their mark then the creature would have an opportunity to set his own ambush and simply wait for the other one to come his way. I could not see the remotest possibility for our success. Perhaps examination of the creature's frame would yield valuable information. I did not care. The destruction of Golem was more important. I was well aware of the monster's strength, confirmed by the papers of Victor Frankenstein which I stole from Captain Walton. Golem had not a prayer. He would be destroyed! This was the way to finally end Golem's life. The creature would also be destroyed. The fiend would be killed by the inspector and his men. They would hunt him down like a dog and justice would be served. My poor Jane would be avenged.

The cemetery was not deserted at this hour. There were people all about. They might take us for resurrectionists and kill us before we ever found the monster. Fortunately, Trevor had conveyed to me the location of the vault the creature was using as his hiding place, which I then provided to Golem. If the creature was indeed at the Lamar Tomb, Golem would walk directly to his death! His weaponry would not save him. I could not help but notice Golem's face at this moment. In it was both a horrifying determination and fear. The creature stood between him and immortality.

Golem went north and I south, along the perimeter of the graveyard. Within a few moments I was left alone to ponder the futility of his mission and his deserved death. I knew that the creature would kill Golem with ease, and though part of me yearned to be the direct instrument of his dying moment, I would accept the secondary function of sending him to his certain death at the hands of the creature while I survived them both.

I knew from Frankenstein's account that the creature was a master spy. He most assuredly had knowledge of the workings of the kryo-units and intended to use it to secure his escape. But while Golem and the creature fought I would return to the laboratory, board my vessel, and lower myself down. I would be secure, since the vault could not be opened or seen from the outside. I would then be able to set the timer for a short period, allowing for the life span of a man to pass, and reawaken in a world free of my pursuers and this hell. With this plot in mind I left my weapons on a tomb and departed for the laboratory as quickly as possible.

Along the way it happened that Inspector Glennon and his men spotted me. It was an opportune time. I sent the inspector in pursuit of the creature and Golem, informing him that the infamous doctor and a gigantic man were responsible for the horrid crimes in London, and that I had chased them to the cemetery. I told the inspector to double his men and shoot the creature on sight as he was a killer of many. I said that I had lost them and was returning to report them to the police. To my horror, Inspector Glennon revealed to me that William, my mother's mate, was being sought for arson, and was the prime suspect in other burnings which he did to cover various murders. He had been seen in Celestial Cemetery by townspeople. The inspector and his men were searching for the creature and William.

He produced a warrant, together with a list of suspected victims which I snatched from his hands. Among the names was that of my mother, Dorothy Hamel. I was shaken and almost fell. Unfortunately, when Glennon saw the pain of my heart he sent a guard along with me, and I could not object without causing suspicion. I cried all of the way back to the laboratory. What more could happen?

The Creature's Notes
February 1st, 1849

Having placed corpses all over London I grew tired. Before I could fall asleep I heard some noise outside. It was the footsteps of a man. It was William, a fiend that I had seen delivering bodies to Dr. Golem. Slipping out of the rear of the tomb, I surprised him and grabbed him by the throat and would have killed him without a thought, but he persuaded me to listen. He wanted to exchange information for bodies that were still in my wagon. I choked him until he murmured that my life was in danger. I eased my grip and told him that he would receive the bodies in exchange for the information. He told me about Golem's plot to kill me and the weaponry that he was going to use.

After William conveyed the information I knocked him to the ground by breaking his leg with a swift kick. I kept my promise to him, for as he lay on the ground next to the wagon I overturned it, crushing him with the bodies and the weight of the wagon.

It was time for Golem to seek me out. He would most assuredly search the Lamar Tomb and the recesses of the Lamar Walkway. I would lure him to the center of the Celestial City, to the Alam Tomb, a crypt dedicated to a murderous family; they were a filthy lot who fought in wars of conquest, their existence but a tribute to the inhumanity of men. Golem thought of them as shining examples of his kind. They are revered and their tomb has become a monument. Buried there in this filthy place are the remains of slavers and drunken scoundrels whose true villainy is yet to be told.

I seduced Golem up Lamar Walkway, toward Branfels Way. He was pulled along by his own obsession into the clutches of death. I took him on to the main walk, Howlton Walkway. It was a path named after a "benevolent" slaver — a man who supposedly treated darker people with respect, but never fully released them from slavery. He was a fine representative of the hypocrisy of mankind. I toppled over Howlton's fantastic monument on the way to the Alam Tomb.

I took Golem past the Timothy Maver and Phillip Shultz tombs, markers for a solicitor and a property owner. Shultz was Golem's business partner. Maver's legal expertise worked and conspired to throw Hamel and his family into the streets of London. Unknown to Hamel, I had surreptitiously gone to his mother's house on the night of his revelation. Oh yes, Shultz had cause, the rent was due, and of course Maver was only fulfilling his responsibilities to evict them. The solicitor was only executing his legal duty. His duty of course was to seek out human misery for a price.

In later years Shultz contributed to the poorhouses and even paid for small stone tablets for the dead at Bully's Acre. His guilt-ridden corpse lay in my path. The Maver grave also lay along the way. Maver was, in addition to being a solicitor, a historian. He was an ardent defender of the "benevolent" slavers and saw to it that the "good" qualities of slavers were defended in the local papers and elsewhere. I toppled over their horrid tombs, crashing them to the ground. Golem would recognize their filthy graves. He would see their bones which I exhumed and impaled upon a cross.

Golem's dogged spirit led him past Tayer's Tomb, Ward's Tomb, Thompson's Tomb, and those of other hypocrites. They were his accomplices. He would see all of their gravestones crushed to the ground. These graves held orators and resurrectionists alike. All were vile and evil men whose graves soiled the landscape. The great liars were represented there. Tayer and Ward were grave robbers, as was Thompson.

I considered destroying the tombs on Commerce Walkway. This part of the cemetery held the remains of fallen soldiers who died in the interests of England. They died defending England's vulpine grip upon the Americas, which strangled its populations and enslaved millions. I did not carry this out, however, for these men, though guilty, did not cry out from the grave to be memorialized for their mistakes. A man forced to do the evil bidding of others should be left in peace, for if he has realized he was wrong, he would not want historical glorification. Men in defense of slavery and oppression are morally and historically doomed, and as such it is unfit to glorify them in death. Hypocrisy rules this filthy world!

I left those tombs as they were. They held the remains of the misguided. Instead, I destroyed the tombs of those who sought to glorify their evil deeds. These were the historical societies whose aim was to glorify the men who carried out the horrid murderous crimes of the empire. It was in this section of the cemetery that I swept aside their tombs. The men they glorified should have been left to rest in peace. The Historical Society had a plot which I completely obliterated.

At the Hays Tomb, Golem caught sight of me and fired a shot which missed. I ran toward Howlton Walkway and turned west. It was cold and growing dark as the sleet rained from the sky. My body was easily able to withstand the cold. I knew that I could set the pace by allowing Golem to get close enough to me to fuel his fire, but staying just far enough ahead to lessen the accuracy of his aim. I did not see Hamel. I did not think he came along.

At the Fannon Tomb I paused to reflect upon another hypocrite — another soldier of darkness. He had been a military man who commanded troops to enslave millions. I looked at the elaborate structure and thought it a waste for so much time and finance to have gone into it. I ripped the doors from its entrance and entered its dark recesses. In a dark niche I found a tomb which I shoved off of its slab. It crashed to the floor and shattered.

I moved on but made certain that Golem was still in sight. He was slowing. I saw an advantage. I ran past the Olive and Hackle Vaults. The sleet was coming down now. At the Cherry Tomb I paused again as Golem was no longer in sight. I looked around and noticed that many of the stones were small. Tucker's Tomb was barely visible. It was small and covered with dead twigs and brush. According to the records, this area and the surrounding Cherry Field Cemetery was where many of the destitute were buried.

Here, at this potter's field, I saw the common people's graves . . . the people from whom I was surely made. I looked at each stone carefully, walking between them, reading the names — Anderson, Lewis, Williams, Green, Prade, Johnson, Calvert, Emerson, Percy, Sanders, Watson, Gardy, and on and on. For a moment I lost control of myself and ran faster and faster past each grave. I ran so fast that the names whizzed by, and soon I was lost in a frenzy. I held onto the hope that perhaps a name would someday be mine. Tears streamed from my eyes. I was constructed from the bodies interred here, any one of which could be the remains of my ancestors.

I wanted and needed a name! I thought of choosing one from these remains, but I did not know which one to use. From the records I thought it might be possible for Hamel to determine which cadavers were appointed in my construction. From the notes of Victor Frankenstein I might be able to determine my lineage. Filthy Hamel was now in possession of them, having stolen them from Captain Walton. Victor Frankenstein put me together and animated me, but my body, and hence my lineage, remained unknown. I desired to discover my origin and my name. It was my aim to retrieve the records of my creation from Hamel.

I paused at this place and looked around at the barren wasteland made possible by the smallness of the monuments. At this location I knelt down on both knees to reflect upon the sorrow of these lives. Farther west I could see another potter's field and the remains of a slave burial ground. The shrubs and grass were grown over them and many of their markers had toppled over from lack of care. Some of the small headstones were sunken down into the earth and many were tilted in odd ways. The slanted stones painted a picture. It was a strange cascade of death, like crooked teeth in the mouth of some monstrous fish. Some of the stones were very old and blackened by time while some were recent, but all were in disarray. They were half hidden under overgrown brush and shrubs. Many had simply fallen over, creating the appearance of a walkway. There was poverty even in death! A cold mist seemed to hang above the ground here, and in the distance over the vastness of tombs the scene grew faint.

I looked west at the gray horizon. Where the sun would be positioned there were only gray clouds. The cold rain wrapped an icy robe around the cadaverous landscape. I looked east, and in the distance I could see my foe approaching once again. His distant shape appeared elongated as he ran. I stood once more in the middle of the walkway. There were tombs on both sides. With my legs spread and my arms high I screamed for Golem: "Join me! Come to immortality!" I turned at once and headed for the walkway and the Travis Tombs. Travis was yet another one of Golem's heroes. I led him south and then back east toward my final destination, and his!

This section of walkway was narrow. I thought its path would be appropriate, for in the dark recesses of the catacombs fear would play with Golem's mind, and if not fear then apprehension or doubt. The hideous statues of death would stab at him, for these tombs represent the futility of permanence. At the Alam Tomb, Golem would die by the instrument of his own creation. At the Methodist Churchyard I rushed on once more to compensate for the distance between us. I spied his figure on the horizon and turned to run again. It took but a few seconds to traverse the distance. Once at St. Mary's Walkway, I decided to go no further. The ends of the cemetery did not extend past Flowers Path which was only a short distance away.

I turned east down the dark narrow cobblestone walkway and ran past many majestic tombs along this corridor. I would topple and batter them all! I looked back but it was too dark to see Golem's figure. He would soon be lighting a torch. He was sure to be slowed down by the nooks and niches of the catacombs. The desire in his heart would propel him to follow me to realize his wretched dream. I proceeded directly to the Alam Tomb. Along the way I toppled more stones for Golem to follow.

Finally, at the Woolworth Tomb I toppled the high monument to the ground. Its monolithic structure crumbled as it struck the stone walkway. I crossed Alam Walkway and walked up the steps of Alam's Tomb, through the Roman columns to the double doors. Fortunately, lightning flashes showed the way, as the niche of the doorway was dark. I could not proceed until the next flash. When it appeared I entered the structure. I lit a torch that I had used to engrave at night and held it ahead of me. There were several tombs before me, two that I had read about: R. Stein and L. Burke. They were both soldiers, politicians, and writers whose work oppressed many. I slid the Burke Tomb off of its slab so that it crashed into R. Stein's grave. The bones of the vile men slipped from their death crib and shattered on the dusty floor.

The Alam structure itself held various corpses. It was a memorial to several men who had shown courage, or desperation, in wars of bygone days. All of these evil, biased men, hailed by Golem and his ilk, were immortalized in this vault. Nothing was more fitting than the ceremony I now held for them. I looked to my right and there was a vault with the name Travette on it. I had heard of his valor in battle, but what he was defending was unjust; this fact was overlooked by the distorters of history. Travette was often eulogized and lauded in a false symphony of praise with parades of people who held ceremonies in front of the tombs.

I had a task ahead of me. I was once the fallen angel, once in another frame of mind. I will not destroy myself as Werther did. I have read *Pilgrim's Progress* and liken myself to the sojourner who rejected all to accomplish his task. My journey ends in the chariot of life. I went to the Travette Tomb which sat on a slab. I heaved it over so that his bones mingled with those of his filthy comrades. I furiously kicked and scattered the bones over the floor. I tossed skulls and bones out of the door and onto the steps.

And So It Was

Golem looked back for Hamel but once. He imagined his form in the distance. He thought that Hamel would most probably be destroyed because he had not the heart nor the mettle to carry out the creature's destruction if he discovered him.

From Hamel's report, Golem thought the monster should be near Lamar Walkway. These tombs were large. Some were big enough to provide a hiding place. He was now walking in a northwesterly direction. Lamar Walkway had hundreds of tombs, and as he walked ahead he saw a vault in which the front door was ajar. He did not notice a name but it was dated 1527. He peered inside, opening the door carefully. It was dark, but there was still enough light to see a short distance ahead. There was an open trapdoor and opened crypts in the wall. The monster had been here. He had discovered a tomb with books in it.

Golem looked at the buried books. Some of them had been opened. He thought it ridiculous that the creature found some presumed importance in reading them. "A monster, created raw and unformed, could only mimic from ignorance the higher thoughts of these mighty authors," he said to himself. The monster left a copy of Shakespeare's works on the steps. "I cannot fathom the deductions the creature would have mistakenly made. What diabolical reasoning emerged from reading the works of Shakespeare?" There were other books strewn about which he did not bother to investigate.

Before he could descend into the crypt he heard a blood-curdling scream — a scream like the howl of a monstrous apparition, a howl of rage and pain combined. Golem turned and rushed out the door and saw the monster ahead of him, toward the west. He pulled his musket from his shoulder and raised its long heavy barrel toward the misty figure. He fired. He thought he saw the creature fall. He raced up Lamar Walkway toward Branfels Way and turned south but the creature was not there. He stopped just long enough to reload the musket. Up ahead, at the Travis Tomb, he saw the creature again, waving and taunting Golem to continue the pursuit. Earlier, Golem had thought his will was of a single-mindedness, believing that he could not be swayed from his determination, but now his steps toward immortality became measured.

He proceeded down Branfels Way past the Travis Tomb and toward the Burnet and Nolan Tombs. Golem spotted the creature again to the south, at Howlton Walkway. He thought that Hamel should have headed west by this time. "We should now have the creature caught in a crossfire," he thought. He peered through the icy mist toward where the creature was standing wide-legged with his arms spread out. He was a perfect target. Golem quickly raised his musket and fired. The creature appeared to fall once again. Golem was now waiting for Hamel's shot. It never came.

Suddenly the monster was running toward him with incredible speed. Golem pulled his revolver from his coat pocket and fired, but the creature's speed was incredible. He avoided the shot and then let out another wild scream as he turned about and headed once more in the direction from whence he had come.

The trees and hedges shook violently and shuddered like some dark haunted phantom from the cold winds. Sleet and ice struck the bare branches and within a short time accumulated in patches at the tips and on the trunks. Golem looked back south and could see a small but growing wall of snow and ice accumulating on the back of the gravestones and on the trees and hedges.

The howl of the wind haunted his soul. He thought he heard a dog bark and whine in the distance, which, owing to the task at hand, brought up an ancient fear in his being. He listened for the sound of the dog again, but the howl and crescendo of the wind soon took over. The wind rushed past his face like a ghostly mist. Whether his imagination had taken control, or reality had become a phantom, he could not say. As the mist cleared in the distance he saw the monster appear out of a cloud. As the low ominous clouds rolled away from the creature's head, he began taunting Golem once again. The creature raised up straight, and then bent down. His monstrous hands were touching his knees in an apparent mimic of blowing and bellowing. As the wind rose his bellowing coincided with the wind gusts. It could not be real! Golem began to think that he was going insane.

Golem raised his revolver and fired at the bellowing monster. The shot cracked like thunder as it left the muzzle and plunged through the cold air. As he fired, the creature bent down to bellow again. Golem guessed that he had missed. With another blast of wind he heard the horrid gale of the monster's laughter. He looked in the direction of the scream but the creature had taken flight again and disappeared beyond the hill on which he had stood.

Golem reloaded the musket as quickly as possible, fumbling with powder and rod. He could not stray from the quest of his heart.

He stiffened his resolve with bloodthirsty passion. He put his weapon across his shoulder and headed for the hill as fast as his heavy legs could carry him. Golem ran past names that were now blurred by the frenzy of his pace. Christian, Cooper, Milton, Frost, Wolf, Allister, Dermott, Shafe, Wagner, Richardson, Greene, Lewis, Jackson, Dancy, Boyd, Phillips, Leeks, Dorn, Rice, Alexander, Amos, Lamb, Darwin, Coleridge, Bunyan, Gairy, Reagan, Agrippa . . .

He frantically ran up the hill trying not to read or hear, but the stones spoke to him. Their inscriptions spoke repeatedly and echoed loudly in his ears:

Tis no matter of consequence as to the choices
of men, all must end in death.

Tis no matter of consequence as to the choices
of men, all must end in death.

The passing stones and shrubs were now becoming embalmed by the falling sleet which the wind sometimes plucked at like a vulture. The shrubs themselves, packed with ice, now resembled pallid tombs. The hope of immortality was being drained from him like a liquid from a receptacle. He had to destroy the monster or all was lost. The dream — his precious dream of immortality that would replace the uncertainty of heaven and hell with life everlasting — was threatened.

"I *must* kill the creature," he thought over and over. With all of his will he pushed on to deliver the death blow. He thought now about the possible future. If the creature lived on, the world would come to know his terror. It was not just himself or his life that was being considered — he knew the fate of all others rested with him. "If Hamel and I are destroyed, the secret of my experiments will die with us.

One of us must kill this monster!"

He pushed on through the sleet. His hat was now frozen to his head. His face was blanketed with white death. The icy rain on his face glistened like sweat. The desire in his heart to kill reduced the noise of crunching ice beneath his feet to a whisper. In between the howls of the wind he could hear the demonic screams of the creature, taunting him, inviting him to destruction.

"My right to everlasting life is being jeopardized, and that of all future generations!" he cursed. He thought now of himself as a warrior, a hero, of a future yet to unfold, of a man committed to an ideal, to a dream, to the greatest achievement that men could ever hope to obtain! He was the thing between now and forever!

He rushed to another hill, and among the tombs in the valley below, at the corner of a mausoleum, the creature stood, waving him on. Up above him on yet another hill was a row of catacombs. The creature ran toward the stone entranceway and disappeared into the street that separated the structures. Golem ran toward him as fast as his weary legs could move.

At the top of the rise, Golem looked east but Hamel was nowhere to be seen. He called his name several times in the sleet and mist, but there was no reply. As he was about to call out again he heard the horrible sound of the monster's voice; "Here I am, Sir Astley! Here awaits your immortality!"

He turned and saw the creature at St. James Walkway. The creature was again taunting him. Golem resumed running, and as he did, the creature again began to flee. They passed the Palmetto gravestones and Monumental Passage. Golem tried desperately to close the distance between them, but the creature stayed just beyond his range. Golem discarded his heavy musket, hoping to lighten his load enough to gain the ground needed for a good shot with one of his pistols.

At Pine Path, Golem could see that the creature had gained more ground, for he was now at the Cherry Tomb. Golem's lungs were about to burst. "Hamel must have heard the shots," he thought. Perhaps if he waited a moment he would catch up. Finally it occurred to Golem: "God, what if he is not coming? What if I was right about Hamel after all?"

Golem sat on a stone retainer at Pine Path to rest. It was getting darker and it was bitterly cold. He could not understand what had happened to Hamel. "He must have heard my shot!" he said aloud. He looked back toward the east and cursed at the cold misty distance, cursed at Hamel for not being there.

"Perhaps the police found him or some other fate has befallen him," he thought. In any event, Golem was determined to go on. His precious goal was in his hands. At this thought he jumped to his feet and ran on through the sleet and cold wind.

He ran past grave after grave. These stone monuments seemed but a waste now, for he was on the threshold of never needing the services of a stonecutter or a grave digger. He ran past them and soon they became just a blur that no longer mattered. His will was rekindled.

He headed west into the setting sun. He was now parallel to the center of the cemetery and the Alam Tombs. The Alams were said to be a heroic family, committed to justice and freedom. "It seemed that the monster would proceed here owing to his misconceptions about man's greatness," Golem thought. But before he could turn on to Alam Walkway he spotted the creature once again. His back was to Golem now and he was running at an unbelievable speed. The creature raced up to Jefferson Walk and Golem quickly followed. He was once again almost close enough to fire.

Golem ran past old gravestones too old to read and stained black with age. Even in this cold the sweat poured from his skin like water as he tried to maintain the courage to carry out the task that had befallen him. The creature slowed his pace, purposefully, always reappearing on the grave-littered horizon just when Golem had become unsure of his direction.

There were moments when, as he paused to catch his breath, he actually feared the creature. Golem tried to maintain the spirit to kill him. To do so he tried not to think at all. He was running, running among the dead, desperate to end the life of the creature, running through the deadly landscape, past tombs of all sizes and shapes, falling, struggling to regain the chase, chasing life and death in an endless graveyard. The stones were set in a hopeless maze. He fell several times, but immediately the thought of letting the monster live, or escape, drove him onward. His spirit left him and raced ahead of his body. He imagined that his spirit caught the creature and shot him through the head. He desired to shoot him through the head, to totally destroy the cursed creature. While the monster struggled with his wounds Golem imagined using his knife, stabbing him through the throat and then choking him with all his might.

In his mind's eye he did all of these things. The imagined climax of these acts did not produce a feeling of relief, for the end result was the terrifying thought that the monster could survive his most savage attack. He could see him wounded and in pain with several bullet wounds and a knife in his neck, but still with enough strength to overpower Golem and destroy him. Golem's fear grew with each yard that he ran. Soon the gravestones became dreadful obstacles, cursed demons standing in his way. The cemetery took on a life of its own that now resented the treading upon its citizens. When he came to a large stone it appeared to move in front of him, blocking his way.

Now it was passing through his consciousness that immortality did not power his drive, but rather fear, dreadful fear for his own life if he were to fail. Fear and passion made a frantic mix, tossing his will about. He took deep measured breaths, trying desperately to fuel his one desire — to kill the creature. Graves came upon him as he rushed by. The path ahead was like a tunnel enclosing his existence. He imagined the creature's form on the horizon, painted like a grotesque figure upon the deadly canvas of the chase. He ran and ran, never letting go of his passion. He knew that his will would be robbed if he relaxed the intensity of his thoughts.

He came upon the graves of his family, hardly remembering that he had been here recently to say goodbye to them. Horribly, he saw that his father had been exhumed and his rotting corpse impaled on the cross of an adjacent grave. Golem looked at the scene in utter shock. He could hardly believe the ghastly scene before him. He ran once more, attempting to quell his growing terror.

A short time later the graves became unimportant once more. The plundered tombs did not stick out even though his eye caught their inscriptions. These graves and corpses were but pebbles in a sea of stones, none of which had an independent existence, all of them standing like trees in a forest. The path of the chase resembled a great snake, weaving between graves, weaving in and out of the forest of the dead. He fell down once again and struck his head on a gravestone. The stone was loose and toppled over. He stood, hardly remembering what had just happened, and raced toward the creature who was now standing within range.

Golem fired his revolver, blasting the cold air. The shot appeared to strike the creature's left shoulder. His body jerked to one side but instead of falling he raced on to St. Mary's Churchyard. The creature once again disappeared on the horizon. Golem wiped the cold moisture from his brow with his forearm and took a deep breath to regain his determination. He proceeded once more. He ran up to a large tree which had a partially covered gravestone under it. He thought it was a strange grave marker for it was partially buried. For a moment it tempted him as a possible resting place.

He slowed his pace, his chest heaving for air. His brow dropped sweat into his eyes. Just then, Golem saw the tree move away from him. It backed away at a steady speed until it was as remote as when he first saw it on the horizon. It flew away from him as a scene does from a galloping carriage. It resembled a picture, cut out and pasted on a background of graves, a huge cut-out that receded from him as if being carried away by invisible men.

He rubbed his eyes and the tree was as before, large, fully grown, offering some protection from the sleet underneath its canopy. Then the tree appeared as a darkened apparition of death. The limbs and branches shook and twisted into the phalanxes of a human-like hand. This phantasm continued as he frantically began running, trying to escape the grasping branches of the tree. He screamed and closed his eyes, desperately hoping that the sight would disappear. When he opened his eyes once one more it was gone. He was terrorized.

He staggered to the location where he thought he saw the creature recoil from the shot. He searched frantically for the body. Nothing was there. He ran on. Just then, up ahead, the cursed creature stood again, motionless, facing Golem straight on. Golem raised his weapon as quickly as possible, but the monster ran again as the shot missed its mark. Golem clenched his teeth and screamed into the wind, temporarily dispelling the terror. There was still fire in his heart. He ran on. The graves struck glancing blows at his flanks as he ran past them, tearing his trousers into shreds.

Golem thought he was closing the distance. At the western edge of the cemetery, the creature turned south. Golem was now right behind him, but before he could get off another shot the creature turned east back on to Howlton Walkway. Golem came upon the horrid structures too quickly, for the vaults were built closely together and the pathway narrowed. It was here that Golem was thrown into a hellish city of catacombs shaded by trees on both sides and the approaching darkness. He had to light his torch. His progress was slow and tedious. He must look behind each stone column and down the alleyways as he carefully walked along. He came to an intersection in which the creature might have fled in any one of three directions. Golem chose to go east, walking along this dark and dreary avenue of death.

Though he was sure of his purpose he could not sustain his focus. In a hopeless way he wished that the creature had underestimated his resolve. "His foolish taunts only prolong his moment of death," he thought, attempting to recapture his waning courage. A horrible thought crossed his mind, producing more fear than all of the experiences before, that perhaps the monster did not care if he lived or died!

He managed to forget himself for a time. He calmly weighed what he wanted to do—to take aim and fire. There would be no discussion.

His courage was now false, but he did not know it. "The monster shall learn how dangerous a man can be! It would be fitting for him to be dissected by one of my students at St. Thomas for the world to become acquainted with a dissection more famous than the Irish Giant. Perhaps, before this day is over, I will ride into history, having accomplished such an event, the greatest achievement!" He tried desperately to recapture the iron will that he had always possessed.

Now he believed that he could do without the monster's corpse and did not need to study the superhuman frame constructed by Frankenstein. It would be beneficial and would perhaps shed light on cell survival and destruction, but he no longer cared. He forced back obsession once more. "If the constable and his men discover the vessels in my basement all will be lost. We will surely be arrested. Our equipment will be confiscated and we will be hung. If I could kill the monster and bring back his body, we could leave this time and place and resume life under more favorable circumstances. In time, we could awaken, dissect the creature, and investigate its cells."

Here in the vaults of the rich Golem had once contemplated purchasing a plot. The walkway itself was paved with cobblestone, and many of the tombs resembled ancient catacombs with deep niches and underground vaults. It would be easy for the creature to hide himself and lie in wait. Golem would have to proceed slowly now, tomb by tomb, if he were going to succeed. Hamel was no longer important. Golem did not know what had happened; he looked around and ahead one last time, thinking Hamel might yet come.

"If I could only kill the creature! The police could be convinced of his guilt with ease owing to his monstrous appearance and fiendishness. I could convince the inspector that the creature murdered Shadwick and Cooper and the carpenters I had to dispose of who built the vault. We would then find ourselves in an optimum position," Golem muttered aloud to himself.

There was a chill in the air — a coldness — of panoramic proportions. It was stronger than his will. Its effect was generalized upon his body, but singular in his mind. The foreboding wind became like an odious razor cutting his flesh beneath his clothes. He began to shiver.

"My precious project of life is in jeopardy. I have to fulfill the dream of all men! I cannot leave the responsibility to Hamel. It is something that I must do!" he raved aloud. They had discussed all of the possibilities. If one of them were killed by the monster the other would try to destroy it. If escape were possible then the constable was to be notified of the murder of the other. The body of Golem or Hamel would be returned to the laboratory for revival in the future.

If the monster was killed by the police the body should be dissected for analysis. Later Golem could renew his efforts and leave this age. If either one of them were caught before they could capture the creature the other would deny all and keep secret the underground vault and the kryo-vessels. Whichever one of them remained free was to hide until cleared by the police, or if one of them were executed the other would carry out the plan. He had thought of all the realistic possibilities.

As Golem turned down Howlton Walkway he saw the Hertzburg headstone. It was designed in the shape of a clock. Looking at it troubled him. He looked east. The sleet was now falling more consistently and the distance was blurred ahead. He walked in the center of the walkway for a time until it occurred to him this was unwise, for the creature could surprise him from either direction. He moved over to the right side of the walkway, and slowly, tomb by tomb, he proceeded with the death hunt.

He passed silently through alleyways of tombs, down the dark corridors of death, with the howl of the wind sounding like distant melancholy screams whose depths were immeasurable. His walk was slow and steady like a cat stalking a bird. He took care not to crackle the dead, dried, fallen leaves, or snap dead twigs that littered the path. His head pivoted nervously like a praying mantis whose wide eyes sweep the landscape for its prey.

Obsession gave way to fear. His confidence slithered away. Beads of dirty sweat bubbled on his brow and his heart palpitated. His limbs grew weaker with each step on the cobblestone walkway. The look on his face turned to what was clearly absolute fear.

He walked slowly and kept a sharp eye. The wind was cold, and as he walked it grew in strength. At first it rose slowly, but within a moment it became a stiff constant wind. His weight had to be shifted constantly to compensate for the swelling battering wind.

He thought of the wasted efforts and the futile attempts by the people in these tombs to gain immortality. Lightning flashed in the sky illuminating the landscape and pounding the graying darkness. Golem passed the dark recesses which concealed deadly hiding places. With each step he grew more fearful, and although his thoughts were the same they began to waver. "I cannot entertain any idea that separates me from the task at hand," he thought. He needed above all else, above all other considerations, to stay focused on the task.

He could not maintain the coolness of heart as he had done before entering this walled city of death. The smooth turns of his head now turned to jerks on the stalk of his neck. His breath was held in, oozing out in a cold vapor with each spasm. The sounds of his walk, of leather upon stone and brush, were now too loud to tolerate. When he breathed, the loudness of his exhalation brought a terror which he strained to quiet.

These sepulchres in this city of death haunted Golem's every move. He could not drive the fear away with any thought or movement. His spirit was being dissected by the force of this place. His will was being torn apart. He stopped at the side of one of the stone buildings and turned his back to its wall. He looked behind and ahead and slowly his knees crumpled, forcing him to slide to the ground. He held the trigger of the revolver so tightly that it went off. The thunderous clap echoed throughout the walls and raised his hopes. The sound of fear was shattered and his energy was temporarily renewed. It could not last.

As Sir Astley Golem sat on the ground, he realized that cowardice had engulfed him. He could not reload his weapon, for the clatter of steel would surely alert his enemy of his vulnerability. "He would surprise me and kill me while I fumbled with my bulky weapon," he thought. He let the pistol fall gently into the snow. He had another but could not remember if it was loaded. He stood and made his way around the corner of the building, turning toward a large mausoleum sitting in the center of the city. He walked toward it, in the middle of the walkway, fear walking with him.

The sleet came down in hard waves and lightning flashed here and there. There was very little thunder about, despite the electricity dancing in the heavens. The lightning seemed subdued and strange. When it thundered it was crisp and inconclusive; it did not roll to a definite end. Lightning flashes lit the way as darkness now cloaked these surroundings. He stumbled along from tomb to tomb toward the center of the cemetery. There was a deadly chill beginning to creep upon him. As he approached Alam's Tomb there was still one more gigantic vault, the Woolworth Tomb. Golem had known Mr. Woolworth, and indeed had built the monument for him. The huge pillar now lay toppled across his path. When he turned at the Woolworth vault he saw the high Alam Tomb in front of him. The steps to the structure were covered with icy sleet, black and cold.

It resembled an ancient Roman palace, with several stone columns raising its overhang. Its recesses were dark and foreboding. He crossed the cobblestone street and headed up the stairs toward the entrance which was shrouded in darkness. In between the lightning flashes he saw Hogarth's engraving above the threshold. All was there, but when the lightning flashed again he saw that instead of Elijah ascending in the chariot toward heaven, the engraving had been altered. In the place where Elijah should have been there was the hideous figure of the monster, his face turned, with a horrible grin, and teeth bared through stretched skin, a face horribly disfigured. His heart sank. He was frightened and shaken at the sight, for what creature would go to the trouble to carve such a ghastly form. Fear now tore at him. He wanted to escape. The lightning flashed on the recesses immediately in front of him revealing two large double doors. As it grew dark again he heard them creak open. He seized his remaining pistol and readied himself for the next flashing.

To his surprise the next lightning revealed nothing but an open door. It took but a few seconds to realize that his foe must be at his flanks. Golem quickly turned right, toward the Menger Tombs, and almost simultaneously he felt a numbing blow to his hand, the hand that held the pistol. The weapon fell. When the lightning flashed again the creature stood before him, wrapped in rich clothes, cloaked in a fluttering, long, blood-red coat. He was on the step above Golem towering over him, laughing. Golem knelt down moving his hand slowly across the ground, searching for the pistol but to his dismay he could not find it. The creature spied his movements and with a piercing stare froze Golem. The creature moved slowly forward until his form was entirely visible.

The wind died, but little distant whistles of wind and death pushed their way into Golem's mind. An icy vapor rose in the shadows under the creature's flowing cape. Between the ancient columns a horrible apparition appeared before Golem's eyes — the specter of death cloaked in his dark habit, but without his scythe. He appeared to be holding an eolian harp from which haunting whispers of wind emanated. Golem blinked his eyes in disbelief and the terrible vision vanished in an icy vapor. The gigantic creature's form returned.

As Golem looked up he was filled with terror. His heart palpitated at a deadly rate. He could not help but look up again at the doorway of the crypt. Immediately behind the creature, engraved in stone, was a winged skeleton who watched an hourglass that no longer ran. It was at that moment, while caught in the grip of fear, that Golem heard the soft step of shoe to stone. His attention was drawn back to his nemesis. He remembered that he still had a small derringer in his pocket and he quickly grasped for it.

The creature stood before him like a block of stone, legs spread below a heavy chest. His face seemed even more hideous than before, and in the dark shadows of this battlefield he seemed as bulky and solid as a warrior before his enemy. Golem could see the power in his limbs and in his heart.

Then the creature spoke. "You have come to destroy me," he bellowed. "You tramped through the icy fog and freezing reefs of death to find me. Your aims will never be achieved! You can only think of killing me. You wanted to discover the effects of cold upon my stolen tissue! You need not dissect me, Golem, I will tell you. My heart has turned to ice for you and your kind. I had thought of myself as a fallen angel, but now I see myself as a pilgrim on a long journey."

"You are not a pilgrim yet!" Golem screamed. "This is your final journey!"

The creature lowered his voice and spoke seductively. "Listen to me, Golem. I hold the secret to your dreams. I have been shot and beaten. I have been forced to flee across frozen wastelands and have endured the coldest regions of the earth. My blood still flows! Will not your experiments and studies be greatly enhanced by having a living willing subject? My tissue still breathes. Examination of my frame while life still surges within me will be of greater benefit to you. I will tell you what I know of how the glycerol works! I will tell you what I know of my creation, how it was made possible. In turn you can see for yourself the superstrong frame with which my creator endowed me. Your microscope can see the living wonder of my cells which could provide you with easy access for your endeavors. Just give me the book of Victor Frankenstein so that I may read of my creation. Hamel is in possession of it."

Golem was taken in. "And how do you suppose the police can be diverted from their course? They are at this moment trying to find me, to arrest me for the crimes you have so skillfully attached to me."

Having secured Golem's interest, the creature continued to tease him. "It will be easy enough for you to leave here, to return to some safe haven. I will reveal myself to the authorities with a daring raid on their quarters. Word will reach you that you are no longer being sought and that I am the culprit. We can then arrange for a surreptitious rendezvous in which I will submit myself to your examinations."

Golem knew that it was time for sweet words. "What proof do I have that this will be the case if I spare you? Oh, the plan sounds good, but you are a skillful player of deadly games. In your rage you have blinded yourself. You have spied on my work and know of the responsibilities. Even in your sickened mental state you have a chance of renewal. Do you understand! Go with me! Submit to me and your misery can end. Time will destroy the memory of your crimes and with treatment your mind can be made well. I will find a cure for your state of mind and awaken you to live among men as a human being! You will know the sweet sounds of spring, perhaps with a mate that I would create for you. Your misery will be over."

Golem was now prepared to reach for his derringer and was about to begin again when the creature spoke thus: "To be as you? To be as Wolf, or as Price, or as Hamel! To be as man, or as the destitute? To be as the hypocrites in authority, or as the confused in ordinary life! To be as the best of your kind!? I think not! I have seen where your ideals take you. I have seen your weakness and find it quite amazing that your kind has been on the earth this long. You are careening toward destruction. I have read your great works and have seen your Hadrian Wall of brotherhood, your vast regions of poor who I have seen selling the clothes off their backs while you have too many. I have heard your protests of resurrections and yet I was lifted from my icy grave.

"I have seen wagon-loads of corpses on the lonely backroads from Glasgow to Edinburgh and from there to London. I have walked Hadrian's Wall and have roamed hundreds of miles up and down the Thames. I have seen your children die from forced work in factories. I have seen you brag about making it illegal for children under nine to work in factories, but those who are nine, ten, eleven, and twelve continue to suffer. You cannot make leaps or bounds but must destroy before you can learn. You are not capable of advancing to the point needed. It is easier for your kind to kill and maim thousands and then gloat about 'advancements.' What if you were to make it illegal for children to be enslaved — all children? What if you were to stop oppressing the poor — all at once! What if you could see beyond one step?

"Your kind cannot take more than one step at a time, and even then you take two steps backward. Look at the great works of literature. Did not the great Lord discuss the significance of life? Did not Bunyan point the way to salvation? You are incapable of salvation, a flaw that will lead to extinction. Already your species is moving to destruction. You have begun to destroy your very surroundings, which will result in extinction. You will not be able to bear your young with enough frequency to survive the ravages that are destined to come. I will see to that.

"You have come to kill me, this perhaps being the most important battle of all time. Here in this place of death you seek to destroy the last obstacle in your quest for eternal life. How do you feel, Golem? Do you feel at all? Your frozen determination will be thawed tonight in this place!"

Golem tightened his grip on the small gun still in his pocket. He said, "You have no rights in this world. You will not stop me from my historic task. The fate of the world lies here with me at this moment. All of the future rests on what I do here today! As horrid and as monstrous as you are, I shall not fail!"

Golem withdrew his weapon from his coat. As he did, the creature pronounced sternly, "You shall fail, Golem! Death awaits you here! Your kind has extended itself beyond reasoning and nature will rebel against your existence. The proof lies here!"

With lightning speed the monster pulled from his waistband the kryoprobe, the frozen wand that Golem had invented. As the creature raised the kryoprobe to strike, icy vapor slipped from its handle and down the wrist of his striking arm. Golem was frozen with fear and unable to raise his weapon in time. Then the creature thrust the wand into Golem's chest. Golem let out a scream in disbelief. His blood did not drip to the ground for it was frozen as it mingled with the vapor that oozed from his body. Golem fell to his knees clutching the probe with both hands. One of his fingers fell off as it came into contact with the liquid nitrogen. He screamed as he watched several other fingers freeze and fall to the ground.

He looked up into the monster's eyes and yelled, "No! No!" His head fell forward and on his face was the look of fearful rejection. His head moved from side to side in a silent gesture of dissatisfaction and refusal. He began to fall backward with the pain of the frozen wand wrenching his body. He grabbed his face.

These words were in his ears as death pulled him away. In his half-conscious state he heard the creature say, "I have given you peace; your wand, the instrument of death, it is of no consequence, for all of man's efforts signify nothing in the end. Enjoy your wand. It stabs at your heart!"

The Creature's Notes
February 2nd, 1849

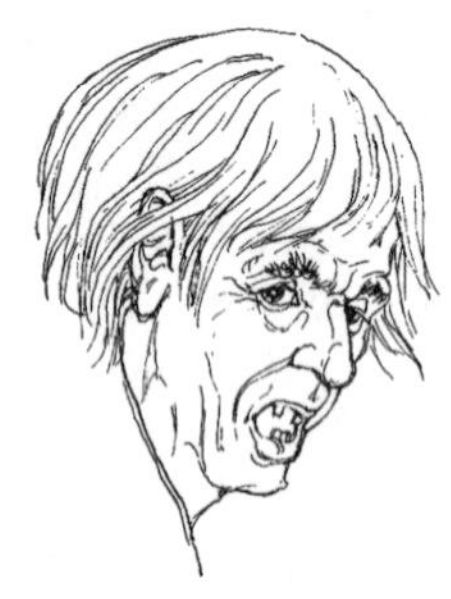

As I approached my dwelling I spied the police inspector and his men searching near my place at the Lockhart Tomb. There were more than fifty armed men with the inspector. To my surprise, I overheard Inspector Glennon say that Golem had lived a short time. The inspector informed the newly arrived men that his own hand was frostbitten as a result of touching the kryoprobe imbedded into Golem. He was horrified at the icy smoking instrument. He reported that Golem had demanded that his laboratory be destroyed immediately. He said that Golem had told him that there were evil forces seeking immortality, and that they must be stopped by burning the laboratory. So Golem did not care about Hamel — he wanted only to stop anyone else from discovering his inventions.

I noticed that the inspector threw some notes on top of a grave. It was the journal notes that he had confiscated from Golem for evidence. Seeing an opportunity to take the account, I surreptitiously snatched them and swiftly headed toward my hovel along the northern edge of the cemetery. I heard the inspector tell his men, "Take the torches! Golem's cursed laboratory will be burnt to the ground!"

When I arrived at my hovel, I picked up the woman that Hamel loved and put her over my shoulder. As I was leaving I saw what I thought at first was a grave robber. He was about to enter the caretaker's shed when he saw me. He looked very old and seemed quite ill. I approached with the intent of destroying him but before I could he said, "Stop! I mean you no harm.You are but the creation of a madman. It is not your fault that hell has been your constant companion. Do not destroy me. I have a task that must be done. Let me see the woman."

I gently placed her body before him. She was still alive. The old man went to her side and held her in his arms. "My dear Emily, my sister. You are Emily Wallace. I am Trevor, your brother. Speak to me."

Her eyes fluttered open and she gazed at him in wonder. "It is true, my brother. My lost brother," she said, with a smile so beautiful that my hard heart cracked a bit.

"I am your brother. It was our father who died in the flood. We never found his body or you. Hamel loves you. He knows who you are. He was my childhood friend. He thinks you are dead now."

The old man turned toward me. The anger in his eyes was strong.

Trevor turned to his sister and she explained, "I was trying to give that evil man Golem money so he would release my dear Joshua."

"It was not right that Hamel should have a loved one," I said. I tried to say more but my lips would not speak. I felt something that would not allow me to continue. I was unable to say anything else.

Just then the old man fell to the ground grabbing his chest. As he lay beside his sister, I listened with sorrow as he told me his story. He related how a man named William had tried to murder Hamel when he was a child. At the conclusion of his story he revealed his plan to tell Hamel this secret but said he needed first to rest, as he felt his strength failing.

"I know the men you speak of," I said to him. "I have killed William. Fate delivered him to me. I can get word to Hamel tonight as I will be going to London before this night is over. I have a date with destiny."

The old man started to cough violently but was able to whisper these words: "Please tell Hamel what I have told you. He needs to know this to ease his pain and loneliness. And tell him that . . . Trevor loved him." Having said this, he fell back, and his sister put her arms around him. They both smiled, it seemed, holding each other and looking into each other's eyes. She stroked his brow, and as he closed his eyes for the last time, she put a soft kiss upon his lips and laid her head on his chest. I stared at them, leaned over them, and realized that they were both dead. I cried for them and fell to my knees in sorrow.

I was now in possession of the secret of Hamel's lifelong quest, and though Hamel deserved to die, I vowed to deliver this message to him. I wanted to bury Trevor and Emily, but as I thought about it, I strongly desired to build a most glorious funeral pyre. I prepared a gigantic mound, splintering the wood from freshly exhumed coffins. Two of the coffins, which came from wealthy merchants were quite elaborate. They had soft white silk pillows with fine embroidery of gold trim. I used them to set the poor creatures in after tearing the lids from their hinges. Around the base of the funeral pyre I stacked at least fifty coffins, upright in a circle, with the bodies of Trevor and Emily in the center. I used a torch from the wagon to set the pyre ablaze, to give the poor siblings a funeral. These poor souls was more pure than the ilk I had destroyed.

The flames rose all about, licking the cold air, and the sky was lit up in a splendid scene. As the flames kissed the seat of death the fire consumed the corpses. I was glad to have given them a proper funeral and final peace.

The fire was sure to attract the police. I almost tarried too long watching the magnificent flames burn and swallow the remains of Trevor and his sister. The fire hypnotized me for a moment. It cleansed my mind of all earthly woe and released my pain. When death comes to my doorstep it would be most soothing to know that my body would be consumed by fire. I pray that fate will deliver me to such a magnificent end. I could not stay long enough for it to continue its magic, for immortality and revenge loomed ahead. If I had stayed but a short time longer perhaps the police would have rid me of my nagging misery.

I quietly returned to my hovel and withdrew inside. I wanted to gather my belongings for the journey ahead. I could get to the laboratory ahead of the inspector with my great speed. Gathering my notes, my Bible, and my copy of *Pilgrim's Progress,* I placed them in a small sack. I wanted to take along and preserve these works in the icy coffin. Then, removing the candle from the tomb, I went to the stairs to commit to paper the events that had transpired. I wrote furiously, and with great speed, until, after a time, the task was completed. I would still be able to dispose of Hamel at the laboratory even if he lowered himself into the icy chamber.

I turned to retrieve my sack and moved up and out of the entranceway. When I arrived at the top of the stairs I reached for the chain which held the door, while balancing the weight of the door on my shoulder. I caught the chain and slipped it off of the hook on the top of the door, then descended into the chamber, closing the slab behind me. The stone door would be too heavy for the inspector and his men to lift if they happened upon it.

After gathering a few more items for the journey ahead, I raised the slab, catching the hook with the chain. When I did so, some of my notes fell from my sack. As I bent to pick them up, a gust of wind blew one of the pages down the steps. I sat at the top of the stairs with my legs resting on the second step, and bent down to pick up the paper. Suddenly I heard a terrible wrenching sound.

I raised myself and looked up in time to see the chain breaking from the ceiling. I tried to move my legs out of the stairwell before the huge stone came crashing down, but alas I was unsuccessful. I managed to slip one leg out at the moment of impact but the other leg was crushed between the floor and the slab. I cried out in agonizing pain and almost lost consciousness . . . but worse was the prospect of death and not being able to retrieve the writings of Frankenstein.

I struggled under the worst pain I had ever experienced. I screamed to drive the pain away, but it was no good. I could not move. After a few moments the realization of defeat began to creep into my mind. I looked around and saw that I had left an axe within reach. In great pain I stretched for my salvation. I tried in a frenzy to raise the stone but could not muster enough strength to lift it from the position that I was in. I looked at the weapon and without further thought raised its deadly blade above my head, striking my leg just below the knee. The first blow was insufficient, and while I screamed in agony, my only thought was to free myself.

I was as wild as I had ever been. I raised the axe again and delivered a more solid blow. I looked at the shattered flesh and could see that one quick final blow would release me from my foot, which I now viewed as a chain holding me back from my task. In haste I made a tourniquet by tearing my upper garments off and twisting them around my upper leg until the flow of blood ceased. A few shreds of muscle bound me to the lower leg. I screamed in agonizing pain with each blow. It took four blows to rid myself of it. I pushed myself back away from the vault, and immediately began to tighten the cloth around my leg. The blood was flowing profusely, but soon, as a result of my tightening, the blood again ceased to flow. As I rolled over in great pain I checked the tourniquet to make sure the blood was trapped. After a few moments I raised myself. I took the torch and burned my stump until all of the blood flow was sealed, screaming the while in utter agony.

After a few minutes, I stood and found that the axe made a good crutch, and I headed out into the night for the laboratory. The pain was ghastly, but my purpose drove me on. I thought that Hamel would be there by now, and if I was going to catch him before he placed himself into a kryo-unit I would have to make haste. Despite the pain, I hobbled toward the town as fast as my condition would permit.

It Came to Pass

A few miles past the cemetery a river ran deep and fresh. The water was warm even though the air was cold, as it bubbled over the taupe-coloured rocks. It slid to the east, sparkling in the twilight of the setting sun before reaching the North Sea. The river flowed out of the soft hills and curved over multi-coloured moors and around lush strong trees. On the way east life along its bank was plentiful. There were mice sitting near the bank whose fur was being gently rustled by a breeze from the north. There were rocks strewn along the ground, placed there, by some unknown force of nature. The rocks seemed to listen to gurgles of water rushing over their marble neighbors embedded in the river.

The wind did not abate as the creature made his way toward the laboratory. Hamel imagined he heard the creature's cry reverberating through the cemetery and out into the countryside. The residents of London also heard these sounds but they dismissed them out of hand and turned over in their beds to sleep.

The pain of his leg was great. It forced him to pause at a stream, partly frozen over. He looked deeply into the water, into his reflection. "Was this arm of mine that of a man or a woman? Was this leg that of a philosopher or a laborer?" he thought. "What did the owner of these eyes see before they were mine? Who did this heart belong to before it was commanded by myself? Did these eyes help a surgeon complete his filthy dissections? I have heard Golem proclaim that organs and body parts may be exchanged one day between bodies, but would anyone want their arms to be given to a murderer so that his task may be accomplished?"

He pondered deeply. "What of the heart? A man whose philosophy embodies hate for the disadvantaged could obtain a new heart to continue life. Perhaps the heart will come from the very person his philosophy has helped to destroy. Golem has called this science. But I want to know the names of the unwilling donors that make up my being. I must have an identity!

"And what of men who cease to propagate? Golem wishes to have the power to inseminate whom he chooses! Will not the offspring of such a hideous idea have the right to know who gave them the fluid of life? They will be named yet unnamed, which seems to me a worse condition than my own. For to plan offspring in this manner will inevitably suck from nature its intended long-range future. This future will remain unknown though they have tried to plan it."

As he looked into the sky he wondered where nature intended this spawn to go. "Can it be that life is here for a reason not yet speculated upon?" The killings by Golem raised another question. "I once heard Golem talk about assisted death for those in great pain. If, during the time I contemplated death — for the pain was powerful, a pain terrible as any disease can inflict — I had chosen to take my own life, I would not be here now, renewed, and with goals in mind. The pain has been so great that death would have been welcome. I requested death! At that juncture in my life I would have responded affirmatively. But in retrospect, I can see that it would have been a mistake, for when pain is at its highest point, a man will agree to anything, including self-destruction."

The creature thought on the matter further. "Golem has focused his energy in a direction that suits his own purposes while hiding behind the cloak of mercy and progress. When a man says he does not want to live anymore, Golem wants to help by killing him. What kind of a fiend derives pleasure from the death of a man in misery? The *misery* should be eliminated, not the being. If science were to put its energy to eliminating pain, suffering, and misery, then the birth of such ideas could never have come to mind. To simply take a man's word for his desire for death, without fully knowing that person, is a fiendish crime. Even if the death assistant is familiar with a part of the complex webbing of another's mind, can he know the end beyond all doubt?" The creature raised himself and stood on the bank of the river.

He looked up at the stars and said: "I am ready! Hamel now stands between me and my future."

BOOK VI

THE PASSING

Hamel's Diary
February 2nd, 1849

Upon arrival I immediately began to prepare the kryo-unit for my departure. I needed to make sure that the liquid nitrogen levels and glycerol additives were in proper working order. I knew that the timer had to be set, and that it would be best to set it for at least five hundred years. In this way perhaps science will be at the levels anticipated, as Golem has said. If not, then I would travel on.

I shut off a valve that controlled the flow of glycerol to the kryo-unit that Golem would use. Within one year his body would be beyond repair. He rarely checked this device and would thus board the vessel unaware that his fate was sealed. I placed a gun in my vessel in the event Golem survived. He would die immediately upon my awakening. I thought about Trevor as I went about my work, hoping that he would return before I left.

I anticipated that if Golem, by some fortuitous circumstance, succeeded in killing the creature, he would want to know why I had already started my journey. I wrote a note which said,

I was detained just a few hundreds yards after we separated by the constable and his men. They asked where you were, to which I replied that you were onto the murderer and culprit of the London crimes, and with great diligence were seeking him in

the cemetery. I informed the constable that I was attempting to help you, but he was suspicious of the amount of weaponry found on my body. I was able to convince them that the murderer had run in the direction in which I was walking and that owing to my tiredness I had fallen back. The constable bought my story, as he had heard reports of the creature and its hideous appearance. He nevertheless instructed me to return, accompanied by a guard, to the laboratory.

Upon arrival the guard was posted outside and I have now quickly descended into the secret vault. I have set the timer for 500 years. I pray for your return, but if for some reason you are detained, as God is my witness I will give you full credit for the efforts that will be realized then. I have placed a copy of this letter in my pocket, frozen with me in time, to verify your work in the event I never awaken. Your notes are also with me, preserved in frozen time for future generations.

God Bless.
Joshua Hamel

I made a copy of the letter and put it in the secret compartment which held the lever to open and close the vault. Golem would look here for any messages. I felt warm inside as I imagined it turning to dust. I went to his files to gain access to Golem's calculations, his notes that detailed all of his work on the project. I bound them in a pouch and placed them in the foot of the other vessel. I looked around for a few of my own notes and my watch which I wanted to take with me.

The power I will have will be my own. I will be able to condemn Golem's work! My place in history will be secured, and the practice of grave robbing will be condemned. With the greatest authority I will also condemn Golem, who will be reduced to the status of a medical charlatan. Golem — if anyone even remembers his name — will be reduced to whatever is my personal account of him, and my personal account will reveal that Golem was a poor surgeon, a pitiful grave robber, and inept in our experiments with cold. News has already implicated him in the terror in London which I will confirm. There was no monster other than Golem.

The Creature's Notes
February 2nd, 1849

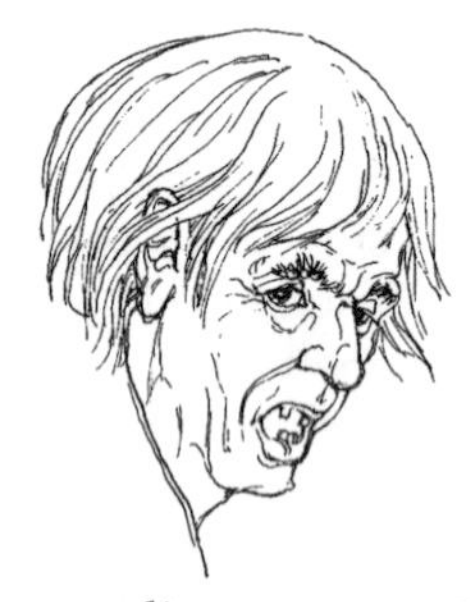

Hamel often spoke aloud about his philosophy. When I arrived at the laboratory and quietly forced the entrance after choking the guard, Hamel was delivering a most hypocritical diatribe about God's will. As I listened to the eloquent soliloquy of this devil I knew he must die as soon as I am finished with his services. Much of what I needed was in Golem's notes, but I would need Hamel to make my mate. I needed his assistance until I could become experienced in the preparations and functions of the vessel. I would need him for my education. I would need his expertise to calculate the populations that must be destroyed, and how this might be accomplished. After which his service will be terminated! I will then have satisfied my revenge. If death comes then it will be with pleasure that I depart. The sweet juices of my plan make me thirst for it to begin.

The fool had not considered the temporary nature of the holy ground upon which he stood. He could not have known that I would still be here now to confound his righteousness. Hamel has undone his own life. Evangelical hypocrite! *I will grant you death!*

Hamel was now beginning his descent into the vault. I secretly followed him. At the entrance of the sunken floor, I approached him and spoke thus

"Vile devil," I shouted. "Your companion is no more! He has

gone to where evil goes.You will not need the note you left! It is now your turn." I jumped down into the vault as the door closed.

Hamel responded by pleading. "Wait! Wait! Please let me live!" he begged.

I grabbed him by the throat and squeezed him until his veins popped up to the surface of his face. "You want to live? Why of course, devil! You may enjoy the prestige of such a great accomplishment! You could not let such an evil ungodly man gain all of that power! Could you?"

Hamel again pleaded. "Wait! Please do not kill me!" he said.

I did not cease my discourse. I spoke with fire in my heart. "I am sure it would be the best thing to do! You have let your companion die. Together you might have destroyed me. I am the product of man's science. I was made from the scraps of your brethren, from the scraps of your Christian neighbors! You are without courage and honor! Is it fitting that two devils should destroy one another while the third lives?"

I was filled with rage and spoke even more forcefully. "I seek revenge, Hamel. I seek vengeance! The giants on whose shoulders you stand have informed me that revenge is a desire to return evil for evil. It is an opportunity for satisfaction, for punishment inflicted in retaliation for an injury, for an offense! This is what your books say."

Hamel was bewildered for a moment but soon spoke. "Let me breathe, please, and I will tell you where you went wrong!"

I let him loose so that he might make the argument. "Re . . . retaliation means to return like for like, from the same book. You did not read far enough!" He tried to plead with me for understanding.

"I read enough, Hamel! What have you done but make me the instrument of your actions! Vengeance is mine saith the Lord! This is what your Bible says!"

Hamel was lost. He could only mutter this: "It also says that there is a time to live, and a time to die, a time to hate, and a time to love."

"You speak the truth, Hamel. It is my time to hate and your time to die!" The look of fear returned to Hamel's eyes. Though I knew he was horrified, there was something else in his eyes. He made no further protest. He seemed resigned to death. I loosened my grip.

"You have said yourself that evil must be destroyed," I said. "You are evil, and so what must be done? You have let Golem die and yet feel justified! Was he more evil than yourself? What sort of evil are you? What sort of evil was Golem? You tacitly agreed with his philosophy while hiding behind an evangelism you never practiced. You have made a mockery of your own philosophy. You wear a false garment. You have wrought your mind with the hammer of selfishness. Do not plead with me further or I will kill you now."

Hamel was quiet.

"You will go with me into your future and mine," I said. "I will help you rid the world of sin and evil, of body snatchers, of the evil men of science, of those who have defiled God's will! I am the one who will help you smite evil. You will help me mend my leg — perhaps you will give me yours! Your prayers have been answered, devil!"

I pushed him aside and hobbled to the controls of the kryo-vessel that I would use. I reached for the timer which I set at 499 years.

"You will go to sleep now, Hamel. I will awaken one year before you. That will give me enough time to contemplate whether or not to let you live. If I decide not to, then I will simply overturn your coffin and watch your filthy remains turn into rot!

For some reason my mind faltered. I thought on Hamel's sorrows. I spoke once again. "I have read your notes. In my heart I have felt compassion for what you have suffered. You have been cast aside as myself by those who brought you into this world. I have cried for you, for your situation, and have raged against you, against your cowardice. For men talk about justice in the world and then relinquish their responsibility. You are unlike the monster Golem in some ways, but still you are a man! You are weak. You are able to reason away what must be done.

"As a result of my readings I have obtained a deeper understanding of the pain I have within. Understanding does not help me, however. It changes nothing! Only revenge will satisfy the injustice done to me. You, however, are different. Before we leave I shall give you the answer to your heart's desire.

"You were alone in the world. I have read your diary while you slept. You had no friends save one. You had no one to love you. In the garden you sat lonely and fearful of the terrible things that were swirling around you. You had no one to share with, to hear your pain. It gnaws at you even now for you do not know yourself. You are like me! The workings of fear, loneliness, and desolation should have destroyed you. You need only reflect on these things. They result in oblivion and emptiness, in swirling thick clouds of doom. William — do you remember him, your mother's friend? — tried to murder you by suffocation. He tried to smother you with a pillow. Trevor told me this before he died. His sister lived long enough for them to be reunited. There, you have it! You cannot free yourself, however. You can only do so by dying! Perhaps you can forgive; it is your only other choice. For me, only the cleansing fire of revenge will give me freedom! That is all."

Hamel had gone white in the face, gasping as he absorbed this knowledge, seeking to fit these facts into the hollows of his aching Void. He fell to his knees and sobbed uncontrollably.

Then I remembered to add, "Oh, yes. And Trevor said with his dying breath to tell you that he loved you. My leg pains me beyond my anger. We must go!"

But there was more I had to tell him, despite my agony. "Hamel, I have read your miraculous efforts to understand yourself contained in those sorrowful pages. You have come to understand that oblivion is the master. Oblivion is the wellspring of man's life, for men try at every gate to obstruct it, so that owing to his evil nature he can continue to ruin the world. Why? If men want immortality why do they corrupt their surroundings? Why does the stench of the Thames overpower Sunday strollers? Why are men so hypocritical? They want everlasting life first and foremost, before making any worthwhile attempt to ensure that their world will still be here in the future."

I went further. "Well, they shall not have it! For I will destroy them all. I will build a race of supermen that will outlive the scum that inhabits this earth. Immortality will be mine and revenge everlasting upon the earth. Humans will never be happy again! Golem's dream of a kryo-population to inhabit the earth will never come to be."

I thought for a moment and continued. It was then that my mind turned. "I will spare you for now, for your plight has touched my heart. But my heart will not hold its calmness forever. I will need you to make my mate and reshape my horrid face. A mate will provide me with offspring to conquer this filthy world. You must agree! No human is worth saving. You know this with greater insight than me. I have destroyed Golem, a task which would not have been so easy if I had to battle the two of you. You allowed me the opportunity to live, by an act of cowardice . . . or wisdom. Your Jane is dead but she lived long enough to meet her brother. They talked and Jane was able to know who she was. This I allowed.

"I will let you live. You will join me in the future. If, after my goals have been met, you wish to leave, I will allow it. We will both be free of man! Here, add these pages to the account. They are the record of Golem's end. Make our book complete. Slip these pages into your diary so that the history of what has happened will be properly recorded. It tells of how Golem tried to kill me to continue his evil experiments, of how you abandoned him, allowing me to kill him, and of how my kind had its beginnings. Freeze these pages with you, Hamel, and when we awaken doom will be the future of your race, doom and death, and life everlasting for my kind!"

There was nothing more to say. "Now, get in the vessel, or I will destroy you now!" I demanded.

As Hamel turned and moved toward the vessel, he spoke words that I shall never forget. "How did you lose your leg? It is bleeding! There is a way to repair it. I know the secrets of reattachment! We have a cadaver that I could use. I can replace your leg."

I was taken aback and did not know what to say. I spoke quickly. "You would do this for me? What trick is this? You are shrewd!" I demanded an answer.

"It is no trick. Yes, why not? I would do it for anyone! And for you, to thank you for allowing my dear Emily to know her past and to see her brother. I will need more bone and flesh to replace such a large leg but I can craft it. With my technique and your strength you will not have to be sedated. With the liquid nitrogen you will feel nothing."

I could never describe how I felt at that moment. I could only answer thus. "Begin then — go! Begin, I accept your offer! I do not need sleep for the procedure, but I will watch you closely. Attach the leg! Make me whole again!"

Hamel worked carefully, and after many hours succeeded in attaching the leg. He explained to me that use of it would take time, and that perhaps much of the healing could take place while we slept if the temperature were raised slightly. I was not so sure why Hamel did this. I thought it but an attempt to gain my sympathy, but I agreed.

Hamel took Walton's notes and his diary off the table and handed them to me. I sealed them in with the cadaver and then he climbed into his own kryo-unit. I sealed Hamel's unit and adjusted the controls. Hamel looked at me and tears filled his eyes. He started to scream. I could not clearly hear what he was saying as the thick glass muffled his voice. I ignored him at first, thinking he was only raving. I was about to adjust the controls on his unit when I glanced at him. He was pointing at something. I followed his pointing finger to below my kryo-unit where a glycerol valve was closed. I would not survive the trip with this valve closed. Hamel had warned me. He could have destroyed me. I would not have known about the valve. Why? I killed his beloved Jane! I reached beneath the vessel and turned it until it was in the proper position. As the icy fog covered Hamel's face he stared at me. I never felt what I was now feeling. I looked at him and felt different. I turned away and lowered myself into an adjoining vessel and set the timer. The timer activated the device. The units were automatically lowered into the basement of the laboratory, slowly descending into forever. The heavy stone slab sealed us in . . . I can write no more as my body grows cold . . . Perhaps this is the end . . . There may be no awakening.

Diary of Ransom McDonald — A.D. 2351

Nothing could describe the sorrow and the darkness that began to close over me after reading the story. This miserable world, now almost done for, would again be plunged into horror. I looked upon the accounts of the story as an omen, an evil that had led to the circumstances in which we now found ourselves. Science had doomed us all.

The tombs lay beside me. Other than our clan I had seen no other human beings for over five years. As far as I knew our small group were the only humans left in the world. It would be an easy task for the creature to rid the world of its last inhabitants. My mind never wandered from the vessel that I sat next to. I was only distracted from this reading by the sound of the howling wind. A corner of my eye never left the cold design of the monster's tomb.

I read like a frenzied spectre unable to separate myself from the pages that lay before me. There was the ever-present thought that I would have to summon sufficient courage to open the icy vessel and destroy the creature. My eye often slipped to the axe that lay before me.

That he should survive to destroy the last of mankind was unbelievable. Yet, the sins of man against himself and his world had to be punished. We had done more than enough to seal our own fate. The day of doom was upon us. I continued to read, ever aware of the menace to the last of mankind.

I thought that it would be easy enough for us to leave the site and let the monster roam the earth searching for victims that he may never find, until he at last would succumb to the dreadful heat that streaked across the sky. It is now the end of the third day. As the red streak in the sky declined towards the evil darkness I concluded my reading. I felt sick and heavy as I was overcome by fatigue. Despite my state of debility I am reconciled to whatever is to happen.

I would pry open the tomb, wait for its gas to evaporate, and strike the creature with every ounce of strength, with my axe. I thought it best to destroy Hamel also. His ideas have caused what we are witnessing today. I was not very optimistic about the chances of survival for the last of our kind, but with such a monster loose we would most probably not last long. The passing of the world is upon us, and as much as we deserve our end I feel the need to preserve life for as long as possible. I have finished the last collation of the pages and have read again what I have written. I am now ready for what is to come.

And So It Was In The End

Golem most probably never asked himself, "What if I fail?" It was only a short time until the world forgot about Frankenstein and his monster. The truth became legend and stories for writers. The world saw many great inventions — flying machines and tranportation vehicles. These advances produced industrial waste and the oppression of people. Devices of destruction were mass-produced for killing one another and great wars were fought in which the body count was ritual.

Nations divided and cities were bombed. Starvation and stagnation were everywhere. The rich learned to live with "acceptable levels" of poverty and acceptable body counts. The appearance of calm, tranquility, and peace was but a fleeting dream for those who looked only at the microcosm of their individual existence. Great nations were overturned by angry populations as authorities fell one after the other.

Scientific truths also fell. Historical stages of development did not follow the ordered paths. It was discovered that there is more than just matter in motion and that chaos is part of all dynamic systems. Science left social science so far behind that social scientific theory was quashed before it had time to catch up. Capitalistic and socialistic theories had to be rewritten, but no one was willing to do so. Many socialists were afraid of losing their religion and capitalists wanted to continue with oppressive measures.

As a result, socialist forms of government collapsed and capitalist forms grew more brutal and hypocritical. The world went to chaos as the populations of all countries revolted against governments of the left and the right. Ethnic wars of hatred became the norm. Class analysis ruled theoretical discussions while ethnic and racial strife ruled the streets.

England and the rest of the world first went through imperialist wars. The two main camps then experienced periods of cold confrontations in which the under-developed world came out the biggest losers. Unemployment, racism, and injustice ruled in the industrialized countries, while bigotry, elitism, food shortages, and leaders "appointed" or "elected" for life inspired revolts in the socialist world.

The capitalist world came out of the chaos in the dominant position but it was short-lived. Racism, riots, military repressions, and new wars against "acceptable" enemies dominated the world. All of this took place within the framework of great technological advances. Buildings were destroyed, set ablaze, people scrambled to destroy one another.

Not only did men gain the knowledge to freeze and revive humans but also their sperm and ova. Scientists extracted from life what they thought was not essential; they felt that emotion, curiosity, and other human elements did not lend themselves to their goals and objectives. Experiments led them to incorrect conclusions about the inferiority of certain races and hence only those of the "desirable" race were allowed to continue. Frozen embryos of the "most intelligent" beings were preserved while those of "lesser" men and women were thawed out and washed down into the sewer systems. All cryonic devices not approved by government inspectors were destroyed, and only those meeting specific race and IQ requirements were allowed to survive.

The cryonic devices were stored and preserved in secret holding places under government protection, and those privileged with preservation were chosen by secret committees empowered to preserve the security of the race. The world had no knowledge of Golem's experiments with freezing. Cryonics was developed independently of him.

Under the growing heat, science spent most of its time seeking ways to preserve life. By the time of the great dust there was no longer enough time to develop suitable environments on the other planets. Life began to diminish and colonization of other worlds was now impossible to pursue.

The work of these men included a plan to eliminate most of the populations of the world by germ warfare and to begin again with an acceptable population of the new world. The scheme of these men was put into action, and while bacteria specifically designed to resist treatment ravaged world populations the new population rested. They were protected from the Black Death in their icy sleep. What the germs did not destroy, the extreme heat did. Populations rose up after discovery of the scheme and emptied thousands of vessels in refuse dumps and rivers.

The earth bled under the heels of war, disease, and famine. The "things" thrown into the rivers and streams poisoned the earth. Damaging elements from all phases of industry filled the air and water with a film that darkened the skies and rivers, and decreased the plant life. One by one, species of animal life were eliminated, as the range of their life-giving sustenance decreased.

The waters were filled with substances that made it impossible for the creatures of the sea to breath. The large fish and mammals lay upon the shores of the earth in great blankets of death. The creatures of the air, both birds and creatures of a more delicate nature, fell to the earth in great numbers. Their corpses littered the roadways of the earth, crushed beneath the vehicles of the day. The insects thrived for a while, eating on the massive amounts of carrion lying all about. They too grew scarce as the carrion was consumed.

Crops began to dry up, and where there were once soft cool breezes, blowing dust conquered the earth. The dark soil, desiccated from the dry wind, became like sand and blew across the countryside in thick smoke. Famine increased, and in the underdeveloped parts of the world populations were reduced. In the large city centers there were food riots and family raids upon other family centers. Fighting to the death for food was the rule.

People by the hundreds of thousands perished within a year. The polar regions grew warm. The melting ice raised the levels of the sea, only for it to be evaporated by the terrible heat. Nowhere on the earth was the temperature below one hundred ten degrees Fahrenheit. The rains never came; it was too hot and dry. By the twenty-third century most of the life inhabiting the earth was gone. The billions of people were reduced to a few hundred thousand, roaming the earth in search of food. No government existed or civil authority. Each person and family struggled for itself.

In the darkness of chaos, in the ruins of a building whose ground level structure had been blasted away, there remained a vault, hidden away, sealed into ancient ruins. Inside of these ruins were the kryo-units invented by Golem but no one was left to know.

And in the ruins of cemeteries, amid a few readable epitaphs shone these words:

Death conquers all, and time's subduing hand
Not tombs nor marble statues can withstand.

The dust in the sky was measured in the billions of tons, in how many parts per million the dust occupied in a cubic foot of air. The air was so filled with dust that one night the stars completely disappeared. The moon was reduced to a dull streak, a shadow of its former self. The day never brightened, and it grew darker with the years. The sun became a glob of dull orange red light. It was on this darkened day in the twenty-fourth century that what was left of mankind struggled out of the hills and on to the remains of a graveyard, and into forever.

The earth had pushed itself together. Parts that were once separated by greater distances closed together. It was a heaved section of earth — once a great city — that was pushed and crunched across a dried riverbed toward a cemetery.

An outcrop that rose high above the stones, and into the upper levels of blowing dust, showed three boxlike and mechanical-looking coffins sticking out from the side of a cliff. There was also part of the edges of a structure of stone around the sides of the coffins, like a large room, but filled with dirt and debris. The earth had shaken, causing part of the ceiling to collapse, breaking one of the vessels.

As the dirt began to slide, from the top of one of the coffins — the result of the blowing wind — a gaseous vapor leaked from a tube that was cracked, and cold smoke escaped into the fierce blowing wind The vapor oozed out, slow and cold. Soon the coffin burst open. After a time the smoke cleared and the head of a corpse fell back from the front end of the tomb. A head with some flesh dropped out of the coffin. Its eyes were rolled back into its shriveled sockets.

The wind was full of blowing dust, dry and howling to the notes of an unknown player. It sounded like music, haunting, dreadful, laden with sorrow and despair, blasting across the remains of tombs, once monuments to the lives of those who passed, now passing themselves into eternity. There were no plants or animals, no water or life in any direction. Only these few humans left, the last of their kind on this world about to become dust. It was too late. The earth was in its death throes, and those that survived hung on by the slimmest of margins. Small groups of life wandered the dry hot earth in search of food. It was the McDonald Clan, one of the last human groups, that wandered down a hill and on to the remains of a cemetery. They faced a sunken destroyed city, and an outcrop with frozen tombs smoking in the rock bed. They have looked for food for days, gnawing on scraps of dead rotting flesh, dead bark, dried leaves, and berries. Their trek has brought them to this place, once a graveyard, now pieces of stone without meaning.

Frost formed under the coffins, dripping water — enough to last a few days perhaps, until the end overtook them. The leader was excited, thrilled for the hope of water which dripped from underneath the coffins.

The time had come. Ransom McDonald held his axe firmly and walked to the vessel. When within striking distance, he tried to balance himself for a mighty blow. Finally, he managed stability and raised the axe.

The axe struck the box but it resisted. On the second blow the vapor began to escape, and before the third blow could be struck the coffin burst open. The smoke cleared and a hideous face appeared. Its eyes were open and staring into the face of Ransom McDonald. McDonald raised his axe again, but before it found its mark it was stopped in midair.

The axe was caught and thrown to the ground. The creature rose from his frozen sleep to exact revenge on the last of their kind. He looked at what remained, at the sun, now barely visible behind the blowing dust, and realized that his end was near. The creature bent his leg, barely able to stand, and cried out to the empty world "Why? Why?" His screams echoed and then faded into the howling winds of forever. The dust rose high above the planet, finally to the watchful stars which had seen all of this before. As the creature screamed, Hamel's unit burst open. Hamel fell out, confused at the events before him.

After a short time Ransom McDonald spoke thus: "There is no one left that we know of! This is all! There are no others! The cities are destroyed, no water, no other life, we are all that is left!"

The creature pushed Ransom away and stood up and screamed into the wind. "What was all of this for? Why did this happen? What reason could there be for this ultimate oblivion! Why did we come to be at all?" His screams echoed across the windy landscape and rose above the dust to the quiet calm of the cosmos as he ran from the scene.

Up from the dust-laden air and out beyond the emptiness and fullness of space, one tiny speck of dust called the earth is lost in the vastness. Its importance has been obliterated and lost as if it never existed.

Diary of Ransom McDonald

Therefore did my heart rejoice,
and my tongue was glad;
moreover also my flesh shall
rest in hope: Acts 2: 26

I am filled with joy. The creature brought a Bible with him which he left when he ran. I now can read it. Thank God! My prayers have been answered! All that has been brought to me is for a reason. Hamel filled in many things that the papers had left out. He was extremely fearful when he awoke from his long sleep. The creature ran from the site and was not seen until some time later. Hamel was taken in by our community. At first he was reticent, but as time wore on he became reflective. He was depressed about what had transpired, even more so when a part of the wall collapsed and the bones of the three carpenters crashed on to the floor. They had been under contract for constructing the basement and were murdered by Golem to maintain secrecy.

I saw the creature many times after that. Once, when I had grown tired of fear, I walked toward him and said, "Kill me! Kill all of us if you want, otherwise I must continue my search for water!"

The creature said nothing. He simply stared at me, and then turned and ran at an incredible speed. Nevertheless, he continued to stay near us, but just beyond our reach. I thought it no longer mattered after a time if he destroyed us; there was little hope for us now. Perhaps there was a shred of compassion left in us. Each time we moved on I left him some water and what little food we could spare. I paid no attention to Hamel's initial objections. He still did not understand.

After a time Hamel became concerned about the book I had compiled. He wanted to finish the story. I gave him all I had recovered from the icy vessel and my notes as well. Perhaps it will mean something someday. It was a blessing that I learned the name of the author of my book. After I saw the name memories flooded my thoughts. I remembered hearing the name of John Bunyan but never associated it with my book. My mother had told me. I remember now.

Epilogue

Hamel's Diary

By and by I lost concern for the creature. Water became the focus of my life. Though the thought of the creature was always there I could not concern myself with it. I wanted to resolve my troublesome thoughts. The creature lay at the core of my thinking, separate from me, but affecting — infecting my thoughts. I wanted him to either kill us or forever disappear. I could not now think of destroying him. I had not the strength to hate the creature any more. All was changed. Our situation was too desperate to think of hatred. He is a part of me, a part of us all.

Everyone I ever knew has now turned to dust, yet they are still with me, painfully so. When I close my eyes I can see the fiend that murdered my mother. I can remember William's eyes the night he tried to murder me.

There is always hope. The emptiness that once completely dominated my soul is dissipating. So too it was with the creature. I am trying very hard not to let the Void return and overwhelm me. These thoughts represent an immense tidal wave that can fast engulf me, and everything that has come to be. If only I had listened to Emily! We would have been happy and I would not now be in this hell. God, please forgive me.

Final Entry — Date Unknown

I was at a gathering one night with the community. The creature never approached a gathering but we were always conscious of his presence. At first I had tried to persuade the group to destroy him, but they were not interested. In fact, Ransom McDonald said to me; "He would probably be doing us a favor, Hamel, if he destroyed us. We have inherited this hell from you. Maybe it would have been better if he had destroyed us the day he rose from the tomb. Forget it! It is a miracle that you are here and alive. I wanted to destroy both of you. You owe God that much."

Later, I proposed that I attempt to construct a device to produce water from the surviving kryo-units. From the shadows the creature watched us. He did little to hide his presence. He listened to our worries and our concerns, and once when the conversations concerned the needs of a dying child, he was moved. The leader was always aware of his presence and one night invited him in. I was fearful of his coming until I saw his face. Despite his horrid appearance I saw fear in that face. He had developed a slight limp, most probably from the attachment I had made.

He looked frightened and meek as he came to us. A small child offered him a seat on a large rock, which he took, and for some reason the child called him Jacob. It was on this night that the creature was given a name. The child was trying to read the Bible that Ransom was teaching him from. It was the Bible that Jacob had brought from the past.

He sat for a long while, saying nothing, listening to the leader speak to us; we paid little attention to him. After he heard that we were desperate for water, and that I could not produce any more, he finally spoke. He had become familiar with the territory and he offered to bring back water to us. He said that with his tremendous strength he would be able to travel the distance despite the heat and unearth water. On this night he said to us: "I once did not know whether it was better to live with the blood of my creator on my hands or to die by my own hand. The grave was a better alternative than a life of utter loneliness. I stood against the devil, as Bunyan did, in the valley of the shadow of death. I have been freed!"

Soon thereafter Jacob went away for several days and returned with a large container of water. A small child went to him and held his hand. He said nothing but only sobbed and embraced the child. Then he spoke, "Beyond the horizon, due east, is an underground water source, covered over by rocks. We must go there if we are to survive. There is water for us all. There is also plant life and things to eat in a valley. The earth trembles constantly and fissures of fire erupt across the path. Come, follow me! I have destroyed the beasts that have hunted you. I have lain in this stinking dungeon of despair too long. As I look across the faces gathered here I see hope, not doom. There, with us, is Joshua Hamel, a man I once vowed to destroy; now all are leveled to this, to this wasteland."

He continued. "My vision is that we will see the Celestial City. We will see the sun and the stars, and feel the warmth of joyful thoughts that will dwell in our hearts. We will enjoy love and friendship. I have been taken away from evil, and though I do not expect to live long enough to see these things, I know it will be!"

Jacob became a prophet, for he found for us a valley unscathed by the blowing dust. He found an oasis of hope. I never referred to him as "the creature" again, but as Jacob. After a time we looked into each others eyes, and for the first time I perceived a distinguishable smile on Jacob's face. I could not help but return the smile for he had delivered my liberation.

We followed him at a distance. He carried two small children too weak to walk. It was on this day that Jacob, finder of water, disappeared. He had put the children down so as to spy what lay ahead over a ridge. One of the children wandered away toward a chasm. The earth shook and shifted and almost swallowed the child, but Jacob, with the speed of a God, pulled the child away from the fiery chasm to safety. In doing so he forfeited his own life, for he disappeared in the fire and hot gas that belched from the chasm before us. His eyes met mine as the ground sank and the flames swallowed him. I cried.

We found the water and the garden that he had discovered. We will live out our lives here. Many times I have wept thinking about what has happened. We saved the words of Jacob and over the years produced a book about the story that brought him here. I was given another chance to right what had been done. I remember once being told, by my mother, that we are in part made from all of the people we have ever known. That we are just pieces of all of the people we have encountered.

Jacob finally accepted peace despite the fact that never was there a creature more justified in exacting revenge. His life has meaning for what is left of the world. I am old. I could still repair a kryo-unit but I have no interest in knowing what lies beyond. I am only thankful for what has happened. I pray that what has happened does not become myth or religion. I pray that we will always know what occurred. I can write no more, enough has been said. May God forgive us all. . . .

Acknowledgements

I thank God that I am still alive and able to write at this time in my life. I thank my wife, Edwina, for her stability and love. I most probably would have never written a book without my wife's love. I love her dearly. My children have been a blessing: Marcus, my son, and two beautiful daughters, Elena Patrice and Angela Christine. They are blessed children whom I love dearly.

I would like to thank James Goslin for his reading of the first rough and for his optimism. He has been a good friend offering humor, insight, and friendship. I would like to thank Alice Geron for her expertise and wisdom as an editor and publisher. Although my parents did not live to see this accomplishment I think they would have been extremely proud and uplifted that something came from the ashes. I thank my mother for her gift of reading and my father for his determination.

I would also like to thank the English Department at the University of Texas at San Antonio and the professors who taught me. Special thanks go to the University of Texas Health Science Center at San Antonio through the Office of the President for their research of issues related to the novel

Thanks to David Starr, the Honorable Bobby Perez, Jasmine Azima, William Kaufman, the Honorable Edward D. Garza, Howard Anderson, John H. Sanders, and Carlos Richardson for their assistance and sponsorship of my book, and for believing in me despite the negative burps fired off by hobgoblins and small statesmen.

Finally, I also wish to thank Mary Shelley for producing a masterpiece that will endure for all of human existence. Mary Shelley's work inspired me to attempt, in a most humble way, a sequel to her story of Frankenstein. In many ways her work is closely tied to my existence.

M.S.

PALO ALTO COLLEGE L R C
3 6171 00164629 5